# I Once W

I Once Was Lost

Based on a True Story

by

ROGER DOWIS

# I Once Was Lost

## PROLOGUE

John Newton bolted upright in his hammock and sat there for a moment. The concussion had driven him from a sound sleep to acute awareness. Something is terribly wrong, he thought. He rubbed a fist across a sleep-filled eye when a warning voice came out of the darkness. "All hands to the main deck. The ship's foundering!"

He dropped over the side of his hammock and found himself knee-deep in a layer of cold seawater. His eyes adjusted as he looked about the crew's sleeping quarters, then up toward the main deck. He could just make out Captain Swanwick's pale face. He's terrified. He's never afraid, not in any crisis, and now he looks like he's seen death itself.

"Get up, lads," thundered Swanwick. "All hands to your duty stations."

Newton sloshed through the black liquid and climbed the stairs. He reached the hatch and the wind carried a furious chorus of voices to his ears. The ship was listing so far that waves lapped over the broadside. Swanwick, positioned on the quarterdeck, waved his arms like symphony conductor.

"Get the main sail tied down," he roared at three men bailing water, only to have it blown back against them. "And have the carpenter repair that hole in the side. Seal it off or we're going under."

Then the captain pointed at Newton. "You," he bellowed, "get below and fetch me a knife."

Newton immediately carried out the order. This was no time for defiance. His feet gingerly located each step beneath the water. He

4

stopped when he was half-way down the stairs, and for reasons he could never explained, looked back over his shoulder. At the top of the landing, in the very spot he occupied only seconds before, stood another sailor. Eyes paralyzed with fear, the man stared into the abyss and could neither move nor look away as a mountainous whitecap crashed onto the deck. Newton watched the wave sweep his shipmate into the dark oblivion. One moment he was there, and the next he was gone forever.

Newton shook off the brain-searing image and forced himself forward. Fumbling in the darkness, he groped beneath the water, found his sea bag and the knife inside. Clutching the tool, he worked his way back to the main deck, pushed through torrents of rain and grabbed hold of a bowline. Soaked through, he offered his hand up to the captain.

Instead of taking the instrument, Captain Swanwick glared at his subordinate for a long moment. Finally, he said, "For months you've been stirring things up, trying to convince the crew that God's no more than a myth. Well, boy, God is real, and this is His retribution. I've a good mind to throw you over the side as a peace offering."

Newton searched the deep lines across the captain's forehead, his narrow eyes and clenched jaw. This was no idle threat. His hand dropped the wind flapped through his clothing and time stopped.

"Well, do something. Start bailing," said the captain as he turned back to giving orders to the rest of the crew.

The captain was right. Newton looked down at his feet and recalled all the times when he'd pushed God aside. He lifted his head and spoke into the wind, "God has no reason to offer me grace, not after the way I've lived. No, this is the end for me. I'm lost."

Chapter 1

Wapping, London

July, 1732

"For my thoughts are not your thoughts, neither are your ways my ways," declares the LORD. Isaiah 55:8

John Newton wedged his small body between the large stone fireplace and a dark green sofa in the living room of the small house. It was his favorite place in the world; at least, when his parents were arguing.

The quarrel was one he'd heard many times, mostly just before his father was about to return to sea. The captain's voice was as large as his body, a fearful presence, dressed in his black uniform. He waved his hands about as he spoke and his heavy boots thumped as he paced across the kitchen floor.

His mother was just the opposite, small and frail. She often coughed during the conflicts, caused by inflamed lungs. But she was a woman with strength of heart, and John knew she would remain calm without giving into her husband. She sat in a rocking chair and was holding some yarn, which she used to knit while she talked. Her light blue dress matched her tired eyes, and a black shawl covered her shoulders. She often complained about the cold, even when others felt the temperature was too warm.

"Hush now," she scolded, waving an airy hand at her husband. "I don't want him to hear."

Nothing pricked John's ears more than the possibility of hearing one of his parents' secrets. He leaned forward, just far enough to dip his head around the edge of the couch. Still in his pajamas, he knew his parents would send him off with a scolding if they discovered he had slipped out of his bedroom.

"I'll say it outright," said Elizabeth, leaning back into the cushion of her rocking chair, "our son afraid of you. And why wouldn't he be. He's only four, but you treat him like he's one of your sailors."

The captain stopped his pacing but made no effort to answer until Elizabeth impatiently looked up from her needlepoint. Her husband's only response was a resigned shrug.

"That's just my way of talking," he said. "I do it with everyone."

"Exactly," countered Abigail, "and John is not everyone. He's sensitive, and he needs you more than ever. You're gone for up to a year at a time, and he thrives on your attention when you come home. Why don't you try to be more of a father instead of the master of the ship?"

John sat so still his breathing seemed louder than his parent's tiff. That was what his mother's word, a tiff; they never argued.

Elizabeth held the socks she was working on up against the light, inspecting them for flaws. They would match her husband's favorite decades-old sweater, the one he refused to give up. He could be so stubborn about some things, she thought.

"I want you to teach the boy about the ways of life. If you don't, who will?"

The captain exhaled a stream of smoke from his pipe, filling the air in front of him with gray billows. He shook his head back and forth slowly, making sure his wife was finished speaking.

"And how is that to be accomplished? I'm at sea more months than I'm at home?"

"That's up to you, but if you want to influence your son, you'll have to be around him more when you *are* here."

The captain took another draw on the pipe clenched between his teeth and stuffed his calloused hands deep into his pockets. It was easier to think if he walked, much the way he commanded a ship from the quarterdeck. His frame was lean and erect, his features angular, and his eyes black as flint.

"I just don't want the boy to be too soft. He stays inside most of the time and rarely plays with the other boys."

"That's because they bully him." Abigail stiffened as she spoke. "He's different, and they think that gives them the right to torment him."

John rubbed the hollow of his shoulder absentmindedly. Only a week ago a larger boy had threatened to beat him up. John was small for his age, and the odds of winning a fight were nil. He knew that because he's always lost fights. He wasn't ashamed, though. The kid who always started the fight was at least a head taller and more muscular.

Anyway, John knew he wasn't a fighter. He tried making up for his size by using big words. The last time, a boy had walked up and pushed hard against his shoulder, knocking him off balance. "You think you're better than the rest of us, don't you," he said. "Keep it up, *boy*, and you're going to get an honest to goodness beating."

After that, John only went out when the street was clear.

The captain stopped talking as if he'd run out of words. His index finger jabbed as he began to speak. "Let's talk about the real issue here. You want to turn him into a preacher. There, now. It's out in the open."

Elizabeth never looked up from her work. The unrelenting groan of the rocking chair filled the silence as if filling in for its mistress. "The Lord's work is an honorable profession."

Without meaning to, the captain's voice grew loud again. "I've never interfered with your involvement in the church. Just the opposite, I respect you for it. But I don't like the idea of him joining the ministry; at least, not with your church."

Elizabeth's hands dropped to her lap as she sighed. "And what would a man who'd never darkened the doorway of *any* church know about that?"

"Well, for one thing, those people, present company excluded, are pious. Regular folks can't stand being around them." The catch in the captain's voice a failed effort to control his booming voice. "For goodness sake, the whole congregation is full of Reformers. It's a poor religion in my estimation."

One side of the shawl slipped off Elizabeth's emancipated shoulder, and she took a moment to return the wrap. She was constantly cold these days, sometimes causing her to shiver when everyone else found the temperature comfortable. She ignored the despairing remark and continued to defend her hope for the future.

"John's bright for his age. He can read as well as any adult, and he has memorized long passages of the Westminster Catechisms, not to mention several classics. He reads and understands them all."

"'Liz, we both value a good education. The Spanish Jesuits certainly taught me well, but there's more than reading books when it comes to being a man."

"On that we agree," said Elizabeth, her tone steady, "but he's young and would be little more than a cabin boy at his age. I'll not have him scrubbing the deck of some ship taking him to God knows where or consorting with crude sailors. I've worked too hard to abandon him to such wastelands."

John watched the captain start to say something. Instead, he tightly clenched his jaw and walked over to the hearth. As John moved his head back behind the sofa, he could hear his father tapping the bowl of his pipe against the fireplace wall. Then he refilled it with fresh tobacco, tamped it down and held a match to it until the glow was sufficient to continue burning.

"He'll be of age in a few years. Sooner or later, you're going to have to let go."

"Yes, but only when he's ready."

Without warning, a spasm emerged from deep inside Elizabeth's lungs. She hunched forward and waited for the contraction to pass, but it only became more intense. *I'm suffocating*, thought Elizabeth. But instead of panic, she was inordinately calm. *I wonder if this is my time.* It was her last thought before losing consciousness.

Captain Newton wasted no time in reaching his wife, helping steady her as she bent forward. "John," he yelled to the back of the house. "Stay here with your mother till I bring back Doctor Riley."

John bounded out of his hiding place in time to see his mother doubled over in her rocking chair and his father dashing out the front door into the darkness.

Minutes later, the captain returned with an elderly man wearing a plain woolen black coat. He was stooped over with age and slightly tilted to the side that carried a small black medical bag. Quickly assessing the situation, the doctor disengaged himself from the outer garment, handing it off to his friend and leaned over the sick woman's side.

"There, there, Mrs. Newton. The worst is over now."

The captain stood out of the way and watched, helpless to do anything more. "John, he said, "it would be best if you waited outside."

John ached to stay in the room but knew better than to ask. He slipped into his coat and stepped outside on the large wooden porch that encompassed the entire front of the house, and examined the surrounding houses. Finding the street deserted, he turned towards the adjacent window, cupped his hands over his eyes and peered inside, being careful not to breathe on the glass.

"No wonder you're not feeling well. Living with this old salt is bound to make anyone ill."

It proved to be a poor attempt at humor. Everyone in the room understood that Elizabeth's condition was serious. And, her condition was getting worse each month.

Rhylie set his black leather bag on the table, unfastened the clasp and laid out his instruments.

"Please remove your shawl, Ma'am."

Elizabeth did as instructed. The doctor placed a cone shaped device against her back and was listening to her lungs. He moved the device twice more and then seemed satisfied.

"Sounds like a bunch of old rustling leaves," he said and proceeded to check her eyes and throat. "Has the honey tea helped any?"

Elizabeth shifted backward and settled back into the rocker. "Sometimes it keeps me from coughing long enough to get some sleep," she murmured. "Those are my best days."

The doctor replaced his patient's shawl and patted her shoulder. "Just relax for the time being, my dear. You'll start to feel better soon. It wouldn't hurt to have your husband fix some more of that tea when I've gone."

While returning the instrument to his bag, the doctor's steady gaze signaled Newton to follow him outside. The captain trailed after his old friend into the crisp autumn air. He pulled the collar of his coat up around his neck, stuffed his hands deep into his pockets and waited. He clearly was not used to being a spectator during a crisis.

"How bad is it?" he said.

"I've found it better to be straightforward with patients and their families, so please don't take what I'm about to say as being insensitive. Her condition is deteriorating faster than expected. Her condition has worsened."

The old man took a breath, giving the captain a moment to process the information before continuing. "As you know, there's no cure for Consumption. You can expect the frequency of these episodes to increase. If you can't be here, you'll have to find someone to look after your wife. I'm afraid she might have another attack and slip into unconsciousness. Without the aid of someone else, she could choke to death. Have you got someone who'd be willing to help out?"

The captain scratched his chin as if thinking. "She has a close friend. Perhaps arrangements can be made. I'll look into it straightaway."

"Good, then. Between my other patients, I'll check in as often as possible. But mind you, it won't be enough."

"Doctor," said Newton, "do you know how much time we have left?" The words sounded like a defendant pleading to the judge for a stay of execution.

"Two months, two weeks, two days. Who can say? Most of the time these things end with the patient slipping into a comma and passing away in their sleep." The doctor's voice took on a softer, more respectful tone. "That's God's blessing, Captain. Less suffering that way. We want to hang onto our loved ones forever, but eventually, we're all going to pass on."

The two men nodded without saying anything more. Captain Newton escorted his friend as far as the picket gate that guarded the small yard. Then, he turned on the heel of his polished black boot, and ambled back to the house, where he would prepare the tea.

When the front door clicked, John meandered out from behind the ancient Oak tree that presided over most of the yard. He stared down and watched his shoes stir up a blanket of fall leaves. The shoes would get dusty, and his father would scold him, tell him to clean them off and that he hoped John would take better care of himself in the future. But none of that bothered him. In a matter of weeks, winter would come, and the colors would change from green to gray, putting everything to sleep. John understood that plants and trees would return in the spring, but humans, when they died, went away forever.

He took two great little-boy strides towards the gnarled trunk of the Oak and kicked it, and then he kicked it again, only this time, hard enough to sting the ball of his foot. The pain felt good, made him feel alive.

"This shouldn't be happening," he exclaimed as if talking to an invisible friend. But it *was* happening. The doctor had said as much. His anger worked its way through his immature mind until he clearly understood that it was God who was responsible. He was taking away a woman who faithfully read her Bible and prayed each day, a woman who loved her family and took care of her son. God, he concluded, was doing something evil, so God must be evil.

John's conclusion defied all his mother's teaching; nevertheless, it burrowed itself in his very core.

Chapter 2

Aveley, England

July, 1734

"Where can I flee from your presence? If I go up to the heavens, you are there; if I make my bed in the depths, you are there. If I rise on the wings of the dawn, if I settle on the far side of the sea, even there your hand will guide me, your right hand will hold me fast."
Psalm 139:7-10

John knew something was wrong. From his bedroom, he could hear his father's boots as the captain walked between the sitting room at the front of the house and the back door of the kitchen. He'd been listening to the footsteps for the better part of an hour and could not go back to sleep.

It was his father's habit to rise at dawn each morning and swim a mile in the cold ocean water not far from their home. He said the ritual served to clear his head. After the swim, his new wife Thomasina served him a breakfast of ham and eggs with fresh baked bread slathered in marmalade. He normally went to the dock and watched the crew work on the ship that he would take out to sea in only a few weeks. But not today.

For months, his father lived in the house but said little and spent long hours during the evening sitting by the fireplace, just thinking. She was my mother, too, thought John. I have feelings. But nothing seemed to make any difference. Each time he tried to get close, the captain closed himself off.

Having no choice, John tried to wait out his father's separation, but nothing changed. Then one day his father came home and called John over to his side. The captain remained standing, looked down and said, "I've met someone, John. She's an Italian lady with two sons of her own. We're going to get married."

But things did not go well. John did not like his new brothers, and he got out of the house whenever he could sneak away. Thomasina, as he called her, did little to correct him, and soon he was staying out after dark.

It was morning when John stumbled down the hallway, spooned himself a bowl of porridge and sat down at the kitchen table. Still dressed in his wrinkled gray nightshirt, he had not yet washed his face, or given any thought to what he was going to do that day. Sleeping late was a newly acquired luxury. Only two months ago, Thomasina shook his shoulder in a futile attempt to rouse him from bed. When he refused to get up, she simply decided not to disturb him.

Sleep was like medicine. It permitted a respite from his stepmother's constant badgering. The more she pestered him, the more he felt the need to insulate himself. If he had to be home, he was only there long enough to eat and go to bed. He spent as much time as possible reading in his room, or outside with some of his newly minted friends, a group of boys whose parents looked the other when complaints of mischief.

This morning the captain was stewing about something. Perhaps one of the neighbors had complained upon his return from his last voyage. If John stayed at the table any longer than it took to eat, he was sure to get another scolding. Still pacing, the echo of the captain's boots slowed until his father stood in front of him, motionless and silent. His hands remained clasped behind his back, but his eyes rose slowly from the floor and rested on his son. "John," he began, "I have something to tell you, and there's no way to make it come out easy, so I'm not going to mince words. I'm sending you to boarding school."

Although it was direct, John's foggy mind did not immediately grasp the implication of the message. When it did register, his jaw fell slack for several seconds. They were putting him out of the house, the home where he was born and lived for the last eight years.

At first, his entire body went numb, with the same kind of feeling as when he accidently banged his elbow on the table. Then his eyes began stinging, and there was a high-pitched ringing in his ear.

"It's Thomasina, isn't it?" said John. "She's making you do this."

The captain sighed and waited a moment before he answered. "You might say that, but if you're honest, you'll see that you brought this on yourself."

John pushed the bowl away and covered his brow with the edge of his hand, still staring at the table. His face felt hot, and he could hardly find his voice. "I brought it on?" he rasped.

"I'm speaking about your behavior during the last six months. You're responsible for at least a part of this situation."

John waited for his father's explanation.

"Thomasina advised me that you've been taking off without telling her where you're going. She doesn't care much for the company you keep, either. When she asks where you've been all day, you refuse to give her a straight answer. Your language isn't fit for mixed company anymore, which is nothing more than disrespect for everyone else in the house." There was a gap in the conversation. Finally, the captain said, "She's just given up on you."

The captain pulled out one of the chairs and sat down beside his son, leaned forward and perched his arms on top of his knees. "For your sake, I wish Elizabeth was still here. I never worried when she was alive, not about anything. But since her death, well ..."

John sat very still. The words were more than he could bear. What if she didn't like his new friends? His stepmother – oh, how he hated the word -- didn't care about him; in fact, she encouraged him to run around with rougher boys. His father called them rabble. And it was all right with her as long as he stayed away from the house. It was her way of getting him out of the way. He tried to get along, or at least he thought he had. She had become a wedge, separating them, leaving his father had the thankless job of telling him that he was no longer welcome.

He choked for a moment, swallowed the lump in his throat and kept his head down. The new baby made him feel like an intruder, but he couldn't bring himself to say it. It hurt when his father doted on the child. I might as well be an orphan.

"She's given up all hope of trying to control you," the captain continued. "Under any other circumstances, a good horse whipping might be in order. I believe you've earned it."

"I didn't realize that things were so bad," John murmured, his voice rising several octaves, frightened and on the verge of breaking down. Worse still was the idea of living with a bunch of strangers in some faraway school. No longer able to hold back, tears trailed down his cheeks, mouth and onto his tightly folded hands.

The captain, feeling very uncomfortable, collected himself and stood up. "I'm sorry, John. I can't continue to referee the two of you when I'm at home, and she refuses to take responsibility while I'm away. The matter is settled."

Surprised, John felt his father affectionately squeeze his shoulder, a final gesture of compassion. Without saying more, the captain put on his coat and walked out of the house.

Chapter 3

Boarding School

Essex, England (1734)

"He stilled the storm to a whisper; the waves of the seas were hushed. They were glad when it grew calm, and he guided them to their desired haven." Psalm 107:29, 30

John Newton came to a stop at the crest of a hill overlooking the Essex School for Boys. His legs ached after walking more than a mile, and he set his bag of clothing down. This was his first time away from home, and although he didn't want to admit it, his heart fearfully thumped against his chest.

Picking up the bag again, he crowded all thoughts of home from his mind, brushed a mop of curly black hair off his forehead, and slowly walked down the dirt pathway. Rounding a bend, he saw the school for the first time. The odd collection of red brick building stood in a half-moon shape. He could see a three-story residence hall, another building of classrooms, a dining hall, and finally, the Administration Building. On a knoll off to the north, a cathedral rested above everything else. The church held Newton's attention for a long moment, and then he murmured, "Reminds me of a sentry standing guard over a prison."

Moving forward, John approached a large iron fence, where a redheaded boy with freckles caked across his cheeks casually leaned against the gate. He wore a red neck-cloth, and a blue waistcoat displaying the school crest on the coat's breast pocket.

"You must be John." The boy extended a welcoming hand. John set his bag down and shook hands just the way his father had taught him. He stood up straight. First time anyone offered to greet me like an adult. "That's right," he said, taking the older boy's hand. "John Newton."

"Good on ya, then." The boy motioned over to the pathway. "I'm James, your roommate. Grab your bag, lad. My job's to show you around."

The two boys walked along a worn path lined by green wild grass, and James began what was obviously a well-rehearsed monologue. "You look about, what, eight-years-old?"

"Nine," said John.

James placed his hands on his hips and gave John an appraising gaze. "Small for your age, eh? That's all right. We have all sizes and shapes here." James stopped for a moment and looked John in the eye. "I'll show you around

in a moment, but first let's get some unpleasant business out of the way. All this is going to seem strange at first. It's going to be different than living at home with your parents, but you'll be an old hand before you know it. The most important thing around here is to learn the rules."

"Yes," said John, agreeing with the obvious, but he was completely confused.

James began walking again, this time more slowly. As if talking to no one in particular, he said, "You'll soon learn that we have both official and unofficial rules in this institution."

John's head tilted to one side. *Don't like the sound of that, whatever it means.* "Not to worry," said James, an understanding, half-smile appearing. "You'll get the hang of things in no time. For now, just remember to stay in the middle of the pack. That's been my philosophy for the past two years and it's kept me out of some pretty tight scrapes."

John looked at his new friend. He started to ask a question but thought it better to wait. His stomach was tight. He ran his hand across the spot that always burned when things weren't going well. That happened a lot since his mother died, more often after his father remarried.

When they reached the dormitory, John followed James up the creaky stairs, down the second floor hallway and through the doorway of third room on the left. Two beds lined the walls on opposing sides of the room. He set his bag down next to the one that contained a thin mattress, and looked around. On James desk were his textbooks, and a small painting of what John guessed was James' mother. The wall walls were completely bare.

Watching his roommate, James said, "I know what you're thinking. That's all we're allowed. The rules forbid any wall decoration.

John's mouth dropped open. *This isn't a dorm. It's a jail cell.* "But why? What could it possibly hurt to decorate the room a little?"

James chuckled softly. "You're going to hear a lot about discipline in coming weeks, and this is part of a program designed to help you grow."

"Grow," said John, his mouth half-open. "Grow how?"

"It's about doing with less. Some things are necessary and some aren't. It builds character." Then James smiled again and said, "At least that's what the headmaster says."

John sat down on his bed and rested both elbows on his knees. He wondered if his father really understood what boarding school was like. Then he remembered that the captain had attended one himself. He'd always said that school was where he'd become a man.

Breaking the momentary silence, James said, "So, what's your story?"

"My story?" said John. "What exactly does that mean?"

"Everyone here has a story. Sometimes it's a father who's ambitious for his son and wants him to have a good education. Could be the death of a parent, leaving too many children to handle. Things like that."

John shrugged resignedly. "I suppose in my case it's all of those things and more. My father wanted me to follow him to sea, while my mother hoped I would go into the ministry. That all changed when she died from influenza. My new stepmother and I didn't get along well. When the new baby came, they sent me here."

"Believe it or not, that story is rather common," said James. "At any rate, fathers want their sons to prepare for manhood early. Many a parent has planned a life for their child, and it all begins here in school.

My father wants me to be a lawyer someday. Thing is, I have no intention of pursuing the law."

"What do you want to do?" said John.

There was a twinkle in James' eye. "I intend to be a pirate when I grow up."

Both boys laughed, and then John said, "Seriously, what do you want to do someday?"

"I have absolutely no idea," said James, his face blank.

John held up his hands, as if surrendering. "Then that makes two of us," and they laughed again.

"I'm already corrupting you. By the time I'm through, you'll have absolutely no character left."

Then James' voice took on a more serious tone. "Let's get back on subject. You'll be attending services tonight. Church is mandatory, of course, with preaching on Sunday mornings and Wednesday evenings. It's not too bad, though, since there's no homework assigned on those days."

The information came all too quickly. John didn't know where to begin with all the questions his mind had collected, so he decided to just wait and watch.

James looked out the window. "Come on," he said excitement in his voice, "the sun is setting and it's time for dinner. We'll get beef with potatoes tonight."

The way it sounded, John wondered how often the cook served meat. Rather than say anything, he followed James down the stairs. Then the boys half-walked, half-ran across the green span of grass to get in line. Half out of breath, James leaned down and whispered, "I forgot to tell you to about mealtime. "Be mindful when the monitors are within hearing range."

John's mouth dropped open and stayed that way for a moment before he recovered his composure. "What kind of place is this?" he said.

"Shush, not so loud," said James as they moved into the line. He took note of a boy who stood a few heads in front of them. The boy smiled smugly, and James warned him off with a menacing glare.

"Just watch your step," he continued. "I'll explain later."

They worked their way through the serving line and took a place at one of the long rectangular tables. The school seemed more like a jail, and although he wouldn't admit it to anyone, John was scared. I'll be glad when we go to church. At least I'll feel safe there.

At the conclusion of what was anything but a leisurely meal, James elbowed his new friend. "Just follow me and do as I do." They fell in line, cleaned off their serving trays and quietly walked out the doors, and toward the chapel. John continued to observe, not speaking for fear he might draw attention to himself. The arches of the Anglican sanctuary met at the center beam, high in the gray, misty air. Tall stained-glass windows signifying various stories from the Bible lined the towering walls.

John seated himself in a hard wooden pew in the third row on the right side of the sanctuary, and watched the pews fill. Then the

Chaplain stood and occupied the pulpit. He looked about seventy and had deep crags across his forehead His eyes, too pale to call blue, were set close together. He wore a black frock coat over a white shirt with a clerical collar.

The minister opened a large Bible and read from the book of Genesis, telling the story of Cain and Able. When finished, he closed the book shut with a sense of finality. "This," he bellowed, "is a story of pride and a rebellious spirit. You newly arrived students would do well to learn this lesson. Obedience is always rewarded; rebellion leads to God's wrath, and the mark of Cain."

James leaned to one side and whispered out of the corner of his mouth, "Not to mention the wrath of the school staff."

John sighed when the sermon finally ended. The minister stepped down and walked to the church entrance, where he waited to welcome each new boy. "I'm pleased to meet you," chimed the old man as they shook hands.

John noticed something peculiar. The old man placed his free bony hand over each boy's during the handshake, covering it. John shuddered. *That's just how my father used to shake hands. It was his way of showing control, marking his territory right from the start.*

The line snaked along, and when it was John's turn, the old man's breath hit him like a furnace. *He's been drinking!* John said nothing, possible.

As the boys ambled back to the dorm, John said, "That's the first time I've ever seen a drunken minister, especially one who was preaching."

"I suppose the old boy has a bit of a problem," said James, his tone neutral and free of any judgment. "He probably drank the leftover communion one too many times."

"Why on earth does the chancellor allow him to stay?"

James looked over his shoulder, making sure no one could hear what he was about to say. "There's one thing you may as well get straight, right from the beginning, boy-o. The school does the best it can with what it has."

"The best it can? What's that supposed to mean?"

"Rumor has it that many ministers apply to teach at religious institutions just before they're put out to pasture."

"Out to pasture?" asked John.

"You know, forced to retire. There are men on staff, but they arrive wanting to save the world. That doesn't last long before discouragement sets in. By then, no other church will take them. Their only way out is to move from the classroom to the ivory tower. I guess they figure even a burned-out minister can't get into any trouble if separated from the students."

"Trouble, like what?" asked John.

"Oh, there are lots of ways," James continued, "but the thing that can hurt the school most is when a teacher goes too far when he punishes one of us. That's why they discourage the town's adult parishioners from attending church here. No adults, no complaints. No complaints, and there's no trouble. In the end, nothing changes. You'll

29

see that the people who like the chaplain are always indisposed whenever any parents visit."

"This all sounds pretty strange," said John, shaking his head from side to side. "The church I grew up in would never have tolerated such behavior, much less encouraged it."

The two boys talked intermittently meandered along. Finally, John heaved a long sigh and asked, "This is a lot to remember. Is there anything else I need to know?"

The older boy stopped momentarily, keeping his hands stuffed deep in his pockets. "I suppose the first thing is to understand the lockstep method works."

John's eyebrows arched. "Lockstep? Isn't that what they do in prisons?"

"It's not quite that bad. It means doing each task the same way every time. The daily schedule, where you sit, when you eat, you'll learn to do them all at the same time, and the same way every time, We're allowed to talk at meals. But mind you, talking can be used as a trap?"

"Talking, a trap?" said, John, and then chastised himself for sounding like a parrot. *This is getting more confusing by the minute.*

"A simple, 'pass the salt,' is acceptable," said James. "You start horsing around, though, and one of the staff will cuff your head before you see it coming. It can also get you a demerit. Too many demerits and you get the paddle."

"How many is too many?" asked John

James looked sideways at his naive friend. "You don't want to know. Like I said, the secret to success here is blending in. That's all you have to remember, don't stand out. The very best and the worst draw too much attention to themselves. Sooner or later, they pay the price."

It was the second time his roommate had mentioned that standing out in the crowd could lead to trouble. "Come on," he questioned, "can it really be that bad?"

"Not completely. There are good things about the school, one of them being a quality education. Once you get into the swing of things, you'll feel more at home." James elbowed his new friend in the ribs and said, "Come on, roomie. I'll race you to the residence hall." All at once, long-legged James bolted ahead of John who tore off after the only friend he had in the world.

The first week was little more than a blur. The rapid learning pace, getting to know his teacher, and reading subjects his mother had never addressed were taking a toll. It all left John struggling to keep up. Even the other boys seemed distant. Finally, one night as he and James prepared for bed, John unburdened himself to his only friend.

"I don't think our teacher likes me," he said, head bowed as if making a confession.

"Mr. Bell?" said James. "He doesn't like anyone, including himself. And, now that you've brought it up, there is something about him forgot to tell you. He likes to single out students who challenge his authority."

Is there no good news about this place?

James stretched out in bed, folded his pillow in half and pushed it under his neck. He looked up at the ceiling as he talked. "He targets the weakest boys. He justifies it by saying they need to toughen up, and that he's preparing us for the real world. No one believes that, of course."

John didn't consider himself weak, but he was small. "Alright then, what should I do differently?"

James licked his thumb and index finger, reached over the top of his bed and pinched the wick of the candle resting on his desk. The room went dark, and their voices suddenly seemed louder. "That's an interesting question.  Not sure you can, other than to show a little humility. But that's the way to beat him at his own game."

"But I haven't done anything. In fact, I try my best to avoid him. You know, keep my head down and stay in the middle of the pack, just like you said."

"That's not exactly true, boyo."

The muscles in John's shoulders tightened as he hung up the last of his clothes and slipped into his nightshirt.  "Okay," he groaned. "Tell me what I'm doing wrong, exactly."

"You remember last week when he handed our test papers back and commented on your penmanship? Said it needed improvement."

John thought back. Right in front of everyone, he said my penmanship needed improving. He could have written it on the face of my paper or talked to me after class; but no, he wanted to embarrass me.

"Yes, I remember."

James pushed into his pillow, tucking it under his neck. He rested against it and yawned. His voice softened as sleep approached. "You gave him that go-to-hell look of yours. Well, you can be sure he saw it. I know because his jaw tightened just before he went on to the next student. He may not have said anything at the time, but he's not going to let it pass. He's just biding his time."

Even as John listened, he felt bile rising up into this throat. James didn't have any authority to talk to him this way, even if he was right.

"You haven't been here more than a couple of weeks, but you're already getting off on the wrong foot. Truly, John, your back stiffens when he looks at you, and you have a way of glaring back. Don't tell me you don't know what I'm talking about. Just in case you don't, I think the word I'm searching for is defiant. It means your attitude is only making a bad thing worse."

"I know what it means," snapped John, lacing his fingers behind his head as he lied down. His eyes had finally adjusted to the darkness and he could see the slats of wood that made up the underside of the ceiling. "I know what you're saying, and it's not fair. He's a bully and keeps coming after me, even when I haven't done anything wrong."

"Fair?" James chuckled softly. "Fair, as in fairytale? There is no fair in life, especially here at Essex." James turned toward the wall, signaling an end to the conversation. "Beware, my friend, or you'll find out the true definition of the Trinity."

"Trinity, like in the Bible?"

"Yes," he uttered, as the urge to sleep overcame his weary body. "Just remember, I warned you."

John didn't answer. Instead, he turned over on his side and stared at the wall.

Chapter 4

The Breaking Point

Essex, England (1734)

"Blessed are you when people insult you, persecute you and falsely say all kinds of evil against you because of me. Rejoice and be glad, because great is your reward in heaven, for in the same way they persecuted the prophets who were before you." Matthew 5:11-12

The school's classrooms accommodated exactly thirty pupils. Each student was required to sit at his assigned desk, fold his hands stiffly on top of the worn wood, and pay strict attention as he waited for the instructions that would signal the beginning of that day. Mr. Bell's large desk rested in front of an even wider blackboard. The morning sunlight filtered in through several windows along the outer wall.

Mr. Bell walked into the classroom precisely at 8:00 a.m. each morning, almost as the minute hand of his pocket-watch swept across the twelve. His height was below average, causing some of the boys to snicker behind his back, making jokes about the 'little man.'"

John could tell the whisperings spoke not only of his stature but his character, as well. His attire never varied. He wore a dark frock coat and a neck scarf bearing the school colors. He often contemplated his well-manicured nails while addressing the class, and the press of his suit was like his manners: immaculate. He took great care to pace his sentences and enunciate each word with exaggerated clarity. So much so that those listening sometimes found themselves wanting to hurry him along by finishing his statements, an act he considered highly discourteous. John hated him right from the beginning.

John also heard that Bell possessed a most peculiar talent. Regardless of where his gaze fell, every boy in the room was certain the headmaster was looking directly at him, and had the ability to read his mind. No one was able to escape this mysterious ability, and by the end of the first week, Bell had evaluated every student, openly identifying those boys who merited his special attention.

"Some of you," he warned early on, "those of you who lack discipline, or who harbor a rebellious spirit, will require additional attention to shape your character." He turned on his heel and glared at John. "Unfortunately, Mr. Newton, you seem to fall into both categories."

Then he broke off the stare and began to pace between the rows of desks. "Each of you must ask yourself, am I a sheep or a goat? Will I be a faithful member of the flock or choose to wander off on my own?"

Bell walked down the aisle between the desks as he spoke, his steps causing the wooden floor to creak. He kept a pointer tucked under his arm, turning it absentmindedly between his fingers. He went up the next row until he reached the student sitting in the first desk. "Mr. Phillips," he commanded. "Stand up, please."

Like the rest of the boys, Phillips had been listening to the footsteps and could hear Bell coming. There was surprise written across the boy's face. His head snapped at the sound of his name, and he jerked up to his feet, like an unfolding stepladder. Phillips attempted to speak, but found he had no voice. After a moment of silence, he said croaked, "Yes, sir."

Bell walked around the boy, slowly turned, and faced him. "How tall are you, Phillips?"

"I'm not sure, sir," he said, voice faltering. "I mean, it's been a long time since anyone measured me."

John noted that Phillips was tall for his age. The boy stared straight ahead, avoiding any hint that he might be so bold as to make eye contact.

"Is that so?" said Bell, his voice even. "I do believe you've not been looking after your uniform. There are loose threads on your coat."

Without thinking, Phillips looked down and could see one of his buttons had a thread hanging from it. He quickly pinched the thread between his thumb and forefinger and pulled. But the string didn't break. Instead, it grew longer, until it dangled from his fingers. The button bounced off the floor and rolled under another boy's desk. Phillips' face turned bright red and John knew the other students would tease him after class. They would not stop until some new victim did something to make himself stand out.

"Attention to detail, boys. You would all do well to pay attention to the small things." Bell continued to pace to the front of the room, turned slowly and said, "Be seated, Mr. Phillips."

Phillips sat down and John watched his shoulders relax. "What they say is true," whispered John to himself. "I could feel Bell watching me during the entire incident, even when his back was to the class."

The next day John discovered which group he belonged in, and it wasn't the sheep. The class had been in session no more than a few minutes when Bell took particular satisfaction in John. A sly smile creased his face as he turned to face his pupil. "Mr. Newton, just look at the way you're dressed. I must say, you've apparently learned nothing from Mr. Phillips' failure to follow the dress code."

John flinched as everyone's attention turned on him. "I'm not sure what you mean, sir."

"Your neck scarf, Newton, straighten your scarf." Bell drew out the last word of each sentence.

"Yes, sir," said John. *Guess it's my turn in the barrel.* He hastily reached up with both hands and struggled to center the garment without benefit of a mirror. His fingers told him the tie was exactly where it ought to be. As always, he had taken great care to press his uniform, and make sure it was free of any loose threads. The last step was a final look in the mirror. His shirt, trousers and belt buckle were perfectly aligned. Anything less drew unwanted attention and demerits.

Bell's heels sounded against the wooden floor as he walked across the classroom and stood over his victim, watching as the rest of the class bore witness to the silent humiliation. The more John fumbled, the more frustrated he got. Finally, his face burning with indignation, he let his hands drop idly to his sides.

Mr. Bell picked up the pointer he was holding. A pall fell over the room as he glowered at John, who looked up and met the school master eye-to-eye.

Bell spoke in a low voice, often leaving the ears of his students straining to make out the words. "Hold out your hand, please, palm up."

John carried out the order, wondering what trick his tormentor had up his sleeve. The schoolteacher pocketed the hickory stick in between his crossed arms. Sometimes he would use the instrument to tap the top of a desk as he walked between the rows, pointing out minor infractions. Some days he used it as a pointer, emphasizing a notation on the chalkboard. And when in public, where the other staff members might casually observe their colleague, it was nothing more than a walking stick used to steady a harmless old man's gait as he navigated from building to building. But today Bell would demonstrate another use, one he kept hidden from the rest of his peers.

With the stick still clamped beneath his arm, Bell waited. Before the boy's hand was completely open, before brain could warn John to pull his hand back, the instructor slashed through the air. A muffled crack shattered the silence, followed by more pain than John imagined possible.

"The Father," murmured Bell in a low, even voice. "Now bring it up level again, boy."

John grimaced, although he followed the head master's instruction. Once again, the cane struck with blinding speed and the crack of second-growth-Hickory against flesh and bone resonated throughout the room.

"The Son," hissed Bell, baring his teeth. He nodded for the student to lift his hand one last time.

John wondered if it was humanly possible to bring his trembling arm back to its original position after receiving such a blow. More than that, he doubted that he could force himself to hold it in place, knowing a third blow was coming.

He needn't have concerned himself. No sooner had he willed himself to open the hand, than the instructor delivered a third and final blow.

"And the Holy Spirit," concluded Bell. He coolly walked back to the front of the classroom, hands folded behind his back, fingering the cane. Then he turned and faced John. "You need a change of attitude if you expect to fit in here, Mr. Newton."

John's throat closed, holding down a tidal wave of emotion that kept him from answering. Then he realized that no one expected him to. The other students had witnessed the cruel punishment many times, and the response was always the same: silently bowed heads. Yet John could see compassion in their eyes. Their sympathy was accompanied by a barely audible sigh of relief. Bell had picked someone else, and every other boy was safe for another moment.

"Let us return to our texts," said the teacher, offhandedly. A rustle of pages filled the silence as each boy opened his book, acting as though nothing had happened.

In the weeks that followed, John was often the target of Bell's ever appraising eye. Each day the little man vigilantly searched for a new infraction. John endured the cane so often that some days his fingers involuntarily curled into a tight ball, incapable of turning the pages of his book.  Because he feared the fierce punishments, he became distracted and could no longer think clearly. When asked a question, he often froze and was unable to speak, even if he knew the answer.

Bell seemed to take all of this in stride. "Daydreaming again, Mr. Newton?" asked Bell.

Is there no end to how many times he will ask the same question? "No, sir, I'm just having a little trouble concentrating this morning."

"Your mind strays too often these days, young man," Bell intoned. He tapped the pointer at the side of his desk, punctuating each word. "Lack of concentration can be a fatal character flaw here at Essex. You must get hold of yourself."

Try as he would, John could not get his nerves to settle down. Each week his apprehension increased to a new and bedeviling level. Nor could he stop his hands from trembling. One morning as he and James sat down at their desks, he said, "I don't think I can take much more of this."

James put a steady hand on his roommate's shoulder. "Look at me," he demanded. "Look straight into my eyes."

John fought an overwhelming urge to keep from bursting into tears, and did as his friend instructed.

"You're stronger than you think boyo. If you're a mind to, you can take his guff all day long, and then ask for more. It's all up here," he said, tapping his finger against his temple.

Encouraged, John steeled himself, praying throughout the day to a God he swore could not exist. When the abuse continued, his thoughts grew resentful. *Is He listening? Is God even there?*

The next night John did his homework after the evening meal. He said little to James, and went straight to bed after closing the last textbook. Sleep came quickly, but he remained restless throughout the night, tormented by frightful dreams. His eyes opened all too soon as the morning sun pushed through the window, robbing him of needed rest. His aching body stretched and pleaded for clemency. Surely, he hadn't slept more than an hour. During those moments when he had managed to drift off, his mind wrestled with terrifying dreams. He swung his feet out of bed and walked across the cold floor to the bathroom. Shocked as he passed the mirror, he saw deep circles under his eyes. I look as though I'm dying.

In the midst of all the frustration and anxiety, there was another voice, one with soothing tones of assurance. It came from a compilation of scriptures his mother had read. "You are of great value, and a child of God, and you were fearfully made in my image. There is nothing that can separate you from my love."

John believed the words and hid them in his heart. I am better than what Bell is trying to make me believe. I won't give in.

But despite his best efforts, John soon reached his breaking point.

The school bell clanged the next morning, signaling the students to rise. Something inside of John told him he could go no further.

"Hurry up and get out of bed," James said, trying to sound encouraging. "You'll feel better after you eat breakfast."

"I can't," moaned John. "My stomach is killing me." He pulled his pillow into his abdomen and twisted from side to side.

James looked down as he tucked in his shirt, buttoned his trousers and stepped into his shoes, almost simultaneously. "Either way," he said, "you'll need to see the nurse, so you might as well get up."

John's muscles worked against one another, and sharp spasms pulsated in the right side of his neck. Getting dressed proved a challenge. He pressed forward, first putting one hand through the sleeve of his shirt, then the other.

"James," he said in a voice that sounded like sandpaper rubbing against wood, "can you pull the back of my shirt up for me?"

James walked over and gingerly held the collar with two fingers, lifting the garment up over his friend's shoulders. "Can you manage the buttons?" he asked.

"Yes," came the voice again. "I can make it."

James looked at his friend with genuine concern. "What about the trousers?"

John's tone carried an air of forced independence. He picked up the pants and said, "Thanks, I can manage. Go ahead now. I'll catch up with you later."

The walk to the infirmary was slow, each step a painful process of putting one foot in front of the other. When he reached the small brick building, he noted its plain unadorned face. Only a faded sign gave any accounting of its purpose. Inside he found a small waiting room where he sat down on a spindled chair with no arms. Not knowing what else to do, he waited until a nurse finally opened the interior door.

"And just what brings you here?" said the nurse, looking down at him, arms folded across her chest.

As was the case with Mr. Bell, many a joke was passed around about Nurse Bosworth. She rarely came out of the infirmary, but John saw her when she left at the end of the day. She was a plump woman who wore the traditional uniform of her profession, a white dress, partially covered by a blue pinafore displaying a red cross in its center. Gossip alleged that her poor work ethic prevented her from finding a proper position. Her previous job at a London hospital ended in disaster. After a pattern of cutting corners, the administrator confronted her. There was, of course, no real choice and she was gone that afternoon. After months of searching, she applied at the school and was delighted when they made her an offer.

James explained that state law required the administration have a nurse on staff; however, the position did little more than reassure the parents that someone was looking after the health of their children. She needed a job, and by and large most schools maintained low expectations when it came to nursing skills. It was a perfect fit. The school saved money by offering a below average salary, compensated by room and board. There was another benefit, at least from the nurse's point of view. There was no doctor on staff, no one constantly looking over her shoulder, no one who would criticize her half-hearted interest in her duties. Best of all, the residents of Essex remained healthy most of the time, permitting Bosworth to take uninterrupted afternoon naps.

She placed a hand along his forehead and said, "We don't put up with any malingering here, son. You've slight fever, but nothing to be alarmed about." Then, cocking her head to one side, she said, "You'll feel better if you just obey the rules."

"Yes, ma'am," John said. He gritted his teeth and walked out of the office and back toward the classroom. He rotated his arm and tried to ease the pain that traversed across his shoulder and neck. I'm at the end of my rope. Can't go on like this much longer.

* * *

The following day the boys filed into their classroom in their usual formation. However, on this morning someone else stood next to the blackboard, watching and nodding as each student entered the doorway.

A man not yet thirty, with wavy black hair combed back, and a smile in his voice, announced, "My name is Mr. Peterson. Mr. Bell has been granted a leave of absence, and I will be taking his place for the remainder of the semester."

There was a peculiar silence in the room, and then the class erupted into spontaneous applause. Papers sailed aimlessly through the air. Mr. Peterson did not smile, but neither did he try to rein the boys in. He let their enthusiasm continue until it lost its natural momentum. With a voice that exuded both patience and calm, the teacher continued, "We shall begin with chapter ten in our history books. I believe that's where you left off."

No explanation regarding Mr. Bell was forthcoming, and his name never came up among the staff, at least, not within earshot of the students. As far as the other teachers were concerned, he was gone and soon forgotten. In their world, his presence had been irrelevant. But John's world changed dramatically, and for the better. He liked Mr. Peterson immediately. This new and younger man loved teaching and energized his methods with humor, bringing out the best in what he affectionately referred to as "his boys." John found his work challenging and the seeds of learning planted early on by his mother took root and flourished.

During finals week of the following year, Mr. Peterson placed each Latin exam face down on the desk of every student. John was the only exception. He looked down at the paper and at once saw a note scrawled across the margin: "Well done, Mr. Newton! Well done!"

John leaned back into his desk for a moment and let the rest of the class fade into the background. I've turned a corner. I don't know if God was a part of this or not, but I survived. Now it's time to move on.

He leaned to one side and whispered, "James, my father has written. I'm leaving school and going to sea."

Chapter 5

Tomorrow Not Promised

England (1736)

"Lord, make me to know my end, and what is the measure of my days, that I may know how frail I am." Psalms 39:4

John was late--again.

He stood on the wooden dock, stained green from the Thames Estuary, and filled his lungs with salt air. His hand shielded his eyes from the hot sun as he strained for a better look at the battleship. The crew was aloft on the yardarm of the main mast, tying down the canvas sails.

Docked a few hundred meters from the shore, the man-o-war was a thrilling sight for a boy of thirteen. And his friends, too far out to hear if he yelled, cut through the waves in a longboat, headed for a tour of the Ajax.

John had followed his father to see the previous year on his twelfth birthday. "One day," said the captain, "you'll command your own ship. And with any luck, you'll end up owning one or two."

Captain Newton spent all of his spare time teaching John the art of good seamanship. Properly reading and comprehending charts, navigation, the complexities and proper use of a sextant were all skills required of an able sea captain. And there were discussions about leadership. At times John was permitted to eat alone with his father.

The captain would share examples of the day. "A soft word will gain you the willing cooperation of your men," he said, poking the air with his fork. "But there are times when a stern hand is called for. That's the difference between a request and an order, and sometimes the difference between life and death."

John was even allowed to steer the vessel, although he had to stand on a box to see the large compass, located just on the other side of the wheel. But there was no special treatment or favor given. His father set a high standard, and expected him to learn, just as he had in school. He also shared in all the lesser duties required to run a ship. A tight well-run ship required that daily scrubbing of decks, the mending of sails twice over, so they didn't rip again. He stood watch and climbed masts that reached up into the blue sky, leaving him dizzy when he looked down. It was a fresh adventurous start in life, and he loved it.

When John returned to England, he made friends with the other neighborhood boys, something his stepmother disliked, thinking them too rough and undisciplined. The idea of becoming a preacher now seemed vague and unfamiliar. He saw himself more like a man of the world, having spent a year with nothing but older men.

Now, standing on the dock, he desperately wanted to join his friends in the boat, but he was late, again.

"Those your mates?"

For the first time John noticed an old man kneeling at the corner of the mooring, tying down a small boat. His brimmed blue hat shaded a leathery face, lined from years of exposure to salt air and the unrelenting sun. It was the man's uniform, the coat and hat of a first mate that caught John's attention. At first, his reflexes almost made him come to attention, but then he caught himself. He was a little embarrassed but still respectful.

"Yes, sir, they are," said John

The man groaned as he straightened up and rubbed his lower back. Still looking out to sea, he said, "So, your friends took off without you, eh? I'll wager this wasn't the first time you missed out. Them that's late once, is late most of the time."

John was willing to bet the man was always on time, perhaps even early but certainly never late. One did not rise to the highest enlisted rank without dedication and self-discipline.

John looked out over the water, able to make out the dark outline of his five friends, etched against the azure horizon. They were half-way to the ship now, and his bones ached to be with them.

John watched as one boy began to roughhouse, pushing against another lad's shoulder. Although the other boy held onto the brow of the craft, he leaned over its edge, laughing and raising his arm in defense. Then he pushed back, only harder, leading the other boy to stand up. Soon, arms tangled together as each contestant wrestled to overpower his opponent.

"Hey, sit down, you blokes," yelled a boy at the end of the longboat. "You're gonna turn us over, you are."

As if fulfilling a prophecy, the weight of the boat shifted sharply to one side, then the next. Terror spread through the occupants like a plague; no one could swim. Small hands reached out for the high side of the craft, which now lifted completely out of the water. Terrorized at the possibility of drowning, one boy scrambled over the others as he looked back at the sea lapping at his heels. Then John watched as the boat flipped into the air, tossing all of its passengers into the sea.

Panic-stricken, John gasped as arms flailed about in the water and hands clawed the empty air. Some tried to cling to the side of the hull, hopelessly struggling to grip the slippery wood. In less time than it took to take a deep breath, their muscles grew weary and the boat slipped below the surface.

In their final moments, only the macabre silhouette of figures jerking about against a dark blue sky remained. John turned to the old man, arms outstretched. "Do something!" he pleaded.

The sailor's expression revealed nothing more than that of a dispassionate observer. He folded his arms and said evenly, "There's nothing to be done, boy. I've seen this before. A merciful God will take them in a moment."

No sooner were the old man's words spoken than John's friends stopped moving. After a moment, only two of the bodies remained of the surface, face down, rising and falling as the gentle tide pulled them out to sea.

Then, in the same way the dawn cracks through the darkness, his mind revealed a stunning truth. I was supposed to be with them.

Had I not been late, my lifeless body would be out there among the others. He struggled to grasp the complexity of it all, but it was more than his young mind could comprehend.

"I know what you're thinking," said the old man, interrupting John's thoughts. The voice seemed to come from somewhere far behind him. "Don't bother trying to make any sense of it, not on this side of Heaven."

Without warning, one of his mother's favorite Bible verses flashed into John's mind, the one she spoke as she lay dying: "Since we are not promised tomorrow, today is the day of our salvation – the day to get right with God."

It was too much to bear and John turned away, his forearm brushing tears from his cheek. He did not understand any of it, and he didn't want to. Why did God allow this? They were no more than innocent boys.

He turned his back on the horrific scene, and then began the slow, thoughtful walk back to town.

Chapter 6

The Shadow of Death

Gillingham, England (1738)

"Yea, though I walk through the valley of the shadow of death I will fear no evil, for thou art with me." Psalm 23:4

Robert held the rank of midshipman, and was a year older than John. They served on a clipper ship bound for the Mediterranean on a two-year voyage. Both knew that regulations forbid fraternization between officers and sailors, but like all young men, they had enjoyed discussing their dreams and common interests. John saw the captain was watching on more than one occasion, but the skipper turned and looked the other way. I wonder if the old man lets us get away with it because of we're young? Or perhaps, the old man just is getting soft.

Careful not to abuse the unofficial privilege, the two spent many evenings on the isolated bow of the ship, where they conversed at great length. Throughout the voyage, Robert displayed unusual leadership skills for one so young, but he also had a well-concealed rebellious streak. He remained faithful in all his duties while aboard ship, never calling his character into question. On land, however, he enjoyed a glass of ale and the company of a pretty woman.

In time, he invited John to come home with him to visit his father's farm. From the moment they arrived, the two young men stood looking out over the view. The emerald green hills rolled endlessly into one another, divided by hedge rows taller than a man on horse-

52

back.

"It's stunning," John said. "You're a fortunate man to live in such country. Your father must be quite wealthy."

Robert ignored the remark. Instead, his mouth turned upward into a mischievous grin. Before they had even stowed their sea bags, he said, "Come with me to the barn. I've been waiting for months to show you something."

The barn door creaked as the two put their shoulders to it and pushed. A shaft of light penetrated the darkness and when John's eyes adjusted, he saw a magnificent black horse leaning over the rail of her stall. She had wide intelligent eyes and sheen across her coat. She stopped munching on a pile of hay, lifted her head, and snorted. The sheer size of the animal left John breathless. "She's splendid," he said, reaching up to pet the animal. But before his hand reached the animal's forehead, she whinnied and tossed her nose high into the thick air. Then she eased forward and tentatively tested the intruder, her flared nostrils sniffing.

"She's a two year-old and loves nothing more than to run all out." Robert fished a carrot from his coat pocket. He saved the treat for this moment. He handed it over to John. "Here, she can't resist a good bribe."

The horse eagerly dropped her soft muzzle to John's palm and munched loudly on the delicacy.

"I can't wait any longer," said Robert, pointing to the tack room. In no time, the trio walked the saddled horse along the grassy trail that led to an open field. Skeptical of the animal's temperament, John walked to one side. Using his friend as a buffer, he watched the horse snort into the air and rock her head up and down.

"She knows what's coming," said Robert, handing over the reins. "She'll run like the wind. But mind you, she's just a youngster and still a might skittish, especially on wet grass."

John nodded. They came to the top of a knoll and he worked his foot into the stirrup and pulled. Settling into the brown leather saddle, it took him a moment to adjust to the height of the horse, which looked back at him with a judgmental eye. Then, without any signal from its rider, the mount unexpectedly stepped forward and broke into a trot. John, surprised at the sudden start, lifted the reigns, leaned forward and prepared himself for what was sure to be a day to remember. "Haw!" he yelled, and gave the animal her head.

As if anticipating the command, the horse stretched out into a long, easy rhythm that was as natural and fluid as the wind. The cool air buffeted against John's face. His balance remained steady and true, giving him an ever-increasing sense of confidence. He kicked his heels against the horse's flanks and felt her launch into an all-out run. Hooves pounded against spring grass, keeping time with the horse's labored breathing.

Far behind, Robert ran to the top of a rise, tracking his friend's direction of travel. Exhilarated, he his heart pounded in time with each thump of hooves against grass.

The scene of his friend racing over the hills exhilarated Robert. He cupped his hands around his mouth and yelled, "Keep her by the hedge row."

John tried to steer the horse more to his right, but she ignored his awkward prodding. Then, without warning, the horse slipped.

Her hooves slid across on the wet grass, and her neck arched as she went down on one knee. The magnificent animal desperately tried to recover, got halfway up, and then slipped and fell once more.

The momentum of the fall hurled John over the animal's head, causing the sky and ground to merge into one long blur. His body vaulted into a slow motion tumble until it struck the ground with a heavy thud, his back absorbing the full impact. He bounced once, and then rolled several times until his torso lost momentum and skidded to a stop.

John lay deathly still, unable to breath. He waited for an eternally long moment, fighting to remain conscious. Finally, as if a spark of life spontaneously ignited, his chest expanded as the atmosphere forced oxygen into his lungs.

Robert ran down the hill and slid on his side until he came to a rest next to his friend. "Are you all right?"

John lay very still, afraid to move, mentally taking inventory of the dizzy is all."

Robert stood, offered a hand and helped pull his friend onto his feet. In a solemn voice he said, "That was more than a little close."

John looked around and saw the horse was standing nearby, calmly she'd broken a leg."

"You don't understand. I'm not talking about the horse. Look at that." Robert pointed in the direction of the hedge row.

John's eyes followed his friend's line of direction. Next to where his body had catapulted into the air, a sharp spear-shaped branch protruded from the thicket. He had literally been within inches of certain death. Had he fallen to the side, instead of forward, the spike would have run him through.

After a moment of silence, both boys burst into nervous laughter. They walked over and inspected the branch, marveling at its iron-like density.

Gone now was the conspiratorial smile Robert usually sported. Now his voice had a serious tone. "Come on, that's enough excitement for one day. Let's get the horse back before anyone finds out what happened."

John took up the reigns and soberly followed his friend.

That afternoon he walked toward home, reflecting on how the day might have ended. The grim reality of his friends drowning remained fresh in his memory. Is this a coincidence, or did God just spare my life again?

Chapter 7

A Slow Poison

England (1740)

"Beware lest anyone cheat you through philosophy and empty deceit, according to the tradition of men, according to the basic principles of the world, and not according to Christ." 1 Colossians 2:8

*Lord Shaftesbury's Characteristics* had a red leather cover and gold inlaid letters. It stood out from the rest of the books, and immediately piqued Newton's curiosity.

A sign above the bookstore read Come Inside. The invitation spoke to an urgent and longstanding need to connect intellectually with a part of Newton that cried out for something more than the humdrum routine of life aboard ship. Although he spent some of his leave drinking in pubs with his shipmates, he longed for a respite from the routine. His mind had an insatiable craving for new and challenging concepts. And on this warm afternoon, he was on the hunt for something to read and some time to himself. Once inside the shop, he examined the book's eloquent cover and turned the pages through the different chapters. It was a book on religion, or so it seemed to be. And although he had struggled with his beliefs, his curiosity got the better of him.

"You're looking at popular book, my friend," said the balding shopkeeper, as he approached. He was a small, slender man who wore a leatherwork apron. "It's a favorite among those who call themselves

Free Thinkers."

The words rang with familiarity. Newton recalled that his mother favored the Independent Church, often referred to as Dissenters, given the label because of their opposition to the Church of England. Perhaps he would find something in common with his early religious roots. He dug down into his pocket, fished out a few coins and paid the man.

"Thank you, sir," said the proprietor, handing back some change with a satisfied smile. "I hope you enjoy the book."

Newton wandered down the street and seated himself on a bench beneath a large tree with branches that provided some welcome relief from the sun. He leaned his back against the trunk and from the moment he began reading, the book began to take effect like a slow poison. Characteristics offered an entirely new way of looking at God, one that allowed men the freedom to indulge in any kind sinful of appetite. Orthodox teachings had become unfashionable, it purported. Lord Shaftsbury professed that God was unconcerned about the insignificant events of a man's life, nor was He the great architect of some plan for humanity. Instead, the Creator kept his distance, inserting himself in the affairs of the world only when He deemed it necessary.

Newton found the theory fascinating and absorbed one precept after another; and, the more he read, the greater the appeal of its message. He reflected on his own life and soon concluded that God had in fact shown no care or mercy for young John when his mother died, or when his father sent him away to boarding school. God can't be bothered with worrying about a little drunkenness or carousing with women. John concluded that there was no need for a Heaven or Hell. Sin only existed in the minds of those willing to submit to the slavery of the Anglican Church, where greedy leaders leached off the donations of weak-minded parishioners, veritable sheep who allowed the pastorate to do all their thinking for them.

The concept of total freedom inflated Newton's sense of self-importance and pride, a sin that appealed to all men since the beginning of time. For years, his anger at God had dominated his thoughts and, therefore, his conduct. Now he could justify his roiling without fear of any consequence. This fantastic new theology permitted him to act on any impulse, whether it was anger or lust, and remain right with God.

The book explained that mankind was free to live however one chose to live, without consequences. In the end, God would forgive everything.

Chapter 8

Temptations of the Flesh

London, England (1742)

"For by means of a harlot a man is reduced to a loaf of bread: and the adulteress will prey upon his precious life." Proverbs 6:26

Newton was asleep, and then he wasn't.

He looked about and realized the morning sun had yet to break through on the horizon. Only the sounds of slumbering men rose and fell in the black darkness of the ship's quarters.

*What was it? What stirred?*

He shut his eyes again, once more seeking the comfort of deep slumber. After a few moments, he stretched and looked up at the ceiling. It's hopeless. I'm wide awake. Then, out of nowhere, he was seized with an overpowering impulse to pray.

Where is this coming from and why now? Prayer hasn't been a part of my life for years. I've always found a solution without relying on God, which in most cases is just a weakness. Yet, there's this insistent pulling, this silent voice urging me forward.

Newton finally strung a few words together, stumbling as he spoke. Guidance seemed an appropriate spiritual request. "Father in Heaven," he began, "be with me and guide me through this day."

Finishing the simple prayer, he felt an immediate release, as if something had literally let go of his soul. I'm not sure what just happened, but something did. Most days I don't believe there is a God.

Other times I believe he exists but is cruel. Now I find myself praying.

He slipped out of his hammock and started dressing. None of this makes sense, and I have more important things planned for today.

By mid-morning, the men restlessly milled about on the main deck, waiting to receive their liberty chits. Each one signed his pass, saluted the officer-of-the-day and the ship's flag, and then cheerily padded down the gangplank that rested on the edge of the dock. The town and all its pleasures awaited him.

As the men collected into small groups, one of them called out, "John, come join us. I know a pub that offers seafaring men a good time and serves something better than the rotgut you'll find at most taverns."

Newton shifted his weight, holding back till he could find the appropriate words. Up until now he had avoided carousing with the other sailors. There were other places in town he preferred to visit. Having to live with the other men while confined to a ship was one thing but subjecting himself to their crude public behavior was quite another. The watchful eye of any officer held their behavior in check while aboard ship, but in town, they were free to act as they pleased.

"Come on, Johnny," said the old seadog, his arm beckoning. "It's time to find out what life's all about."

Newton looked at the weathered seafarer. He probably thinks it's his duty to break me in, the old salt teaching the kid the ways of the world. Truth is, I'm just as weary of officers as they are. They're always ordering us about, acting like they owned us. Suddenly, all his resistance faded, and his chest expelled a large swoosh of air. The others wanted him to come along. Why shouldn't he experience the rough side of life just once? He walked over to the man, looped an arm around his neck and beamed. "Lead the way, your grace, and show me your worst."

The pub was two streets over, and soon the men ducked through a low doorway and down into what appeared to be a former cellar and now a tavern. The air was dank and the walls slick with sweat. Newton followed the men as they snaked between sailors from other ships and sat at a long wooden table with one unsteady leg badly in need of repair. The establishment anticipated the needs of its patrons and met them with all due haste.

"Ahoy, mates," shouted the bartender, as he fanned an arm through the air. He was a short man, oblivious to the stains on the white apron joined around his generous middle. Anticipating the needs of his patrons, he shuffled over to their table, arms laden with mugs of rum.

"Welcome, boys," he continued in a voice that rang with false amiability. "You've come to the right place for a good time, you have."

Each man lifted and drained his glass without pause, and just as hastily landed it back on the table, signaling the call for a second then a third round. The coarse language of the worldly men grew louder and more loutish with each additional refill. Newton, who was still learning how to hold his liquor, looked around to see if anyone was watching. The man seated next to him elbowed him in the ribs and muttered, "That's it, John. Won't be long before that warm glow takes hold of ya."

Newton had to admit that he did feel more relaxed. Each vulgar joke grew funnier than the one before. In all the frivolity, he scarcely noticed the silhouette of the large woman perched on a stool in the corner shadows of the bar. She patiently examined her nails, waiting for the right moment to make her entrance. It was only when she slowly strolled into a shaft of light that Newton caught sight of her.

Mandy tested the limits of her white blouse. Her hair was coal black, drawn back on the sides and held in place by two red ribbons. She rested a hand on each hip and gently rolled into each step.

"You strong lads need your glasses refilled," she said, beckoning to the barkeep with a lazy tilt of her head. Although she addressed the group as a whole, her dazzling eyes lingered on the youngest and most vulnerable in the crowd.

Embarrassed as he was, Newton met her gaze, looked away, then back again. He found himself staring and simply could not resist the woman's unspoken invitation.

A chorus of laughter broke out as the closest man reached up and pulled the wench to his side. "Give us a kiss, lass," he said with a liquid voice.

Without hesitation, the woman leaned forward and gently kissed the man's cheek before whispering something in his ear. Both erupted into laughter, and the sailor swatted at the woman's prominent fanny, only to miss as she swirled out of reach, dodging the good-natured blow. Her teasing smile encouraged each man, making him feel as though he was the singular recipient of her charms. She brushed one seaman's hair back out of his face, graced another's jaw with sensuous fingertips, and still leaned over toward another, seducing him with a peek at her substantial cleavage, all of which fueled the group's exhilaration.

Newton's gaping jaw dropped in astonishment. Never before had he witnessed a woman display her body with such abandon. He gave up all hope of averting his eyes.

She continued to maneuver between customers, savoring the moment of spellbinding control. Working her way over to Newton, she met his admiring stare and held it for a long inviting moment. "You're a fine looking young one, you are," she entreated. "I'd fancy taking you for a roll in the hay."

The other men chortled away as Newton remained mute, his eyes glazed over. For the first time in his young life, he could not think of a response. One of the cluster reached across the table and grabbed the boy's arm. Half rising out of his chair, he challenged, "Come on boy, this is your day. It's time to become a man."

The straightforward invitation was unnerving, and Newton burned with passion. He looked around the table of onlookers, who reminded him of thirsty dogs lapping up the delicious moment. Regardless of what happened next, this instant would monopolize the ship's gossip for weeks to come.

The barmaid was an old hand at the game of seduction. She leaned forward even further, took the young boy's face in her hands and held it in front of her. In that still moment, her captivating eyes melted any last vestiges of resistance.

"You *are* a clever boy," she said, reaching down and clasping his hand.

Newton lamely attempted to beg off. "I'm not much at socializing, miss."

Another burst of laughter erupted from the crowd, and Newton shifted nervously in his chair, looking first at the woman then back at the men.

She gingerly placed her free hand around Newton's neck, came close and whispered in his ear. "I've a room on the upper floor. Come with me, love, and I'll take you to paradise."

Without waiting for an answer, she pulled Newton onto his unsteady feet, but like a man clapped in irons, he was unable to move. She seemed to sense his reluctance and pulled his face down to her breasts.

Newton opened his mouth in protest, but a rapid assortment of lurid remarks from the men drowned out any protest.

"Go on, Johnny, have some fun on us," said one man, as he took a drink and plunked his heavy glass down on the table, spilling much its contents. He fished out a coin from his pocket and snapped it down alongside the mug. "We'll gladly chip in for your first time."

Mandy pulled young Newton alongside her, pressing her supple flesh into his chest. Even more self-conscious, he turned away in an awkward effort to conceal his obvious arousal.

The woman led him across the floor and up the stairs, pushed along by the cheering throng. Newton's mind pulled one way then another, racing between his lustful thoughts and the memory of the prayer he hastily uttered that morning. He was about to break away, when the woman pulled him into her room and pushed the door closed with a swing of her hip.

Chapter 9

Polly

London, England (1742)

"When I was a child, I spoke as a child, I understood as a child, I thought as a child; but when I became a man, I put away childish things." 1Corinthians 13:11

Captain Newton poured his second cup of morning tea and pulled up a chair at the kitchen table. John, who sat eating some fried eggs across from his father, noted the cheerful look on the captain's face. After a hasty bite of bread and a slug of the coffee, Newton Sr. turned toward his son and broadly announced, "John, I'm pleased to tell you that I have wonderful news."

John, having moments before emerged from the bedroom where he spent most of his time, wiped a hand across a sleepy eyelid. He was still wearing his nightshirt, and too much sleep left him groggy. He was sure the news must be about work since he had been unemployed for months and had no desire to change his circumstances.

"My old friend, Joseph Manesty," his father continued speaking as he brought the cup up to his lips, "has agreed to offer you a position, one with a handsome wage and a wide open future, if you work hard."

The lad of seventeen straightened up and tried to concentrate. "Captain Manesty?" he asked, trying to recall the name.

"Yes, yes, I'm sure you remember me speaking of him. He's going to offer you an opportunity to learn the sugarcane business in Jamaica.

If you do well--and I'm sure you will--one day you'll be the owner of your own plantation."

The captain waited for his son's response, but when none was forthcoming, his patience quickly waned. "Well, what do you say, John?" he asked with an inflection of irritability.

"The idea is a bit daunting, sir. I've never been to Jamaica."

"It's not much different than most of the places you've sailed. If you work hard," he said again, "Manesty will make you a full partner."

John drew in a deep breath and inwardly groaned. The idea of making money was certainly alluring, as long as he didn't have to show too much ambition. But living in another part of the world for the rest of his life was less than appealing

The captain stood up and looked down at his son. "I'm not going to mince words, John. You're scheduled to sail on one of Manesty's ships two weeks from today."

There was a moment of silence when neither of them spoke.

Since John offered no further objection, Captain Newton solidified the bargain. "Good," he pronounced, "then the matter is settled."

"I have one more item of business. I'm sending you to Chatham for a few days." The captain pulled a letter from his pocket and handed it over. "Years ago your mother and Abigail Catlett were very close, best friends, in fact. She was unable to visit Elizabeth before her death, but now she's asking us to join her."

"*We*," said John. "Sounds more like she's asking both of us to visit Come to think of it, isn't this something better suited for you, since you know the family?"

The older man examined the bottom of his mug and swallowed the last of the brew, and dabbed his lips lightly with a napkin. "It might be, but it's rumored that Abigail resented my getting married so soon after your mother's passing. Frankly, it puts me in a difficult position, one I'd rather not have to deal with. You, on the other hand, will be warmly received."

John wanted to end the conversation. A visit to the Catlett's, the training involved in running a plantation, and having to live in Jamaica was too much for him to absorb all at once. Instead, his mind wandered back to the woman in the tavern. It had become his favorite escape.

Although he'd never seen her before, John recognized Abigail Catlett the instant he saw her kneeling on the grass, churning the soil around several red rosebushes in the flowerbed that lined the front of a white clapboard house. She was an average size woman, who wore a blue linen dress covered by a dark apron. Her dark hair was parted in the middle, was brushed back on the sides, and it shone in the light. John estimated her age at thirty, although she looked much younger.

When she stood and noticed John, her fine features broke into a warm delightsome smile. She cleaned her hands on the apron and bustled over to the picket fence that bordered the modest yard. "John," she exclaimed, "at last you've arrived."

Caught off guard, John stopped at the fence line. After all, she had never seen him. He slung his sea bag to the ground.

Abigail reached out for his hands, leaned forward and kissed him on both cheeks. "Come around to the gate and come inside," she said, her voice bubbling with joy. "You must be exhausted. Let me get you something to drink. Oh, I am so pleased that you came. We have a great deal of catching up to do." Out of breath, she caught herself. "Just listen to me. I just can't stop talking."

Abigail led John through the doorway, where the simplicity and order of the living room caught his attention. It had the same quality as a well-maintained ship standing by for inspection. He noticed the family pictures hanging over the dark walnut mantle that lay suspended above a red brick fireplace, the soft brown walls accented by mocha colored curtains, and the blue oval rug on the floor. There was a sofa between a handmade rocker and a blue overstuffed chair. In the corner, a hurricane lamp rested on an antique round table. It was a cheerful house, one that offered a warm welcome to its guests. I've not known the warmth of real home since my mother died.

Newton eased his way into the dining room. For the first time he noticed a beautiful young girl patiently sitting at a spinning wheel. In no more time than it took the young man to draw a breath, his mind collected every detail of the lass. Curly blonde ringlets framed her delicate porcelain features, accented by a soft blush across her cheeks. She was radiant, but it was more than her physical beauty that captured John's attention. There was a pureness about her. And when their eyes met, John's heart melted, and he instantly knew he was in love.

"Mary," said Abigail, walking between the two, "I want you to come in here and meet someone. This is Elizabeth's son, John Newton."

The young girl stood and strolled into the living room, and offered a polite curtsy. "Pleased to meet you, sir," she said, nodding her head slightly.

Although she leaned forward, her captivating gaze never strayed from John, who found himself staring back at the young girl. Catching himself, John removed his hat, which he now wished he had done upon entering the house, bowed at the waist, and said in his most formal voice, "By all means, ma'am. The pleasure is mine." It was the best he could do under the circumstances.

"Please sit down, John," Abigail said, as her hand directed the young man to the overstuffed chair.

Mary maintained a respectable distance on the neighboring sofa. John started to sit down, abruptly caught himself, and allowed the ladies to take their seats first.

"You must tell us the news of your family, John. Your father recently wrote that you are following in his footsteps as a merchant seaman."

"Yes, ma'am," said John, with a prideful lift of his head, although he didn't know why. He wasn't at all sure he wanted to go back to sea. Then the most bizarre words popped out of his mouth. "But the real purpose of my next voyage is to explore the possibility of becoming a plantation owner."

"A man of property," said Abigail with an approving tone. "It sounds as though you'll have a prosperous future."

Newton primarily spoke to Abigail but frequently turned towards Mary, hoping to encourage a smile. His heart kept pounding, and he felt his confidence was slipping away. *How strange that I have traveled halfway around the world, can handle any assignment aboard even the largest vessel, and yet feel like a tongue-tied schoolboy when in the presence of ladies.*

After briefly catching up on the family news, Abigail stood, and said, "Mary, why don't you show John the garden out back, while I finish making dinner."

Without hesitation, Mary stood and took her new friend by the hand. Together they threaded their way through the house and into the dappled afternoon. A white gazebo rested at the center of a well-manicured garden of colorful flowers, where the two sat side by side. A bouquet of large Magnolia blossoms laced across the top of the arbor excited John's senses, and for the first time since his first encounter with a woman, he struggled to find something to say. His ability to make conversation was rusty, and he found himself repeatedly stumbling as he tried to put his thoughts into words. After several false starts, he finally threw out what he considered an acceptable opening. "I would have visited sooner had I known of you, Miss Mary."

"All my friends call me Polly," she said, ignoring the compliment. "I'd like it if you would, too. And I will call you John, if I may." It was more of a statement than a question. John marveled at her confidence and the ease with which she handled herself socially. She made him feel at home, as though they were old friends renewing their acquaintance after a long separation.

"So," inquired Polly, taking up the slack of silence, "you must tell me, is life at sea truly as adventurous as it sounds?"

"There were times when it was, in the beginning."

"You sound as though you've lost interest." She looked at him with inquiring eyes. "Are you giving up the cargo industry for the plantation?"

"Fact is," said John, "I haven't settled on what I want to do with my life. My father wanted me to become a sea captain, and hoped I would one day become an owner of ships. My mother wanted me to become a minister. That seems almost laughable now."

"I heard about your mother's death. Mother said it was Consumption. That must have been very hard on you."

John gazed at the horizon where it met the clear blue sky and shared his most intimate thoughts. "She was the only person that ever truly loved me. She taught me how to read early, even some Latin. As difficult as it was for her in the end, she never missed a day. I'll never understand how God could let such a good woman suffer."

John surprised himself with his unintended candor. Never in a million years would he normally have been so open with someone he had just met. For the first time since mother's death, I feel a genuine connection with another person.

There was a moment of silence as Polly considered her thoughts, as well. "My father says most men find meaning through their work."

John sighed and shook his head doubtfully. "That would be wonderful if I could only narrow down what I wanted to do for the rest of my life."

"I'm a little confused, John. Are you saying you don't want to go to work on the plantation, either?"

"The truth is, Polly, I have no idea if I do or not. The offer of working at a plantation was something my father worked out with the owner. He never discussed it with me. I'll probably end up doing it, but the thought leaves me wanting."

John shook his head and released a sigh of frustration. Then he smiled and said, "Besides, the plantation is in Jamaica. How am I supposed to see you again if I'm half-way around the world?"

"I don't know what I want in life, Polly. Given a choice, I'd like to find work around here, near you." It was as much of a conclusion as John could reach, and he hated it. His life was absent of any real direction, and the relationship could not move forward without some foundation. He knew it, yet there seemed to be nothing he could do about the situation.

"I'm sure you could find something," encouraged Polly. "There must be something you'd like to try."

A half-serious smile formed. "I've spent many nights wondering about the answer to that question. All I know is seafaring, and I'd be at sea most of the time. If I could settle on something that I actually felt good about -- anything here on land -- I could start preparing. If someone was willing to train me, I'd commit to several years of service."

Polly attempted to hide her astonishment. "An indentured servant? Would you that far?"

"Staying near you is all that matters. I mean, I want to find the right kind of work, but I'd do anything to live in Chatham until you became of age." John waited, wondering how Polly would react. His words hinted at an engagement.

When she said nothing, the stillness weighed in the air, and John nervously shifted the conversation back to his past. "My mother's death changed everything for me. My father remarried within a year and had another child. It was as if he started a new family, one that I wasn't a part of it. His new wife and I bickered constantly. When she couldn't take it anymore, she convinced my father to send me away."

"I can't imagine what it must have been like," said Polly, her voice filled with compassion, "not having a mother at such a young age."

During the last day of his visit, John made his intentions known. As the couple sat on their bench beneath the arbor, he looked straight ahead as he spoke. "I'm only sure of one thing in life, Polly. I love you and want you to wait for me." Newton stopped, hoping for some sign of affirmation. A word, a sigh, or even a squeeze of his hand would be enough. When nothing happened, he faced her and asked again, "Polly, will you wait for me?"

Without answering, Polly reached up and tenderly placed her hands along the sides of John's face, reached up and lightly kissed his cheek.

"I'll wait, John," she whispered in his ear. "I'll wait for you as long it takes."

Time quickly passed, and while many areas of Newton's life remained unclear, two were cemented in his mind. First, I must report to his ship; and second, doing so will means leaving Polly for at least a year. She has filled a large void in my life and parting seems unthinkable. After all, hadn't Abigail offered an extended invitation? "You're welcome to stay as long as you like," she had said. How sweet the words sounded. Encouraged, John gave up any intention of becoming a plantation owner in some distant country. It was not that simple, however. He still had to return home and face his father.

* * *

Captain Newton paced back and forth between the parlor and the kitchen of his small home, his heavy boots thudding louder with every measured step. He started to speak to his son, who was standing stiffly at attention, then held back. After several painful minutes, the captain broke the silence. "Not only have you embarrassed me," he began, a tremor in his voice, "but you've let down one of my closest friends. By all rights, I should disown you."

John had expected his father to be angry, to yell and possibly punish him, but never this. If he did anything to displease his father in the next few moments, he knew he might be banished, penniless and with no expectation of any inheritance.

Looking straight ahead, John watched the vein in his father's neck throb. "Have you any idea what would happen if you abandoned your post while at sea?" The air weighed heavy as the captain waited for his son to answer.

John cleared his throat. "I'm not sure, sir."

"Well, I am. Captains do not tolerate such folly and would likely have you whipped or keelhauled as an example to the rest of the crew."

Unable to get any words past the thickness of his throat, John only nodded. Defending himself would make things worse. He had been a sailor long enough to know that captains had complete and indisputable authority over their crews, even to the point of death.

Captain Newton stopped pacing and locked eyes with his son. "You will this very day," he declared, over-enunciating every word, "go to the docks and find another ship. You will sign on as a common seaman. Once aboard, you will faithfully carry out your duties under another pilot. You will do nothing to bring further shame on our name. Is that clear, John?"

"Yes, sir," said the lad. But the idea was not to his liking, nor did it match the plans he'd been hatching. Nonetheless, if he found a ship that would return within the year, his father might soften. Then Polly would be within reach.

Chapter 10

A Season Apart

Chatham, England (1742)

"To everything there is a season, and a time to every purpose under the heaven." Ecclesiastes 3:1

Polly helped her mother clear the table of the remains of the evening meal. She was learning to cook and already had three recipes her father added to his list of favorites. "Daughter," he said as he pushed away from the dinner table, "your roast beef is the best of the best, aside from your mother's, of course." He winked at them both as he patted his stomach with both hands. He watched his daughter glow as she accepted the compliment. He fished his pipe out of a side pocket of his vest and went to the back porch to smoke.

Polly cleared the plates off the table and stacked them in the sink. As they did every night, her mother would wash, and she would dry. The house, her family and the meal all gave her a sense of security. She hoped that one day her own home would provide the same peace of mind. And it was her future home that was on her mind. "Mother," she asked, "how does a person know when they are truly in love?"

Abigail smiled warmly and gave her daughter a reassuring hug. "One usually associates a question like that with love. Are you, Polly, in love, that is?"

Polly poured some hot water into the washbasin and let three plates slide beneath the water. Thinking about her answer, she picked up another and began washing it with a soapy rag. "Honestly, mama, he's all I ever think about."

Abigail pulled her daughter in close as they talked. "I remember how your father filled all my waking moments when we first met. Love, especially in the beginning, can take your breath away," she said, rocking back and forth. "But that doesn't mean your first love is the one you ought to spend the rest of your life with."

Polly stepped out of her mother's arms and returned to the basin. "How else would you know love was real except by your feelings?"

"Listen, young lady, and hear this well." Abigail's voice combined both love and firmness. "There are plenty of unhappy wives who let their hearts run away with them before they got married. They spent all their youth trying to find the right person to marry, and then spent the rest of their lives trying to figure out how they could get out of it. That's why above all else listening to your parents is important."

Polly gave her mother a puzzled look." You and father approve of John, don't you?"

"Truthfully, we aren't sure yet."

Polly caught a wet dish just before it slipped from her fingers.

Carefully, she dried it off and placed it in the cupboard.

"John comes from an honorable family," Abigail continued. "But he's still trying to find his way,    and he can't take care of someone else until he makes up his mind about what he intends to do with the rest of his life. I don't quite know what to make of him."

Polly held her breath, afraid to speak. She wanted and needed to have this conversation, but not if it meant having to break off corresponding with John. She speculated that her mother was just about to make such a demand. "He's honest and sincere," she inserted.

"I believe he is sincere when he writes and says he loves you." Abigail dried off her hands on her apron and took note of her daughter's surprise.

"Have you been reading my mail?"

"No, of course not, although as a parent I have every right to. But I've a pretty good idea of what he says in those letters. Polly, it takes more than romance to make a marriage work, more to make it last a lifetime. It takes maturity and right now John has no way to support you."

"But he knows that, mother. He's hoping to find work here on land."

"There's more to it, dear. He has to come to terms with himself, has to do more than get up in the morning, go to work, then come home and eat dinner. You two have to sort out what you have in common. There are children, money, and even religion to consider."

Polly's voice took on a defensive tone. "I'm comfortable going to any church John chooses."

Abigail spread out her apron with her palms, and then her dark eyes searched until he had daughter's full attention. "It's not the denomination that concerns me. It's his belief in God, or rather, the lack of it."

"He does believe in God, Momma. I'm certain of it."

"I'm not sure he knows what to believe right now," countered Abigail. "Even if he does believe,      I'm not sure he fears God and that makes all the difference in how a person lives out his life. It also tells me something about how John will treat his future wife."

Polly's forehead creased. *"Mother,"* she said, drawing the words out. "John would never mistreat me."

With the last plate returned to the cabinet, the two women walked back to the table and sat down.    Abigail pressed her daughter's hands between her own. Leaning forward, she said in an even tone,    "The Bible says a man is to treat his wife in the same way Christ treats the church. Do you understand what that means?"

"Yes, he's to treat me with respect."

"Yes, respect is part of it. There's more, though. The passage also means he's to put you before himself. Right now John is struggling with how he feels about God. In fact, he's a little angry with him."

Polly's face registered surprise. "He told you this?"

"Not in so many words. We talked about the untimely death of his mother, how his father remarried and sent him packing off to boarding school." Abigail steepled her fingers as she searched for just the right words. "I think John will be a good man someday when he grows up.

"His father was gone for months, sometimes years, and without his example, John lagged behind most young men his age. My guess is that things haven't turned out the way he hoped, and he blames God."

"That's silly," retorted Polly. "We can't blame God for anything."

"Right you are, my dear. Sounds silly when you think about it.

After all, he is God, and we are not. That's as simple as I can make it. Frankly, I'd be concerned if I could understand God. I mean, think of it. If I could, he wouldn't be much of a God."

"You talked about fearing God. Why does it always have to be about being afraid?"

Abigail stood and placed her arm over Polly's shoulder and guided her out of the house and toward the backyard garden. By the time they arrived, she was swinging her hand playfully. "Your father and I have yet to make a decision regarding this matter. These things are often more about the timing, and we're not sure yet that the time is right. You're still young, and in some ways, so is John."

Polly turned and hugged her mother. "I love you and father with all my heart," she breathed. "I'll do whatever you say."

Abigail squeezed back. *Now if John will only do the right thing.*

Chapter 11

The Dream

Mid-Atlantic (1743)

"And in the last days it shall be, God declares, that I will pour out my Spirit upon all flesh, and your sons and your daughters shall prophesy, and your young men shall see visions, and your old men shall dream dreams." Acts 2:17

Newton stood alone on the deck. It was his turn to stand guard during the third watch, in the dead of night. He did not mind the solitude. He leaned back against the railing, looked up and marveled at the countless stars spread across the spacious sky. He was at ease when alone; in fact, isolation was a luxury aboard ship, and one that he valued. He enjoyed being alone, free from the rigors of life aboard ship.

For every day that passed, he was closer to seeing Polly again. The ship was due to return to port within a week, and he would be back in Chatham, back with his love. He looked forward to rekindling their romance. Often filled with talk of his release date, the conversation focused on a profession that would keep him home. He missed her, so much so that she was on his mind throughout the day. Imagining her helped him fight off the boredom of routine aboard ship, and the unpleasant association with men of lesser standing.

Thanks to his mother, he had more education than most and a better understanding of the world than most of the crew. Visiting other places expanded his awareness of the different cultures; nevertheless, he could walk no further than the edge of the deck. And, having to interact with loutish men who looked forward to nothing than their next meal and a visit to some shoddy tavern left him wanting. Newton knew he was a better man than that. And Polly and her parents expected more from him. He wasn't perfect, but he wasn't one of them, either.

Newton remained lost in the twilight between the pale disappearance of the moon and the crack of light that would soon break over the horizon. All this quickly changed when a stranger stepped out from behind the center mast. He was wearing an iridescent white robe with a hood that concealed his face. Had the man been any closer, Newton could have reached out and touched him.

Startled by the sudden appearance, Newton challenged the man. "Identify yourself, sir, and state your business?"

Without a word, the figure extended his arm and opened his hand. There in his palm lay a golden ring bearing a large ruby in its center. "This ring," he began, "comes with a promise. The person who wears it will have a prosperous and joyful life."

The stone fascinated Newton. He reached out, took the ring and slipped it on his finger. A perfect fit.

"However," the visitor continued, "should the possessor lose the ring for any reason, he will plunge into misery and ruin."

The man stepped back into the shadows, soon replaced by another figure. The second man was quite different from the first. His robe was dark black, and gloominess surrounded his image. "What is that you have there, John?" he inquired.

"It's a special piece, and it comes with a promise that the owner will lead a life of good fortune."

The man tossed his head back and laughed loudly. "Surely you don't believe such folly. Even a child would scoff at such a story. Quickly, throw that fool's gold away."

Newton stepped back and shook his head from side to side. "I can't. You know what will happen."

"Come, come, lad. Don't be silly. Quickly, toss it away before someone sees you."

Newton's cheeks burned with embarrassment. The man was right. How could I believe in such nonsense? He hastily looked around, looking for anyone that might be watching. Seeing no one, he impulsively flung the ring over the side rail. Just as the golden ring touched the water, an enormous rushing sound filled the air, and Newton watched as the entire horizon erupted into wall of flame.

The intensity of the fire cast a light on the face of the figure, and Newton saw a derisive smile etched across a disfigured face. At once, he realized he had been deceived, and now his future was hopeless.

As if acting on cue, the first man stepped out of the shadows and back into the moonlight. Without speaking a word, Newton watched him dive into the water and retrieve the ring. At once, the flames disappeared and calmness fell over the ship.

When the man returned, Newton once more reached out to reclaim the ring. But the man stepped back.

"If I gave you the ring back," he said in a kindly voice, "you would only lose it again. I will take care of it and give it back when you are ready."

Newton opened his eyes and looked around. Disoriented and confused, he realized he had been dreaming. She propped himself up on one elbow and shook his head from side to side. *Did God just speak to me through a dream? Is it possible that I've been wrong? And if God does exist, why is he wasting His time on me?*

Newton rested his head against his hammock and sighed. *After all this time, I'm no closer to understanding my life, or where I ought to be headed. I'm like a ship with a broken compass.*

Chapter 12

The Ultimatum

Chatham, England (1744)

"For even when we were with you, we gave you this rule: The one who is unwilling to work shall not eat." 2Thessalonians 3:10

At this moment of his life, nothing in the world was more important to Newton than his burgeoning love for Polly, and he couldn't wait to see her again. After a year at sea, he wasted no time in returning to Chatham, where he expected to enjoy weeks languishing in the gracious company of the Catlett family. The last days of summer blended seamlessly into autumn with no more fanfare than a slight change in color of the leaves. Like the trees, the two young lovers remained indifferent to the coming of winter.

So John was taken aback one afternoon when Abigail asked Polly to pick some vegetables from the garden and invited John to join her in the parlor for a cup of tea. He pulled up a chair, somewhat uncomfortable with the unusual request. Abigail had never asked him to speak to her alone. He held his cup steady with both hands as Abigail poured, the quietness of the room hanging in the air.

"Having you here has been grand," she began. "At every turn I see your mother in you, and I know you have her heart as well."

"Thank you," he said, looking into the tea. "You're very kind, ma'am."

Abigail sipped the steaming liquid and put it down in front of her.

"I know you and Polly have spent many hours talking about your future," she continued. "I can't wait to hear more about your plans."

John tried to conceal his fear and self-doubt and fear. Under normal circumstances, he might have made something up, but he couldn't lie to this woman. She had come close to taking the place of his mother. "I'm afraid I don't have any plans at the moment," he blurted. "You see, my ship sailed last week."

Abigail's jaw went slack. "John," she said with a disciplined edge in her voice, "this is the second time."

John took a deep breath and held out his palms as if asking for forgiveness. He looked down at his feet and said, "Yes, it is. I just couldn't bear to leave."

"Does Polly know about this?"

"No, ma'am. The time hasn't been right to tell her."

Abigail stood, eyes clear and resolute, and set the cup back into its saucer. "Well, at least she hasn't been keeping secrets from me. However, his changes things, altogether. You'll have to leave for your father's house no later than tomorrow morning," she said, thinking the plan through as she spoke. "And please make it clear to the captain that I had nothing to do with this."

John respectfully got to his feet, but his head remained bowed. "I will, ma'am. It's the least I can do."

Faithful to his promise, John rose at dawn and packed his things. He overheard Abigail in the hallway as she instructed her daughter.

"This is no time for emotional goodbyes. Please remain here in your room." She escorted John to the border of her property where she hugged him, expressing genuine but distant maternal affection.

"John, I believe I understand your feelings for Polly. You haven't asked for her hand. Nevertheless, I'm granting my permission in advance."

John could not have been more surprised. He started to thank her, but Abigail silenced him with a raised index finger.

"There is a condition, though. I want you to settle down at something, a life's work. Choose anything your heart desires, but I won't allow you to see Polly again, not until you commit yourself and actually do something about it. That means a plan, John. You have to show her father and me how you hope to make your way in the world."

Newton's euphoria drained from his body. For a few seconds he could not speak. "Not see her at all?    Isn't that a little harsh?"

Abigail's head took a determined tilt forward. She folded his hand into hers, much as Elizabeth might have done. "Love is often blind, John, and you two are groping in the dark. I need your assurance that you'll start acting more like a man. All the promises in the world will count for nothing if you can't take care of my Polly. It's your actions, not your words that will change my mind."

She exhaled,  and  the heavy condensation drifted a moment before evaporating. "There's work to be done; that's plain enough for anyone to see. Until you settle on a profession and accomplish something with your life, there'll be no marriage."

"I promise I'll do better," he mumbled.

"Don't promise me anything, John. Show me."

Abigail ended the uncomfortable moment with a tender kiss on his cheek. She stepped back, still holding onto Newton's shoulders and said, "Good-bye, and God bless." Then she lifted the hem of her dress, turned and walked briskly toward the house, never looking back.

Chapter 13

Press Gang

Chatham, England (1744)

"Come to me, all you who are weary and burdened, and I will give you rest. Take my yoke upon you and learn from me, for I am gentle and humble in heart, and you will find rest for your souls. For my yoke is easy and my burden is light." Matthew 11:28-30

John pulled his hat down over his eyes. It not only shielded him from the morning sun, but helped conceal his face. He was uneasy, having ventured into the town no more than a handful of times during his visit. Hands jammed deep into his pants pockets and his head lowered, he wandered into the center of Chatham where the working-poor and marginalized managed to survive. Rows of shops where people traded and bought the things required to live lined both sides of the street. The butcher hung his prize cuts of meat in the window, a cobbler's shop revealed an old man working on a piece of leather behind the counter, and a blacksmith pounded on his anvil somewhere in the distance.

All towns had at least one tavern, and Chatham had several. They catered to the needs of sailors when they came to port. John looked around. *A place to sit and some ale, that's all I need to clear my mind.* Just as he crossed the road and rounded the corner of a building, he caught sight of a squad of soldiers. Two sailors held a man by his arms and hauled him from the doorway of a pub to the street. An earring and a tattoo clearly set him apart as a sailor. Then the manacles clicked, and a soldier pushed the drunkard into a line of men standing next to the outside wall. The group murmured their objections in a low cacophony, but all heads remained bowed.

"Press gang!" breathed John. He knew the military harassed the early morning tavern patrons, considering them easy targets. Conscripted into service was allowed by law. He understood that the upper classes considered it a necessary evil required to protect the Empire, while ordinary men referred to it as legalized kidnapping.

No sooner had Newton turned around than a lanky Royal Marine lieutenant, easily recognizable by his red frock, brass buttons and gold braided Pilates, pointed in his direction.

"You, there, stop at once!"

The officer turned to another soldier. "Sergeant," he ordered, "grab that man before he gets away."

The sergeant, a short, blocky man who was plainly at ease commanding the lesser ranks, motioned two musket-toting Royal Marines to follow him. For a split second, Newton considered making a run for it, but a moment's hesitation cost him any hope of escape. Before he could move, the soldiers swarmed him, each grabbing an arm.

"Come with me, lad," commanded the sergeant.

Without thinking, Newton tensed and considered breaking free.

"Don't resist," warned the sergeant in a curiously friendly tone, "or the corporal there will be forced to butt stroke ya."

Newton measured the grimacing corporal who held his rifle at the ready. The determination in his face left no doubt that he would carry out the threat with no more remorse than it took to butcher a hog. The soldier escorted Newton back to the band of men and stood before the lieutenant. "Where are you bound for, lad?" he inquired.

Newton knew the consequences of forced service in the British Navy and said the first thing that came to his mind. "I am on my way to board a merchant vessel bound for Jamaica this very day, sir."

"Then you are a blue-jacket," said the officer with smug satisfaction. He held out a demanding hand. "Your papers, please."

Newton searched his breast pocket and located his pass. Holding his breath, he handed it over.

The lieutenant read the paper, lifted his head and stared into his captive's eyes, searching them for evidence of the truth. "This expired two weeks ago."

Newton failed to offer any explanation, his mouth dry.

"Well, lad, your plans have changed," said the Lieutenant, stuffing the pass back into Newton's pocket. "Instead of sailing to Jamaica, you're going to serve on the HMS Harwich." The officer gave a slight nod in the direction of his subordinate.

To anyone other than the soldier, it was an imperceptible command, but that was not true of the Marine standing behind Newton. Before John was able to make any sense of what was happening, he heard the metallic ratcheting of manacles as they clapped his wrists together.

Newton tried once more to plead his case. "It's true I missed my departure date, sir, but surely I'll find another ship. I'm asking for you to make an exception this once."

"Perhaps you've not heard," countered the officer, his voice cold and aloof. "As of this week, we are at war with France. The only exception for men your age is employment in a job essential to the defense of the Nation. Do you possess any protection papers?"

Newton's chin dropped to his chest.

After waiting for what seemed an eternity, it became apparent that there no documents existed. "Come then," he commanded, half-turning away. "For the next year you will be in the service of your country."

The remark stunned Newton. Only a day ago he had been searching for a way to arrange his marriage. His only choices now were to submit or escape. He looked in the direction of the sergeant. Their eyes met, and it was as though the soldier was able to read his mind.

"Don't try it, boy. You won't get more than a few feet before one of my men shoots you dead. Better to serve honorably than to die a coward."

The Marines half-dragged Newton's body into the line of waiting men and forced him to march toward the dock. He looked around the street and saw he had only been a few feet from freedom. *If only I hadn't stopped for a drink, I would have taken another street and would have missed the soldiers completely.*

"Forward march," commanded the lieutenant. Jostled about, Newton shuffled along at the rear of the loose formation for a few short blocks.

Then the ragged line stopped at the water's edge where a battleship loomed a few yards out.

"You'll be able to write your families and friends once you get aboard, lads," said the lieutenant. "Sergeant, take charge of this mob and show them to the captain's quarters."

Newton was keenly aware of his future's uncertainty. A guard took the line of men below. "Halt," he commanded, and the lose formation shuffled to a stop, each man waiting for his turn to see the commanding officer.

Realizing he was entirely at the mercy of his captors, John issued a silent prayer to a God he wasn't sure existed. When no response or sense of inspiration came to him, his muscles went slack and he hung his head. *The situation was hopeless. Where is God when I need him most?*

He stood in the hallway waiting for his turn. It seemed an eternity before the commanding officer bade him enter. He decided it was of no value to continue the pretense of having accidentally missed his ship. The long detention had provided time to think, and the more he considered his dilemma, the angrier he got. If he had no choice but to serve under threat of imprisonment, he would do it standing up straight, without groveling.

"Next," came a voice and in the next moment Newton found himself standing before his commanding officer.

Philip Carteret sat at his desk, resplendent in a royal blue navel coat bearing the rank of captain. He was a slender man with dark brown hair and wide intelligent eyes. Rumor had it that he was the nephew of one of King George II's Secretaries of State, and had powerful political connections.

"Stand easy, Newton," Carteret said, with a casual wave of his hand. "I make it a point to speak to all the new men when they come aboard."

Newton stood at ease and responded with a simple, "Yes, sir."

Carteret leaned back in his chair and continued his interview. "I understand you've been to sea before." Carteret waited patiently, and then his eyebrows peaked, encouraging his subordinate to answer.

"Yes, sir," replied Newton, his voice firm and clear. "I've been to sea four times but never served aboard a war vessel."

Carteret smiled and folded his hands together, as if pleased with the answer. "The Harwich is a 976-ton ship with a crew of 350 able-bodied souls, many of them criminals and the scum of society. It's unfortunate, but it's the only way we can get enough personnel to conduct the business at hand. Your experience will place you far above that of a raw recruit."

*Recruit. This is the military, all right. I've got more time in service than half the men aboard this tub.*

"We need good men, Newton. I'm going to order that you be elevated to the rank of able full-seaman. It's not what you hoped for, but it is a promotion. Don't take it personally. Consider it a chance to serve your country. We are, after all, at war."

*What arrogance. One-step above basic seaman. Now's there's a real pat-on-the-back for you.* Then he realized Carteret was waiting for an answer and blurted, "Yes, sir, I appreciate your generosity."

"You've still got five weeks to learn the ropes, as they say. Regardless of your experience, it won't be easy. We expect our lads to furl and unfurl a sail in high winds, scour the decks with a holystone, and learn to reload cannon while under fire. Any slacking and you'll feel the Bosman's cane across your back. Is that understood, lad?"

Newton felt his palm grow sweaty as he began to understand the harsh reality of life aboard a military ship during a time of war.

"I expect you'll do fine. That'll be all." Carteret said nothing else. Instead, he kept looking at the newest member of the crew as if waiting for him to respond. Finally, he said, "It's customary for enlisted men to salute officers."

Newton's hand reacted before he could think, offering the standard two fingered salute.

Carteret returned the salute and cut it away sharply. "Dismissed," he said.

Newton hesitated for a moment.

"Well, what is it?" said the captain, clearly annoyed by the delay.

"How long will I have to serve?"

"How long will I have to serve, *sir*!" countered Carteret, his eyes squinting. "You may as well ask how long the war will last. Nevertheless, you can expect to serve for at least two years. Now, send in the next man."

Newton turned and walked out onto the deck and hoped no one saw the shock on his face. *Two more years. Will Polly wait that long?*

* * *

Captain Carteret stood and offered his hand. "Captain Swanwick," he welcomed, "may I offer you some port?"

"By all means, sir. Might as well mix a little pleasure with business."

Captain Carteret bent over a walnut cabinet containing his stock of liquor. He retrieved two glasses and filled them with a dark red liquid. He handed one to Swanwick and sat down across from him in a thick leather chair. Although small, his cabin, trimmed in rich brown walnut contained a small bookcase filled with a compendium of books. In the center of the room was a larger table, used for viewing nautical charts. His sleeping quarters, consisting of a single bed, a chair and an oil lamp, lay tucked into a corner of the cabin. Meager as it was, the room was far more luxurious than that provided for the other officers or senior enlisted men.

"So, I understand you're master of the Greyhound." Carteret leaned back in the chair and offered a brief toast of acknowledgment.

Douglas Swanwick took a sip of the wine and swished the blend of alcohol and grape against his pallet before answering. He was dressed, as was his host, in his uniform jacket, bearing his rank. Although he had never commanded a war vessel, he was confident in his own right. He had held both humble and lofty positions throughout his career, and he was, on many levels, equal to Carteret. And that was enough for him to comfortably present his proposition.

"Yes, I've enjoyed being in command for several years now," said Swanwick. "I first went to sea many years ago as a small boy and worked my way up through the ranks. It's been a good career and I still have a few years left."

Carteret always gave the rules of etiquette their due, but he was not one to delay too long. "I'm sure you do. I hope when my active duty time comes to an end I have as worthy a reputation as yours. And now, how can I be of service?"

The old man sat back and rested the glass on his thigh. "I'm here on behalf on one of our colleagues, and the father of one of your crew."

"Ah, yes, that would be young John Newton." Carteret smiled slightly. "He hasn't been here long, but he's done well thus far."

"I'm pleased to hear it." Swanwick's voice took on a more serious tone. He leaned forward and placed the port on the small table between them. "Allow me to speak plainly, sir. John's father has plans for him in the shipping industry. He requests that you release the boy into his custody. He'd still be serving his country, of course but in a different capacity."

It was Carteret's turn to set his glass down. The corners of his lips crinkled as he considered his answer. He was a fair-minded and impartial man, not given to corruption. "I'm afraid that's impossible, Captain. I would not do it for any of the other men and I'm certainly not going to do it for Newton."

The older man smiled gently and raised a hand as a gesture of self-defense. "The lad's father anticipated your response and wants me to convey that he understands and respects your position." Swanwick spread his hands apart, palms up. "As I said, he has plans for the boy, wants him to advance in rank."

Carteret did not try to conceal his surprise. His eyebrows arched and he tilted his head to one side. Instead of letting his indignation get the better of him, the captain took a breath and responded to what now seemed a game of give and take. "Do you seriously think young Newton is ready to become an officer, to assume a position of leadership and command other men?"

"No, of course not." Swanwick, unperturbed by the critical question, picked up the port and calmly took another swallow. "We had hoped for some position of authority, a midshipman, perhaps."

"A sub-officer?" Carteret's eyebrows again lifted as he considered the suggestion.

Swanwick toasted Carteret with his goblet. "Yes." He drew the word out with affirmation. "A sub-officer in training, so to speak."

Carteret laughed aloud and looked up at the ceiling. "You are a cunning old fox, you are. No wonder the old man sent you to represent him." He leaned forward and held out his hand. "Let us shake on it, sir. Tell Captain Newton we have a bargain."

* * *

Newton had no idea why he'd been summoned. He half-stood at attention in front of Carteret's desk and watched the captain walk over in front of him. When only inches away, he said, "We're going to have to find someone to loan you a midshipman's coat. You're being promoted."

Newton eyes widened. "Yes, sir," he croaked, trying to maintain his composure.

"Don't look so surprised. I can make good use of your experience." Carteret began to pace as he talked, his hands gesturing with each word. "On the other hand, don't let it go to your head. You've haven't done anything yet to show your worthy."

Newton bit his tongue. *Thanks for the vote of confidence. I could run this ship as well as any officer aboard, especially if I kidnapped the crew.*

"I hope you appreciate this," Carteret said.

"Oh, I do, sir," said Newton. "I do, indeed."

Chapter 14

Deceiving a Friend

Atlantic Ocean (1744)

"Do not merely listen to the word, and so deceive yourselves. Do what it says. Anyone who listens to the word but does not do what it says is like someone who looks at his face in a mirror and, after looking at himself, goes away and immediately forgets what he looks like."
James 1:22

The Arctic slipstream turned the air blue as it pushed down from the North. It was the first day of winter, and already cold enough to freeze the hair on a man's head if he removed his cap. Newton mindlessly walked along the perimeter of the HMS Harwich. Most of the crew was on liberty, while he remained behind as aide to the officer-of-the-day. Midshipman was traditionally able to avoid such duty; nevertheless, Newton's attitude during the previous months had branded him a malcontent, and the skipper found the extra duty a fitting punishment.

"You sow seeds of discontent wherever you go, Mr. Newton," Carteret remarked as he rebuked the young man the day before. "While you're alone during the next four hours, consider the morale aboard ship and the example you are supposed to set for the men."

Newton flipped up the collar of his wool coat and cupped it around his neck. It provided little protection against the gusts that cascaded down from the North, and his body began to shiver uncontrollably. A steady wind occasionally pushed him backwards. *Even nature seems to go out of its way to work against me.*

*Seeds of discontent, indeed.* Newton understood that a ship was like a small city, comprised of even smaller neighborhoods. Each found a certain satisfaction by spreading gossip about the other. Still full of anger and resentment over his abduction, he made a commitment to get even with the man responsible for his being there. At every opportunity, he had systematically been attempting to destroy the reputation of Captain Carteret.

The following day he joined a small group of men on a work detail and inserted himself into the conversation. "How's the food been, men?" he asked.

The group of sailors all looked at one another, until one finally screwed up the courage to speak. "No disrespect intended, sir, but I could use a bit more on my plate."

Newton looked around before responding. In a low, conspiratorial tone, he said, "I understand, lad. I've heard talk that the captain holds back the best food for himself. I got it straight from the cook. Says he takes the quality cuts for the officers and leaves the scraps for you men."

In fact, ordering special dishes or having one's food prepared to order was a privilege of rank enjoyed by all captains in the Navy. But common sailors were unschooled in the ways of such things. To them, this was just another example of the chasm that separated the crew from its officers.

Newton walked away, giving the information time to ferment, but he returned the following day to stoke the fires with more malicious hearsay. As he anticipated, the crew registered their grievances through minor acts of insurrection. And Newton watched each incident unfold with a satisfied smile.

One morning he watched as an old sea dog sat patching a sail with some needle and thread. A young midshipman standing nearby watched intently but said nothing. The longer the officer waited, the more his jaw tightened. Deciding the mariner was intentionally ignoring him, the officer blurted, "You've been dallying with that sail for the last half-hour, man. Pick up the pace and finish your work."

What happened next took the inexperienced officer by complete surprise.

"It'll get done proper in its own good time," snarled the sailor, dropping the obligatory sir at the end of his sentence.

Newton had enough experience to know the sailor probably would have never tread on such dangerous ground with a more experienced officer, knowing the penalty for insubordination. But young sub-officers, new to command, struggled to find their sea legs when it came to handling older, and often-defiant sailors.

The midshipman's face registered unexpected shock. He started to scold the man, who was three times his age and known for his salty manner. Newton watched as his peer hesitated, contemplating his next move.

Brittle silence hung in the air, and the crew remained focused on their work, heads turned downward. In the end, youth and inexperience trumped Navy regulation, and the young man simply walked away, as if nothing had happened.

Newton smiled inwardly, knowing he played a silent role in the exchange. Insubordination was a serious breach of conduct. If not immediately dealt with, it could spread like a virus, contaminating the entire crew and ultimately leading to mutiny.

Newton knew the Admiralty Black Book gave commanding officers a wide margin when it came to punishment. The first offense required a seaman to stand at attention while his superior, usually the senior enlisted man, poured a bucket of seawater over the violator's head. The second time, his hands tied above his head, the punisher poured the water down each sleeve. Upon the third occurrence, the senior ranking officer would order the man tied to the main mast with the chambers of heavy guns secured to his arms. After a few hours, the weight pulled on the shoulder, often separating the joint.

Each level of punishment pyramided on top of the other, permitting the ship's commander to order additional penalties as needed. The fourth offense was inevitably fatal. The offending seaman received a sharp knife and a loaf of bread. Then they hanged him below the bowsprit in a casket shaped basket. In the end, the desperate man had to choose between two alternatives: starvation, or cutting the rope and drifting out to sea.

After several months, Newton considered his campaign of retribution a success but found himself wanting something more.

Revenge, while satisfying, did nothing to bring him back to Polly's arms. He secretly questioned her faithfulness, knowing she had every right to change her mind after so many months. Each time he received mail, he agonized before tearing open the envelope, wondering if she might formally ask him to release her from her commitment. When no such request arrived, he continued to ruminate about their separation until he found himself exhausted from worry.

After much thinking on the matter, he decided he was as angry with God as he was Carteret. Was it not God's sovereignty that forced him into service on the Harwich and took him away from Polly? The more he pondered the matter, the more his anger burned. If he could not hurt God directly, then he would hurt Him by proxy, by going after others who believed.

Newton began a crusade to find the weak and vulnerable among the crew. He found his first quarry one night while standing watch on the bridge. He'd heard that Job Lewis grew up tilling the soil and tending stock, a lifestyle that developed a strong, steady work ethic. But the desire to see other lands and different cultures proved irresistible to his young mind.

After months of pleading, Lewis' father gave his son permission to join the Navy and even assisted him in attaining a position as an officer-in-training. Once sworn in, it soon became obvious the lad had leadership potential. But his natural humor and easy smile proved his greatest asses. It ingratiated him to both the officers and the sailors. The captain, who watched from afar, was pleased with the boy's work and his admirable character. It was the commander's secret wish that the boys would one day claim the Navy as his permanent home.

Like Carteret wasn't the only one to take stock of the young man. Newton watched as the younger man acted honorably at all times, refusing to swear, drink or gamble, even when in port. Each night Lewis strolled along the deck, watching the heavens before going to bed. It was an ideal time for Newton to approach the younger man and share the things he had read in Lord Shaftsbury's Characteristics.

Coming up alongside him, Newton greeted his young counterpart. "Good evening, Job. It's a fine night, is it not?"

Newton immediately spotted a hint of half-concealed reluctance in the dark eyes of the sub-officer. It was not the first time Newton had seen the look. By now, many of the men considered him a malcontent, someone who assumed he was entitled to privileges that far exceeded his junior standing.

"It will do," intoned Lewis.

"I don't mean to pry, but may I ask how much time-in-rank you have? I'm just curious."

Lewis decided to say as a little as possible, hoping to end the conversation before it gained any traction. "Not long. Eighteen months."

"Well, that's a start. When do you think we can expect to receive a full commission to ensign?"

Weary of the questions, Lewis spoke his mind. "I expect it will come in God's own time. But it may not come at all if you continue to offend Captain Carteret."

Newton seethed with resentment at the younger man's unrestrained insolence. At that moment, his bitterness and envy gave birth to a new proposition. The young upstart had opened the door, and Newton resolved to pull the youngster off his perch.

"In God's own time?" Newton repeated with a chuckle. "I'll be in this hell-hole forever if I have to wait on Providence."

Taken aback, the young man shook his head at Newton's irreverence. "Are you aware," asked Lewis, "that some of the men are referring to you as the Great Blasphemer?"

"I am, indeed, and I welcome the title," said Newton, his tone unruffled.

"Welcome it?"

"I have my reasons," countered Newton. "If there truly is a God, he's not one I care to worship."

Newton cautiously angled in between the forecastle and a mast, using it as a barrier between himself and anyone who might be watching. "I'll admit the skipper and I have had our differences. Carteret's a hard man, especially if he has it in for you."

"And why not? You ridicule him with jokes and little songs. Not a very decent thing, considering you serve under the man."

"None of my tunes ever mentioned the man's name," Newton said in mock self-defense. "Enough about me, though. I saw you do something quite unusual today."

Lewis cocked his head at a curious angle.

"You prayed over your food. Oh, you were quite discrete, but it was apparent just the same. Is that something you always do?"

Lewis' eyes never varied from the expanse of dark blue water.

"Yes, always." There was a mixture of resolve and irritation in his voice.

"May I ask why?" said John.

"I suppose," said Job. "As you know, I grew up on a farm. My family depended on God to provide the fertile soil and enough rain to produce an annual crop. One bad month could wipe a man out. We understood the meaning of being grateful for our daily bread."

Newton's disingenuous smile transformed itself into a cynical smirk. "I thought it was the farmer who toiled in the hot sun and grew his food by the sweat of his brow that was responsible for the crop."

Lewis briefly weighed his response, reached into the inside pocket of his coat and retrieved a small copy of the Bible. He opened it to the Book of Psalms and read, "You care for the land and water it; you enrich it abundantly. The streams of God are filled with water to provide the people with grain, for so you ordained it. You drench its furrows and level its ridges; you soften it with showers and bless the crops. You crown your bounty, and your carts overflow with abundance. The grasslands of the desert overflow; the hills are clothed with gladness."

Encouraged by the words, Lewis closed the book and put it back into his jacket. "Of course, that's King David praising the Lord."

Unimpressed, Newton seized the moment to advance his cause.

"Have you studied any other books on religion, any besides the Bible, I mean?

"The Bible was the only book in the Lewis household. We would go to church on Sunday morning, come home to a fine meal, then father would read to us from the book." Lewis sighed and said, "It was a good life."

The two men began slowly walking and came to the aft section of the gun deck, a natural stopping point, and leaned against the stern.

"It was much the same way in my house," said Newton, ready to spring his snare. "My mother taught me the scriptures as a child. It wasn't until I was on my own that I found out the truth."

Lewis blinked several times, unable to conceal his surprise. "What do you mean by that?" he said.

Newton nonchalantly folded his arms and measured the pace of his words. This was an opportunity not to be wasted. "Let me give you an example by way of a question. Do you believe God knows everything?"

"I'm quite certain he does," replied Lewis. "He is omniscient."

"Then, do you believe He knew Adam would rebel in the Garden of Eden and eat the fruit his wife offered him?"

Lewis was unsure where the conversation was going and answered with caution. "I believe He knows all things."

"Well, if God knew Adam would rebel, why then man was tricked into committing what we call Original Sin; and if he was tricked, all of mankind has been suffering for something God caused in the first place."

Newton waited long enough for the theory to settle in before continuing. "Seems to me that God played an enormous practical joke on humanity."

Newton could read the younger man's mind. He was trapped, equivocating, and unsure of himself. Finally, he said, "Careful, John, you're talking blasphemy again."

"Blasphemy," Newton shot back, "is a word used by the church when it can't deal with the truth. If there is a God to believe in, it can't be the same one crowed about from the pulpit."

"You're quite the cynic, John. Aren't you afraid of going to Hell?"

"Why should I be afraid of something that doesn't exist?" As he spoke, Newton turned and looked directly at his young comrade. "I believe that when we die, it all ends, just like snuffing out a candle. The light simply goes out."

Lewis blanched and stepped back. "John, this is blasphemy," he said, a tremor in his voice.

"I've shocked you, I know." Newton lowered his voice. His eyes no longer challenged the young man. He leaned forward and whispered, as if sharing a secret. "I'll let you read some of my books, if you like. Stretching your mind can be a good thing, my friend. We'll talk more in a few days after you've had some time to think."

"I don't know that I need time to think, or read."

Newton could see past the wary eyes. The advantage was his, if he pressed lightly. "Think about it, Job. What does wearing blinders say about how you view your faith? God gave you a good mind, the ability to think and make judgments. You ought to exercise that gift."

"I believe the Bible says not to tempt God."

"Think of it as some light reading, something new to explore. No pressure, just follow your heart." Newton saw the tension ease in the young man' shoulders as he warmed to the idea. He even saw the hope of finding a new friend, something rare in the present social climate.

"After all, you're a man now. I have a book on religion that's quite popular among forward thinkers, those with the courage to challenge traditional standards."

Job looked off into the distance while he considered Newton's suggestion. Truth be told, I've never really left the farm, not emotionally. Maybe it's time to try something new. It couldn't hurt to stretch my mind a little.

Chapter 15

Desertion

England (1745)

"Pride goes before destruction, a haughty spirit before a fall. Better to be lowly in spirit along with the oppressed than to share plunder with the proud." Proverbs 16:18-19

Newton had just returned from taking fifteen days leave, and no more stepped aboard his ship when Lewis ran up to him. He stopped abruptly and leaned forward, careful to avoid eavesdroppers. "The captain wants to see you right away."

"I know, I know," shrugged Newton. "I'm late again. Don't look so serious. It can't be all that bad." He handed off his bag to his friend and stood erect as he straightened his jacket.

"I'm not in a position to say how serious it might be," said Lewis, as he helped Newton adjust his shirt, which was unbuttoned to the waist. "Just follow me and for once, show some respect."

Newton followed his friend, who knocked loudly on the door of his commanding officer.

"Enter," sounded a strong voice.

Both men ducked below the doorframe and saw their commanding officer sitting at his desk, leaning over a piece of parchment, pen quill in hand. Coming to attention.

"Midshipman Newton, reporting as ordered."

"Midshipman, indeed." Carteret laid the pen down and stood up.

"Explain your absence, mister," he boomed.

Newton could not admit he had overstayed his leave on purpose. Even suggesting he had lost track of time because of his involvement with a woman sounded foolish.

When the lapse in the conversation became unbearable, Lewis spoke up in his friend's defense. "If I may be so bold, sir."

"Please," said Carteret, "somebody needs to speak for this lost soul."

"No one is making any excuses, you understand, but Newton went to visit the woman he intends to marry. The visit had special significance, sir, knowing he would be away for several more years."

"As will the rest of us," bellowed the captain. The voice was like a warning shot over the bow and cut Lewis off. "I've heard this excuse one too many times."

Carteret exhaled loudly. "Young Newton, I no longer have any faith in you, not in you as an individual or as a sub-officer. You've done your best to disrupt this crew, and you've displayed complete and utter contempt for discipline. In short, you've interfered with my leadership at every turn." Newton looked past the captain, avoiding his piercing dark eyes. "What would you do if you were in command?"

Newton understood that his actions were indefensible, so he said the first words that came to mind. "Company punishment, sir?" It was more of a request for leniency than a realistic expectation.

"Company punishment! Not on your life." Captain Carteret walked out from behind the desk and stood directly in front of Newton. "I'll take into consideration the generally impetuous nature of youth, but I want this clearly understood." Carteret paused, ensuring that Newton was completely engaged. "I've been exceptionally lenient with you. That will not happen again. In the future, you had best follow orders as if the success or failure of our entire mission rested on you alone. Are we clear, boy?"

No one had used such a word since Newton had become independent and able to support himself, and now its application stung his pride. He swallowed hard, forcing the bile back down his throat.

"Yes, sir," he said, thinly cloaking his simmering temper. "It won't happen again."

Hearing the tone, Carteret exploded. "Enough of your impudence! You fight me from dawn to the dark of night. I should take this opportunity to advise you that the Admiralty has changed our orders. Your time in the Navy has been extended from two years to five."

Newton audibly gasped and for a moment could not speak. "Five years!" he finally sputtered. "Do they have the authority to extend my contract?"

"Of course, they do. This is the military and we are at war." Carteret got control of his temper and continued. "Since you're going to be with us for a while longer, I suggest you make the most of it. Get past this adolescent behavior and start acting like a real man."

Newton's pride bristled again. He detested the way his commanding officer talked down to him, so much like his own father.

Captain Carteret gave a casual wave of his hand. "I have nothing further. Dismissed."

\* \* \*

Newton leaned over the edge of the railing on the HMS Harwich. He had been considering jumping ship for days now. His mind raged against the Navy and particularly against Carteret. As far as he was concerned, this was nothing more than legalized kidnapping. If it was not against the law, it should be. No one, not even a government, had the right to round up innocent people, put them on ships, and force them to fight a war.

A hand squeezed Newton's shoulder and he looked up to see Lewis.

"Mate, you look as black as tidewater at midnight on a moonless night."

"I've got to get back on land." Newton kept his voice low, forcing Lewis to lean close to make sure he hadn't misunderstood his friend.

"And how do you propose to accomplish that?"

"I'll swim if I have to." Newton stared at the coast line, estimating the distance to shore.

Lewis cautiously looked around, making certain no one was watching. He turned and pretended to inspect a large sheet of canvas, looking for splits in the cloth. "Put it out of your mind," he breathed.

"We are a country at war, or haven't you heard?"

The words hung in the air. "Job, the consequences don't matter anymore. My motto is …"

"Yes, yes, I know, 'never deliberate.' That's exactly why you should wait and think it over."

Lewis studied his friend's face and tried again. "Three men deserted last week. That's why we're riding anchor more than a mile from shore. Anyone else thinking about leaving had better be a strong swimmer."

Newton picked up the other end of the sail and helped his friend fold it into a square. "There's another way. I overheard the first mate talking. A work party is going into town and to purchase additional supplies."

"And just like that, he's going to let you go?"

Newton lifted his palms in a gesture of innocence. "And, why not?" Lewis raised an eyebrow in amazement. "First of all, he doesn't like you, and second, you were absent-without-leave during your last foray. For the sake of argument, let us suppose you got ashore. Then what?"

"That's the beauty of it," Newton continued. "My father's in Torbay, only thirty miles from here."

"What's he doing there? And what's that got to do with it? He's not going to be able to protect you."

"He's negotiating ship repair contracts on behalf of a company that has vessels being readied for sea. If he hired me, it would be like working for the government, and I'd be able to visit Polly once a month."

It was a jaw-dropping statement, one that Lewis could not begin to comprehend. When he recovered, he reached over and held Newton's arm. "Don't be a fool, John. I'm asking you to reconsider."

Newton pulled free as he stepped away and started walking toward the captain's quarters. Over his shoulder he said, "Thanks, Job, but I really don't have any choice. You're a good friend, just for trying to get me to change my mind. That's something I never do."

A few moments later Newton knocked at the captain's door.

"Come," sounded the traditional command of the captain.

Newton entered and stood at attention in front of Carteret, who hunched over a large map covering a rectangular table positioned in the center of the room. He raised his head and stared at the person who had regularly disrupted his crew. Waiting long enough to make Newton uncomfortable, he finally said, "Well, what is it, midshipman?"

"Sir, the work party picking up the supplies, I'd like to go along."

Carteret raised his eyebrows in astonished surprise then his eyes narrowed with suspicion. "Did this request go through the first mate?"

Newton locked his eyes on one of Carteret's buttons, and kept his body ridged. "No, sir, I'm aware that you alone could honor such a request."

"Tell me why I should," Carteret commanded. He stood up, his considerable height towering over his subordinate.

Newton considered his response before speaking. What was no more than a second seemed like a year. He would have to risk everything. His eyes met the captain's penetrating gaze. "You're right, of course, sir. I've failed you and the men, and I owe you both an apology. I hope you'll give me a chance to start fresh with this assignment."

Carteret snorted and stared back. "You really expect me to believe that, Newton?"

Newton read the captain's level stare and quickly decided the man would not put up with any further impertinence. He was the commander of the ship, an experienced naval officer and from the looks of his face, was about to remove any doubt as to who was in charge.

The captain placed his palms on the table, leaned forward and shook his head. "I don't know why I'm doing this. Pick as many men as it takes to get the job done. Petty Officer Davies is preparing a list of the required goods. He will provide you with the necessary vouchers, which the local merchants will accept as payment.

"Mind you, Mr. Newton. Any further incidents like the last two will get you classified as a deserter. You alone are responsible for this detail and the conduct of these men. Am I understood?"

"Yes, sir, I'll see to it," said Newton, appearing sincere.

Chapter 16

Capture

England (1745)

"Do not be deceived: God is not mocked, for whatever one sows, that will he also reap. For the one who sows to his own flesh will from the flesh reap corruption, but the one who sows to the Spirit will from the Spirit reap eternal life." Galatians 6:7-8

Newton stepped from the long boat and onto the dock. He was the last to leave the boat and he wasted no time in divesting himself from the work detail. Turning to the senior man, he handed him the list of supplies.

He had long ago concluded that Jack McAbby was a man destined to remain at the bottom rung of life's ladder. A two-day growth of whiskers shadowed his face, accenting his badly stained teeth. His eyes remained vacant most of the time, as if his mind were a rusty piece of machinery, always in neutral. When he finally realized what was taking place, his voice filled with a mixture of fear and resentment. Taking the list, he cried, "Don't try to lay this off on me. I ain't no officer."

"Right you are, McAbby, and that's why you'll follow my orders."

"What am I supposed to do with this?" he questioned.

"The same thing you would have done if I remained here. Purchase the supplies." Newton slung a tote bag containing his belongings over his shoulder and started walking toward the center of town.

# I Once Was Lost

The seaman looked at the list without comprehension. Then, looking up he said, "Mr. Newton, this isn't right," he called out.

The surrounding sailors all murmured in agreement, astonished that Newton would abandon them. "We'll all get put on report if you leave us like this."

Newton ignored the warning and picked up his pace. He had no intention of entering into any further dialogue. His plan was to find his father and have him arrange his transfer back to civilian life. He would tell the truth about his absence from the Harwich, arguing that the orders extending his service to five years were unacceptable and justified his decision to abandon the vessel.

The men watched helplessly as Newton crested the hill and dropped out of sight on the far side. A decision was required, but decisions did not come easily to men like McAbby.

Finally, the largest of the crew elbowed his way to the front. "We got our orders, don't we?" he said, as if that settled the issue. "McAbby here will make sure we do as we was told. If Mr. Newton isn't back by then, we'll go back to the ship without him."

"But they'll know he's run off if we go back," said another voice.

"Right you are," said the larger sailor, "and that's just what he deserves."

Newton was making good time as he walked through the center of the city and headed for the main road that led out of town and toward his final destination. He had not forgotten the warning the last time he was absent without permission, and furtively looked up and down the streets, searching for any sign of press gangs. Perhaps, if he had just looked where he was going, instead of paying so much attention to the peripheral alleys and walkways, he might have seen the detail formation of Royal Marines forming up outside a tavern where they had obviously eaten breakfast. One of the men wiped a stained sleeve across his mouth, hurriedly picked up a musket and took his place in the formation.

Newton recognized them as the same squad of men that pressed him into service earlier in the year. Too late to turn back without calling attention to himself, he pulled his collar up, hoping to evade detection. But the weather was not cold enough to warrant bundling-up and doing so only made him all the more conspicuous. Out of the corner of his eye, Newton saw the officer in charge raise his arm and point. "You, there," he ordered, "hold up."

Newton pretended not to hear and started to walk quickly toward the corner of the street. If he could get out of sight, even for a moment, he might be able to outrun them. Just as he lifted his leg and prepared to sprint into an alley, the clatter of metal against wood reached his ears. Out of the corner of his eye, he saw one of the soldiers drop to one knee and level his musket. "Stop or you're a dead man!" he shouted. The situation was hopeless, and Newton slowly returned to the squad of soldiers, waiting for the inevitable questioning.

"Let me see some identification," said the officer, holding out his hand.

Newton reached into his pocket and pulled out his documents. "I'm on business for the commander of the Harwich," he said, lowering his voice an octave and attempting to sound official.

The lieutenant briefly glanced over the papers before he looked back and examined Newton's face more closely. Cocking his head to one side, he said "Didn't we pick you up in this sector once before?"

*He knows.* At once, Newton decided to drop the charade and speak plainly. "Yes, sir, you did. And now I . . ."

"You've deserted the Navy, haven't ya, lad," the lieutenant interrupted. His statement was a declaration of fact, and he was not expecting an answer. He shook his head with exaggerated contempt.

"Sergeant, secure this man in irons and prepare to escort him back to the Harwich."

The noncommissioned officer, a seasoned veteran who had carried out similar orders countless times, retrieved a set of iron manacles from a canvas bag. He placed both hands on his prisoner's shoulders and spun him around. Then came the metallic sound as the restraints tightened around his wrists, cutting off the blood supply. "You stay next to me, boy. Do exactly as I say and I won't have to shoot you."

"Forward, march," ordered the lieutenant. The motley group stumbled forward, each man starting one of the longest journeys of his life. The blade of the sergeant's palm dug into Newton's back, pushing him forward.

The town's people came out of the houses and stood staring as the soldiers marched their prisoners through the streets. *A common felon is treated better.*

"You there," the sergeant commanded, "keep up." He gave Newton a heave push against the shoulder.

"Stop looking around and keep pace with the formation."

Newton monitored the eyes in the crowd. There was neither sympathy nor compassion. It was simply the way things were done during wartime. He felt a great weight pressing against his chest. There's no hope of seeing Polly now. And now, I've got to face Carteret.

In less than an hour, the detail arrived at the port, secured a boat and delivered Newton to his ship. He looked about as all the men stopped working and watched in silence. The first mate muttered something unintelligible as he received the handcuffed prisoner. Normally, he would have directed the men to get back to work, but on this occasion, he allowed them to watch as he delivered Newton to the commanding officer's quarters.

Carteret sat at his desk, pen quill in hand, signing for the rations. Irritated by the noisy interruption, he raised his head. "So," he said, "the Prodigal Son returns, in chains." He wasted no time with questions. His gaze fell back to the papers as he soberly murmured, "Take him below and clap him in irons, Mr. Davies."

Back out on the deck the faces of the men were grim. Each man met Newton's contemptuous glare and then turned his back on the prisoner. As far as they were concerned, he would remain on board the ship but no longer hold membership among its crew.    Without a word spoken, the men collectively decided to cut him off. He was for all intent persona non grata, an unwelcome person. Worse still, the midshipman and officers stood stiffly at attention on the upper level, their faces stern. He hoped to find at least one sympathetic exchange, some glimmer of sympathy, but they remained rigid and stoic, looking out over the sea.

The guard turned Newton around and towed him backwards across the deck, like a piece of used luggage. Deposited in the bowels of the ship, he spent all night and the part of the next morning chained in total darkness. Although he curled up in the darkness and sought the refuge of sleep, the shackles dug into his flesh and rattled each time he moved. So he lay awake for hours, wondering what fate would bring.

The following morning someone lifted the hatch, and a piercing shaft of light appeared. Noisy boots thumped against the wooden stairs. The chains jerked him upward. He could hear the key inserted into the lock. One twist and the manacles fell, banging against the floor. Lastly, the man's burly arms grabbed his collar and pulled him up onto his feet.

"Come on, boy," said the gruff, satisfied voice. "It's time to pay the piper."

Newton lifted an arm, using it as a barrier against the light, and squinted at his escort.

"Ya don't know me, do ya?" said the man, not bothering to address the prisoner by his rank.

"I'm sure I would if I could see."

"Name's McAbby. I'm the man you left in charge of the work

detail. I should say I'm the man you handed the supply list off to and walked away. No one was actually put in charge."

Newton took note of the man's overly broad smile and stained teeth. His memory was vague, and as far as he could tell, there was no reason to try to remember. After all, the man was a basic seaman and had no authority.

The deckhand kept talking as he hustled Newton up the stairs and onto the main deck. "You shouldn't a' done that, old son. It wasn't easy keeping that lot together. You taking off like that might have cost us all."

For the first time Newton could see clearly, and what he saw shocked him. The entire ship's company stood assembled on the levels of the various decks. As tradition demanded, each man wore his hat and stood at attention. Captain Carteret reigned from the bridge, his stoic face impossible to read.

The next senior officer came forward, peeled open a long sheet of parchment and began to read the article of war describing Newton's offense. "The prisoner has been found guilty of gross negligence and desertion during a time of war. The recommended penalty for the said crime is one of the following: flogging, keelhauling, or death by hanging."

He let the scroll curl into its original shape, looked down at Newton and said, "Does the prisoner have anything to say before punishment is carried out?"

Newton's head and shoulders sagged in the silence as he considered the full weight of what the next few moments would bring. Was it possible that he was about to be executed?

"Hearing nothing, the prisoner will disrobe."

Newton unceremoniously pulled off the white cotton shirt and followed the master-at-arms to the far side of the ship.

"Get down on your knees and grab hold of that ratline," he said.

Newton did as ordered and watched as they bound his wrists to the rigging, using double knots. "With God's grace," he murmured, "you won't feel much after the fourth blow. Now, show us your best, lad."

Captain Carteret remained still, letting the silence do its work. When he did speak, it was in low, solemn tones. "Men, you are assembled here to witness the punishment of a deserter, according to the custom of the Service. If anyone else is entertaining thoughts of absconding from Her Majesty's Royal Navy, he would do well to remember this day. Thus far, two men in the fleet have been hanged for similar acts of cowardice."

The captain hesitated long enough for the words to take effect before continuing. "John Newton, having been found guilty of desertion, you are reduced in rank to basic seaman. In addition, you shall receive twelve lashes. Punishment is to be carried out immediately."

The first officer turned in the direction of the master-at-arms and stiffly nodded his head. "Carry out the punishment," he bellowed, and a drum roll erupted somewhere in the background.

The man's muscular arms and back were well suited for the task.

Although he appeared to take no joy in whipping another man, Newton understood that failure to lay into each stroke could cost seaman his own freedom. He picked up the coiled cat-o-nine-tails of the deck and whispered into the Newton's ear, "Stare out over the water and keep your head forward. There's no need to lose an eye, lad."

The words bore into Newton's brain, and he began to tremble uncontrollably. The ocean was aqua blue. The only sound in the air was the rigging as it ached with each gentle roll of the ship.

With a flick of his wrist, the sailor extended each of the straps behind him, and Newton could hear the clatter of leather as it scooted across the wooden floorboards. Then the lash whistled through the air and his muscles constricted just before the strips cut a deep swath into the flesh. His body shivered uncontrollably and his jaw clenched, but he refused to cry out. Again, the whip rattled as it retracted.

His shoulders writhed and twisted as the sound of rawhide announced itself a second time, and the time after that. With each stroke, his nemesis called out the corresponding number.
"Eight," CRACK. "Nine," CRACK.

Newton was largely unconscious by the twelfth blow. His only sense was that of the crew's collective gasp as the last bite of the leather completed a pattern of cross-stitches over his quivering frame. He could no longer hold himself up, and hung heavily from the bindings on his wrists. "Remove the prisoner," the dispassionate first officer commanded. Two men untied Newton and carried him below, where they deposited the wounded body sideways in a hammock. A few moments later, someone arrived with a bucket of salt water.

"As the saying goes, this is going to hurt you more than it does me," said a voice Newton tried to identify. "It's going to be painful, but it'll keep the infection down."

Newton twisted his neck and made out the blurred figure of Job Lewis. He tried to speak, but his throat closed up so tightly it was difficult to breathe. Never before had he been so humiliated and dishonored in front of others. Even his memory of his school days paled in comparison. A mixture of rage at Carteret and self-pity for himself surged upwards from his gut and before he could stop himself, Newton leaned into his hands and began to sob.

"There now, John. The worst is over." Ripples of saltwater squeezed from a sponge rolled over his open wounds and washed away large clots of coagulated blood.

"John, I hate to be the bearer of bad news." Lewis waited, giving his friend time enough to focus through the pain. "The captain has ordered the crew to shun you. Even the lowest seaman will treat you with contempt from now on. One might say it's worse than that. They'll act as though you don't even exist. It's going to be a rough road, I'm afraid." Lewis waited for a moment before continuing. "I won't be able to help you, but I'll remain your friend."

Newton only retreated further into himself as the rhythm of his breathing returned to normal. Still curled up like a child, he withdrew to a place of safety, to Polly. He dreamed she was there, talking in soothing tones, tenderly applying salve to his lesions, and lovingly rocking him.

He winced again as another application of the salt water trickled down his back, the pain pulling him back to reality. "I've just one thing to say, Job." He looked back over his shoulder so that their eyes met. "If I have my way, Carteret will never die of natural causes."

Chapter 17

A Black Heart

Plymouth Harbor, England (1745)

"For out of the heart come evil thoughts—murder, adultery, sexual immorality, theft, false testimony, slander. These are what defile a person." Matthew 15:19

The lacerations stitched across Newton's back were agonizingly raw and open. He lay perfectly still in his hammock, even when trying to sleep. Each time he turned on his side, the flesh split and a mixture of blood and thick clear fluid oozed from the fissures. Then the wounds dried up again, sealing off infectious elements floating in the air. It was the body's way of defending itself as the damaged flesh gradually made repairs. The ship's surgeon examined the back every forty-eight hours, ensuring that wounds were clean and free of putrefaction.    Carteret's instructions to the ship's doctor were explicit. "Make sure the wounds heal properly but free of any medication that might hurry the process along. Pain is a fine teacher, and   Newton's improved memory will linger if the agony of the whip takes longer to heal. He'll not consider repeating his crime so quickly the next time he feels the urge to wander off."

It was still morning and Newton saw sunlight and heard the hatch open, along with the thud of heavy footsteps on the steps leading to the crew's sleeping quarters. Gingerly lifting his head, he looked to his side and saw McAbby. He was holding a wooden bowl.

"Here's some food, Mr. Newton." McAbby's lip formed into a sarcastic curl at the corner of his mouth. "Oh, pardon me! You're no longer a snobbish midshipman. You're just another seaman now, no better than the rest of us. So, plain ole Newton would be the proper salutation."

Newton had been unable to eat for the last two days, and his stomach churned as the aroma of the food wafted through the air. "What's that you've got there?" he asked, ignoring the mockery and trying to sound amiable.

"You can be sure it's not the table the cook would set if you still ate in the officer's mess. The contents of this here's some salt-pork and a hard biscuit, and you'll like it or starve." McAbby was in no hurry to set the bowl down and held it at arm's length.

Newton intuitively understood McAbby's attitude. Officers were an arrogant lot, gentlemen, thinking themselves superior to the underclasses. Newton held out the bowl and took regarded the smoldering resentment in the man's eyes.

"Here now, be careful," he said as he held out the wooden vessel just beyond the prisoner's reach.

Newton reached out. As his trembling fingers touched the container, McAbby let it fall, watching with obvious glee as the bowl bounced along the floor.

"Oh, I am sorry, You're Worship. Seems I've forgotten my manners, not to mention your spoon." He turned, chuckling over his shoulder, and said, "Wish I could stay longer, but I've other duties to attend to. I do hope you enjoy your supper, though."

Newton's expression, the very definition of despair, only invited a great rumble of laughter from McAbby's swollen belly. He continued to mock his defenseless prey between guffaws all the way back up the stairs, where he let the hatch drop loudly into place.

Driven by his hunger, Newton managed to dangle his legs over the side of his hammock. He tried to stand, testing his weight on limbs with muscles starting to atrophy from lack of use.  They held him for no more than a moment before giving way. He crumpled to the floor, and the fall tore open each wound. "Ahhh!" he cried out, then stifled the sound through a clenched jaw.

Once more, he teetered on the edge of unconsciousness. He hung onto the cotton hammock for balance, catching his breath and letting his eyes focus. *What would my father think if he could see me now? Would he be proud that his oldest son had finally reached an acceptable rank, only to find him reduced to the lowest of the low. No, he would be extremely disappointed. Well, what did he expect?*

Newton picked up the biscuit and brought it to his lips. *How can something this plain taste so wonderful?* He broke off another morsel of bread, sprinkled with his own tears.

The tears were not a sign of brokenness or even repentance but symbols of burning anger. Newton's heart had never been so black. *I'd kill Carteret if I had mu knife.*

And then the idea surprised him.

# I Once Was Lost

*Did I really mean that? Would I go that far?*

He contemplated the depth of his ire for a long moment then murmured under his breath,

"Yes, if only I had a knife, I'd get the job done in short order."

Chapter 18

Slavery

Canary Islands, Mid-Atlantic (1746)

"Do not be deceived: God cannot be mocked. A man reaps what he sows. Whoever sows to please their flesh, from the flesh will reap destruction; whoever sows to please the Spirit, from the Spirit will reap eternal life." Galatians 6:7-8

Daydreams of revenge filled the empty hours. His body, while still painfully sore, was starting to heal. But his heart remained an open wound. The ship made its delivery to Madeira and was due to take on fresh supplies. If Newton allowed the first mate to see even a hint of the recovery, the man would return him to full duty, and order him to help carry heavy sacks of meal. He was under no obligation to work, or even mingle with the other men, who now treated him no better than a leper.

He ran his hand across a week's worth of stubble. There was dirt and sweat all over his body. How different from when he bathed regularly, ate with the other officers and was able to leisurely oversee the men who labored beneath him. He looked like a different man now, and he was.

Earlier that morning Newton slowly swung his legs over the side of the hammock, stood up long enough to verify that his legs could do their work, and leaned against a column to steady himself. Then he began to walk. It was twenty steps out and twenty back, a new record.

He had settled back into his bed when a midshipman descended the stairs, briskly walked over and said, "You've overstayed your time in bed, John. Time to get up." The man's tone was somewhere between a jest and a warning."

"What brings you down to the cave?" said Newton.

"Your lack of work ethic." The man's tone did not waver, making it clear that he expected no rebuttal. "The skipper gave me the distasteful task of keeping an eye on you, as if I needed more work to do. Get out of bed," he commanded.

His voice laden with sarcasm, Newton said, "Right you are. I'll be up in a moment." Instead, he turned his back on the man and curled up, expecting to go back to sleep.

As if anticipating the remark, the midshipman gracefully drew a knife from the scabbard on his belt, and with one arching motion, severed the rope that held up one end of the hammock.

Newton tumbled onto the deck with a thud, landing on his hip.

He yelled and then kicked at the officer, who was clearly out of range. He quickly hoisted himself up, ready to fight, when he got hold of himself. Any further act of insubordination would only land him back in shackles and on a diet of bread and water. Instead, he offered a forced smile and waited to see what would happen next.

The midshipman clearly did not care if Newton was capable of returning to duty or not. He had his orders and John knew he would carry them out, even if his charge had to crawl up the stairs to get topside. With the knife still in his hand, he motioned him toward the stairs.

Upon reaching the main deck, Newton observed McAbby loading his duffel bag into a small boat. Cautiously, he approached the man who had expressed deep loathing only a few weeks before. "What goes on, Jack?"

McAbby turned and Newton could see rage burning in his eyes. "It seems the commodore has ordered the captain to swap two of our crew for two on a ship bound for Guinea." McAbby pointed at a vessel now lying only a few hundred yards off the port bow. "And I was selected. Apparently, Carteret thinks exchanging me for some other loafer is the better end of the bargain."

Newton took hold of McAbby's arm. "Under no conditions will you shove off before I've spoken to the captain," he ordered.

McAbby pulled back defiantly. "What goes on here? You've no authority to be givin' me orders."

"Right you are, Jack," said Newton, lowering his voice. "Just this once, do as I ask."

"And why should I do you any favors?" McAbby half-smiled, half-snarled through his stained teeth.

"Because I may save the day for you."

Newton scanned the upper decks until his eyes found an officer. The ensign had once been Newton's friend, but that was no longer true.

Newton worked his way to the quarterdeck and brought himself to attention. "Permission to speak, sir."

The ensign was a tall, slender man, clearly comfortable with authority. "What is it, John?"

"Sir, I understand you're trading McAbby to another ship. I'm asking permission to take his place."

The officer stood silent for a moment while considering the request. "John, at one time or another you've crossed each one of your friends, or the men that used to be your friends," he said. "Give me one good reason why I should forward your request up the chain of command?"

"You're right, sir. I don't deserve any favors. Just this once, I simply ask for your indulgence. My request is for the good of the Service."

The ensign gazed at Newton as he pondered the request. His expression revealed how miserable the man before him looked and smelled. "You're a mess, John, and I'm not just talking about the way you look. Truthfully, I don't think you can last much longer. And that's why I'm going to allow this. Wait here. I'll speak to the captain."

One-half hour later, Newton stepped into the dinghy and found himself a place to sit. His hand held his discharge papers from the Harwich and the Royal Navy of England.

Chapter 19

Bargain with the Devil

Africa (1747)

"For the love of money is the root of all evil: which while some coveted after, they have erred from the faith, and pierced themselves through with many sorrows." I Timothy 6:10

"It will make you independently wealthy in ten years," said Amos Clow.

That statement alone was enough to get Newton's full attention.

"You and I are very much alike," continued Clow. "I once lived hand-to-mouth and had no hope of improving my condition. That is until I relocated to Africa. The trade here can make a man rich beyond his dreams. All that's required are men willing to take a few risks, men who aren't afraid of getting a little dirt on their hands now then."

Newton glanced at the man leaning on the ship's rail next to him. Clow was no more than average height. His frame was heavy, his features aquiline, his eyes gray-blue, and his shoulder length hair entirely silver. His skin, tanned from the tropical sun, never lost its oily sheen.

"The world's got a great hunger for slaves right now," continued Clow. "This is a slave ship and by now you know how to handle its cargo. No other commodity has ever risen to such a high level of demand." Clow smiled, his face the very picture of greed and ambition. "Those who get in now are going to control it all one day.

"So, what do you think, John, are you willing to come work for me?"

Newton listened to the man who was making the unexpected and truly remarkable proposal. He did not particularly like or trust Clow, but the notion that he might become rich appealed to his dreams of financial freedom. He was sure Abigail would give Polly permission to marry once he was on his feet, and his future clear. It was his chance to succeed without his father's help. Slavery was an acceptable way of making a living, even among the people back home. But he needed more information.

"What exactly did you have in mind?" he said, trying not to sound too eager.

"There's not much to it, actually," Clow continued. "I already have raiding parties that go out and capture the black devils. When rounded up, they're held in pens until purchased by one of the ships that pass through. That's where you come in."

"How so?" asked Newton

"My headquarters is on an island near here. I need someone who will keep an eye on these Africans until they're ready for transport." Clow leaned toward Newton and winked playfully. "If you do a good job for me as a jailer, I'll let you start work on one of the other islands, for a fee, of course. It'll be your own business. And if I'm any judge of character, you'll do well."

Newton questioned why Clow would offer such false flattery after knowing him for less than a week. His reputation was no better on this ship that it was serving aboard the Harwich. In fact, he was freer to speak his mind, continuing his blasphemous language against God with even greater enthusiasm.

For the first time, Clow looked away, staring stoically at the horizon. "There's a hitch, though," he allowed, a hint of betrayal in his voice.

*Here it comes. I knew it sounded too easy.*

"The captain has already said he'll release you," said Clow. "But you'll be leaving early and that means with no pay. You'll be obligated to me for the balance of your remaining time."

Newton said nothing as he considered the conditions.

"You can take it or leave it. Makes no difference to me what you do with your life," Clow said with airy tone. "If you stay here, you'll be no more than a humble seafarer. And once we dock, the offer leaves the ship with me. There'll be no second chance."

Like it or not, Newton knew it was true. He had nothing to look forward to, only more time spent at sea for lowly wages. Instantly, he made up his mind to accept the offer.

"I am quite willing to accept those conditions, Mr. Clow, and I will make you a good and willing worker. You have my word on it." Newton knew his word was meaningless at this point. All the same, he meant to keep the promise.

"Good," said Clow, the corners of his mouth rising into a slow, satisfied smile. "I need someone willing to do whatever it takes to learn the trade, and get the job done with few casualties."

Chapter 20

PI

Sierra Leone, Africa (1747)

"Come to me, all you who are weary and burdened, and I will give you rest. Take my yoke upon you and learn from me, for I am gentle and humble in heart, and you will find rest for your souls. For my yoke is easy and my burden is light." Matthew 11:28-30

As the ship's anchor dropped, Newton could see a party of African men waiting on shore. They remained a deferential distance from their mistress, a tall woman, wearing a black sarong trimmed with large yellow flowers. The weave and stitching of the material are far too fine for this part of the world. Someone purchased it for her, perhaps in Europe. And that light skin, she's got a white parent or grandparent in the family tree. She won't look, but I'm sure she knows I'm watching. Newton broke off the stare and back shivered. Newton's back spasmed for a moment. Strange, I feel cold.

He continued to watch as Clow stepped onto the dock, and the woman made a great show of bowing. The slave trader acknowledged her with no more than a slight nod of his head. His approach was slow and lazy, appraising the woman with a lecherous smile. Then he casually slid an arm around the small of her waist, pulled her up hard against his chest, and longingly kissed her. His entire body trembled as if infected with a fever. By any reasonable standard, it would have Been a very private moment, but Clow was enjoying his moment on stage. He broke the embrace. With eyes still fixed on what was obviously *his* woman, he waved for Newton to approach.

Newton hefted his sea bag onto his shoulder and quickly walked over to his new employer. At first, Clow said nothing. Finally, he broke the silence and introduced the woman. "This is PI. I'd tell you what her actual name is, but no white man can pronounce it. So, we just use her initials. She is my second-in-command and runs things around here while I'm gone." Clow laughed and pulled the woman in closer.

Newton might have been invisible, for PI ignored him while she continued to engage Clow with her wanton stare, never once looking in the direction of her guest.

"PI, this is John Newton. I hired him right of the ship."

Newton was quite uncomfortable showing any civility to an African; nevertheless, he nodded in the same manner as Clow. When his head came back up, he noted that the woman was staring at him.

"PI hails from the ruling Bombo tribe," continued Clow. "Without her help I would never have been able to start my own trading business.

PI"s broke off her gaze. She looked over her shoulder, said a few words in her native tongue, and the other servants dutifully picked up Clow's baggage.

Clow set the woman down and walked, talking over his shoulder as they moved toward a cluster of small huts. "We need to get you settled quickly," said Clow. I'll be sailing for Rio Nuna in a few days, and PI will assist you with your work."

Soon they entered a compound of huts, the largest of which was in the center. It contained a makeshift kitchen where food was prepared before it was taken outside and cooked in a large pot. A sleeping mat was rolled up in the corner, and a desk for business was positioned in the middle of the small room. PI appeared holding two clay cups, which she offered to both men.

Newton started to drink but discovered that his cup was empty. Clow, on the other hand, lifted the container and drank his fill, unaware of the slight. PI left once more, this time returning with a large bowl overflowing with bananas and mangoes. She handed the fruit to Clow, who now sat in his chair, enjoying the attention.

Newton walked over to a large jug and dipped his cup in the clear refreshing water and brought it up to his mouth.

"Hold on, son," said Clow, reaching out with a warning hand. "Water around here is often diseased and has to be boiled. Take yours from the smaller jar on the table."

Newton peered down at the cup, then over at PI. She regarded his stare with a dismissive smile, and curled up on the ground next to her master's thigh.

*She would have let me drink that filthy water, and he let he get away with it.* Perplexed, Newton stifled his anger and said, "I'm fine, sir. Just show me to my room and I'll get my belongings put away."

Clow stood with a shrug and followed Newton to the door. "Take that shack over there," he said, pointing to the outer perimeter of the camp.

Newton approached a bamboo hut with a thatched roof. He pushed aside the curtain that served as a door but at the last minute turned and looked over his shoulder. His timing was impeccable. He watched as PI shared a cunning smile with the other servants.

Newton awoke the next morning and found his bedclothes drenched in sweat. He swung his legs over the side of his cot and sat upright, instantly regretting the move. His head swam with such momentum that it forced him to lean over and cradle his forehead in his palms. Penetrating pain surged its way up from his neck to his head. The idea of being sick in a strange land, a place that hosted many unusual diseases, frightened him. I'll bet there's neither medicine nor doctor available on this jungle; at least, nothing more than a witch doctor. What worries me most is that I'm out here all alone, no friends or family on which to rely.

Then, after thinking about what he had just said, Newton saw the irony of his condition. I've done everything possible to avoid friendships, distanced myself from family, and now I'd give anything to have someone, anyone of them, here that might help me.

A moment later, he heard a noise. PI peeked around the flimsy makeshift grass door. What came next confirmed Newton's suspicions.

"Oh," she said with glee, "you very sick." She padded over to the bed and knelt down, low enough that her ample breasts almost spilled over the top of her dress. "Maybe you die soon from fever," she cooed, running her fingers through his hair and wiping perspiration from his forehead.

Newton was too weak to respond and collapsed backward into the bed. His chest spasmed as he tried to re-oxygenate his lung. "Could you call Mr. Clow, please," he said, gasping between the words.

"My man gone to other islands," she said with an air of satisfaction. PI placed her hands on her hips and strutted back to the door. "He gone for long time." She drew the word out to emphasize the length of his absence. "PI boss now."

Newton reached down and gingerly pressed his fingers across his knees, only to find them swollen and tender. "Oh," he groaned. "Is there any kind of a doctor about?"

"No doctor-man here. Only jungle medicine."

Newton draped a forearm over his face, shielding his sensitive eyes from the bright sunlight. "Would you please get me some water? I desperately need some fresh water."

"You sick from water already." PI opened the door and prepared to leave. "You lie down and sleep. Someone check on you later."

Newton tried to speak, but his throat, dry and raspy, only choked on the words. The shapely woman, the one person who clearly had more authority than anyone else on the island, the only one with the power to save him, smiled benignly and swished her hips out of the doorway.

*She is mocking me.* His body began to shiver, and a cold sensation traveled all the way up his spine, into his chest and through his limbs. He discovered a light woolen blanket at the foot of his bed. Pulling it up around his torso, he curled up like an infant. Every few minutes the shivering would subside. Instead of intense cold, his body became hot, and droplets of sweat rolled down his forehead.

*Why,* he queried during the few lucid moments he had over the next twenty-four hours, *does she hate me so?*

The following day PI approached the compound closely followed by two male slaves. She peeked around the door to Newton's shack and called out, "Bring Newton food and water. Not too much, though. He still very weak."

*She's giving me just enough nourishment to survive. What she does not know is that I have a reason to live. Whether she likes it or not, I'll fight to live. If I can make a go of this business, I can return home to Polly.*

For three days he fought, fading in and out of the fog of delirium. On the morning of the fourth day he abruptly woke from a deep sleep. The pain had vanished and the fever broken sometime during the night.

He propped himself up on one elbow and inhaled the sumptuous aroma of roast pig wafting through the humid jungle air. The scent immediately caused his mouth to salivate, anticipating the wonderful food. He rolled his legs over the side of the cot and tried to stand. His legs wobbled at first, and he had to sit back down. On the second try, he managed to shuffle over to the door. From there he stumbled two feet further to a palm tree and leaned against its smooth bark for support.

PI stood in the large open window of Clow's shack preparing all manner of food. *I must look like a half-starved stickman.* He pushed himself over to the hut, the aroma fortifying his will. Eventually, he reached the open door and pulled himself up. Two steps inside and he fell onto a bench next to a crude table.

"May I have some of that, please?" he rasped.

Two male servants standing in the corner looked toward PI before acting on the request.

"Maybe later." PI never looked up, and her tone was as offhanded as someone discussing the weather. "I work for this food. You sleep all night, all day. I eat, you wait." Without further explanation, she turned her back and continued basting the pig. Once the skin of the animal glowed bright red and was ready to split, she carved out several large slices and placed them in a bowl. Exaggerating every movement, she lifted a succulent chunk of meat well above her head and slowly lowered it into her open mouth, making sucking noises as she chewed. It was a silent signal to the slaves, who then stepped forward and their portion of the feast.

Newton was helpless to do anything other than observe. His stomach seemed to protest its condition, audibly growling. After a final helping, PI stood and stretched her arms out, sighing with exaggerated satisfaction. Without saying a word, she picked up the bowl containing a few remaining scraps. "You want?" she said, extending her hand.

Newton could not recall a single incident in which he'd experienced such humble circumstances. He was entirely at the mercy of this mean-spirited woman, who evidently perceived him as a threat. But without her help, he would surely parish. He reached out and took the vessel. The heat of the food burned through the bowl, and his fingers reacted before he could think. It was like watching a dream. The object slipped through his grasp and tumbled sideways to the floor.

"You want food," PI scolded, "you eat from floor, and clean up mess after." Her hand listlessly waved the other servants away from the doorway where they had been silent spectators, the gesture followed by a statement in her native tongue that Newton judged to be an expletive.      He shrank to the ground, picked at the morsels of meat and pushed them into his mouth until it could hold no more. He savored every juicy scrap of the incredible delicacy, chewing until it was finely grated, leaving nothing to swallow. Then he lay on his side on the grass floor, catching his breath and holding his stomach, watching it undulate while grinding down the desperately needed fuel.

Not very long ago, he had been full of pride and arrogance. Now he was nothing more than a beggar was. The story of the Prodigal Son came to mind. Given the chance, I would return home, just as he did.

But will father take me back?

The illness warped Newton's sense of time. Am I in my right mind? Has Clow come and gone away already? My God, I hope not. Without him, I'll never escape the torments of this witch.

For the first time, he observed several newly captured slaves, chained and staked to the ground near his shack. They too, for purposes of keeping them healthy and profitable, were allowed to eat properly. As Newton rose and began to work his way back to his bed, one of the men tossed a handful of meat in front of him. Carefully looking back in PI's direction, he saw that she had turned her back on him, and it was safe to pick up the morsel. He knelt down, feigning weakness while secretly palming the meat.

When he returned the comfort of his new home, he lay back on his bed and enjoyed the gift, wondering at the generosity of the stranger. *And why not,* he concluded, *we're both slaves.*

PI's contempt became even more evident the following morning. She stormed into his hut. Two servants followed in her wake, awaiting orders. She stood over the bed of the only white foreigner within hundreds of miles, placed her hands on her hips and announced, "You sleep too long. You get up now. You walk today."

Newton had no choice but to comply. He propped himself up on one arm and attempted to remain upright. He pushed off the bed with a groan, only to fall to the ground. He tried to get up again and failed once more. I don't have the physical or mental strength to do this. I've got to get my strength back, or this woman is going to kill me.

PI unceremoniously grabbed Newton by the arm and yanked up hard. "You walk now! You walk!"

Newton groaned and struggled to his feet, trembling as he tried to find his balance.

"You walk." she repeated. "You walk now, devil white man."

Newton willed himself to obey, moving forward with teetering half steps. PI said something in her own language and clapped her hands together authoritatively. The other servants began to laugh and immediately set about mimicking Newton's feeble efforts with exaggerated faltering steps, awkwardly stumbling back and forth across the room like some kind of deranged ballet.

She gave a second command, and the servants reached into a cloth bag containing several limes. Laughing in high-pitched unison, both men began pitching the thick-skinned fruit, hitting at Newton's chest and arms.

Newton screamed as the projectiles bruised his skin. The men let go with a second volley, hitting him again, until he fell over.

"Please!" he begged, shielding himself from the next torrent with a raised arm. "Please, stop!"

This time Newton noticed that he did not feel the pain as much; instead, he could tell his face burned bright red with an all-consuming rage. *Somehow, someday, I will find justice.*

In the end, he understood the utter futility of his situation, and a debilitating sadness washed over him. All the fight in him drained away. The more he considered his plight, the more despair set in, until he lowered his head and began to weep.

PI signaled the men to withdraw, and Newton's chest heaved as he fully realized the irony of his condition. *My body doesn't even have enough water for tears.*

* * *

Polly wondered if John was still alive.

151

The sun had risen and no one else in the house was up. After a sleepless night, she sat up, leaned back into a large pillow and fingered a packet of mail that lay nearby. She had been reading John's letters when she fell asleep the night before. It took all her courage not to burst into tears. She had not heard from her beloved for such a long time. It was not uncommon for months to go by, and then several letters would come at once. Now they seemed to have stopped coming altogether.

She untied the string of pink yarn and looked at the most recent post. Sometimes his letters seemed written by a stranger. The words confused her as she reread them:

Dearest Polly,

I love you more than words can express, and daily yearn for the hour of my return. Your letters are the very life's blood that keeps me alive.

God, if there is one, seems to be working against all my efforts to escape those who have taken me find a way to extricate myself from this horrible condition, and will write again soon.

Affectionately yours,

John

Polly sensed a mixture of love and deep-seated anger that went beyond the words. She had matured during John's absence and was now more of a woman than a girl. Her heart told her that John might do something impetuous, something that would end up keeping them apart. And now, the letters had stopped.

She let the correspondence fall into her lap and folded her small hands. "Please, God," she whispered, as tears spilled onto her cheeks, "look after my John." Then she wiped them away with the back of her hand, pushed away the blankets and pushed her way into the arms of her robe. Her mother stirring in the kitchen, and Polly needed her, needed a mother's advice as she never had before.

"Good morning, dear," Abigail said, in between sips of her morning tea.

"Morning." Polly tried to sound cheerful, but her flat response drew a second glance from her mother.

Examining her daughter more closely, Abigail asked, "Have you been crying, dear?"

Polly abruptly turned away and made a second effort to remove any evidence with the sleeve of her robe. "Not really," she said.

"Seems to me a person either has been crying or they haven't."

When Polly offered no explanation, Abigail pressed on. "This has to be about John."

Polly sighed heavily and sat down at the table, her hands folded in her lap. "I haven't heard from him for months. I'm so worried, mother.

"And what is it you're afraid of, exactly?"

"I don't know if I can put it into words," continued Polly. "Several things, I suppose. Lately I've wondered if he's safe, out of harm's way. There's so much I don't know, and so much more I'm afraid I'll find out. Oh, Mother, my mind refuses to stop imagining things."

Polly looked down and realized that she was ringing her hands together.

"Come and sit down," said Abigail. She put her cup down and took Polly's hand into her own. A lifted brow expressed her deep concern. "Are you afraid he's been hurt or is there something more?" she said.

"He might have been," said Polly, her hands caressing her cheeks as she spoke. "There are accidents aboard ships all the time. He hasn't written for months now, and when he did write, such sadness filled his words. I worry as much about his emotional state as I do anything else. He was so lost when he left."

Abigail said, "Look at me, dear."

"Are you afraid John has found someone else? After all, he's been away for a very long time."

The tears streamed down Polly's cheeks once more and this time, she made no effort to hold them back. "I'm terrified that he has. It only stands to reason that he might. He's traveling all over the world with a group of roughnecks who leave their morals at home when they ship out."

"You still love him, don't you?"

Polly leaned into her mother's arms, laying her head against her breast. "I do, Mother. I love him with all my heart." The words spilled out. "He's all I think about. He tells me I'm all he lives for, but the letters have stopped coming, and I can't stop worrying."

Abigail hugged her daughter closer and sighed. "I can only imagine how you must feel. I'll write John's father and see if he's heard anything. But remember, Polly, regardless of what John runs into during this war, he'll return to you if God wills

Chapter 21

Accused

The Plantains, South Atlantic (1747)

"My brethren, count it all joy when you fall into various trials, knowing that the testing of your faith produces patience. But let patience have its perfect work, that you may be perfect and complete, lacking nothing." James 1:2-4

Six weeks after he departed for Rio Nuna, Amos Clow returned to the village.

Newton languished in bed, propped up on one arm and looking out the window. He watched the owner of the Plantains greet PI with his customary lust-filled embrace. As she drew close, PI spoke loud enough for Newton to hear. "Newton almost die from fever. Very sick. Won't eat."

Clow was soon at his new employee's hut. He forced the door open with the heel of his hand, marched into the shack and observed Newton stretched out on his cot. "I understand you've been indisposed, my boy. What seems to be the trouble?" he said, walking over to Newton's bedside. Suddenly, his face revealed his utter surprise. "My, God, lad. We've got to get some food in you. You're wasting away."

Newton knew he was lucky to be alive. The fever had run its course; nevertheless, he grew weaker by the day. He lifted an arm and ran it across his forehead. Every movement still drained his strength.

"I believe it's Malaria, Mr. Clow. As you can see, I've been quite ill."

Clow reached over and lifted Newton's eyelid. "It's the fever, all right. Are you able to keep food down yet?"

A hint of a smile appeared as Newton considered the question. "I would if I could get some. Your woman won't give me anything more than table scraps." A ragged cough worked its way up from Newton's chest, interrupting him. "Frankly, I'm lucky to be alive."

Clow stood back up, his mouth forming a crooked downward line as he considered the allegation. "She knows your stomach can't handle too much this soon," he said, finally. "If you're well enough to eat now, I'll order some food."

Newton was both dismayed and surprised at how easily Clow sidestepped the accusation. It became clear that PI, a mere slave, had exploited her master's weakness for lust. She was now the power behind the throne, and when she spoke, she had Clow's blessing. And she didn't need any competition. That meant she would do everything in her power to kill off the partnership.

"Yes," Newton said, his raspy voice barely audible. "Any food at all would be wonderful."

Clow turned toward his mistress, who was standing just outside of the door, and out of sight. "PI, come in here."

PI pushed the curtain barrier aside and entered so quickly that both men knew she'd been eavesdropping.

"Yes, master?" she said, eyes twinkling.

"See to it that this boy is fed properly. I believe his stomach can handle solid food now."

PI bowed slightly at the waist while backing toward the door. As she turned to leave, half-hidden by her shoulder, her eyes cast a wicked, triumphant glance in Newton's direction.

Newton considered all the events of the last few weeks and reconciled himself to his new position. He was nothing more than a slave, a white slave. And by now, he had given up all hope of ever being anything more. Talk of a partnership was no more than a distant memory, and, after fifteen months saw no way of rising above his present condition. He had no idea why his employer had changed his mind. In spite of his talk of needing help, and an offer to work his way up in the business, nothing had transpired. He concluded that PI had stopped him in his tracks, and there was little or no chance of him ever recovery. He took a deep breath as he realized that he was utterly defeated and without any options. After all, even the other slaves now exercised authority over him.

"If you don't work, you don't eat," was Clow's mantra, and he said it often. One day he tossed Newton a shovel and showed him where to start digging. "We'll plant another row of lime trees here," he said.

Newton had to admit that he was for all practical purposes a slave. He wiped the sweat from his brow with a bare forearm, preferring to work without a shirt in the steamy heat. Standing up from where he was planting a row of lime trees, he arched his back and rubbed a sore muscle with the heel of his hand. Even after three months of hard labor, the work was grueling. He had watched some slaves literally being worked to death. Even if one considered it a loss of profit, one man's death motivated a dozen others to work even harder. The choice was simple: toil with all your might. You'll eat, and you'll live another day.

An hour passed and Newton heard footsteps in the grassy carpet and looked over to see Amos Clow and PI walking toward him. When they stopped within a few feet, he came to a modified position of attention, as was required. He expected them to say something, but they only stared in silence. After a long moment, both turned to the other and broke out in hilarious laughter.

"Newton," sputtered Clow, between guffaws, "look at you. Whatever happened to that arrogant young man who transferred off the Harwich, the one who was always getting himself into trouble?"

Newton was suddenly conscious of his dirty, broken body. More than his physical condition, he was emotionally depleted. The dirt on his chest was smeared with sweat, and he was suddenly seized with a wave of self-contempt. *If I ever escape, I'll come back. They'll remember this day and pay dearly.*

"Perhaps one day you will return here as a sea captain and purchase some of my limes as food for your men." The sarcasm hung on Clow's every word. He turned to PI and said, "One never knows."

"Yes," replied the woman. "One never knows." And they both laughed again.

Chapter 22

A Slave of Slaves

Plantains, Africa (1748)

"Therefore, we do not lose heart. Though outwardly we are wasting away, yet inwardly we are being renewed day by day. So we fix our eyes not on what is seen, but on what is unseen, since what is seen is temporary, but what is unseen is eternal."
II Corinthians 4:16-18

"Behold, Jordan, here stands the only white slave in this part of the world." Clow extended a hand as if presenting some piece of livestock to a buyer. It was a feeble and cruel attempt at humor, just the kind of entertainment in which he delighted. It seemed the more painful Newton's condition, the more his master enjoyed demeaning him. Nonetheless, he stood up straight, still standing in the ditch he was digging and allowed the stranger to inspect him.

Wallace Jordan was a tall man whose height was out of proportion to an all too slender frame. His wavy blonde hair, combed straight back and hanging down along his shoulders, glistened in the light. His skin was dark brown, leaving strangers to mistake him for a native of mixed descent. He wore a traditional white cotton shirt, unbuttoned and tucked in at the waist. Now with disbelief, he gazed in at the poor man occupying the ground before him.

"He's not truly a slave, is he?" questioned Jordan, knowing that only the native population could qualify as another man's property.

"You might call him a field hand."

Newton was familiar with the term. Field hand was simply a euphemism for a slave, so Clow's initial remark was closer to the truth. Such a label would offend most white men, but Newton had grown numb to such remarks. After all, he worked for nothing except the rags on his back and just enough food to keep him alive. Upon his arrival, Malaria brought him to his knees. Even after recovering, there was no escape. He was still too weak to run off. And if he could, where would he go? Only the jungle waited for him, and that was certain death.

"Why not let me take him off your hands?" said Jordan.

Newton watched Clow's eyes light up as he slid his hands into his pockets. He wore a broad-brimmed straw hat, which he tilted forward so as not to give away his hope of making a profit. "Is that a proposition I'm hearing?"

Jordan nodded affirmatively. "It might be. Actually, you ought to thank me for even asking. It's got to cost you more to feed him than he's worth. Just look at him, man. And don't try to overcharge me. After all, you got him for free."

"Ah, but that doesn't mean he's not worth something. As you can see, he's still able to swing a pick. I wouldn't consider letting him go for less than five-hundred dollars."

Jordan laughed. "Just a few minutes ago you told me that this poor fellow is just about spent, not much use to anyone."

Clow shook his head slowly. "You're my neighbor. That doesn't mean I'm going to make Newton a gift. Come on now, you have an educated eye in such matters."

"Perhaps if his health was better. It's going to cost me just to put some meat on his bones. He's not fit to do any real work."

Jordan scratched his chin as if contemplating his next move. "I'll tell you what. I'll offer you two-hundred-and-fifty and not a dollar more. I can see that I'm going to lose money on this deal."

Clow considered having the money, versus Newton, who had become an irritant. While he did the work required of him, the tone of his voice revealed an unbroken and unbending resolve. It was the same mindset that got him transferred by his two previous captains. He turned to Jordan and said, "Have him out of here by nightfall."

Newton stood there silently, astonished that he had no say in the conversation, no more than a silent bystander in a discussion concerning some other than himself. He was about to interject himself when he looked in Jordan's direction just in time to see him wink and offer a veiled smile.

Months passed, and Jordan worked tirelessly nursing Newton back to health. He required no work, and ultimately offered him the same business proposition that Clow had reneged on. He considered him an equal and when they weren't busy, Newton enjoyed walks along the beach. He'd spoken little during his captivity. Now he enjoyed the long moments of intelligent conversation. Jordan made inquiries about Newton during those moments, but Newton could only look away, avoiding anything other than the shallowest of answers. I want to trust him, but don't know if I can. People can use one's weakness as a weapon, just when it's least expected.

One day as they leisurely walked along the white sand of the shore, both men enjoyed the quiet ebb and flow of the ocean. It was a comfortable relationship. Jordan was patient and understood that Newton was in the process of healing.

"Have you any idea how much you've changed in the last few months?" asked Jordan.

"I hadn't given it much thought." It was an evasive response, and not altogether honest. Newton picked up a seashell stranded against a rock. After reconsidering, he said, "Oh, I know there have been some significant changes in my life. I now own some clean and decent clothing and no longer worry about starving to death. But that's probably not what you meant."

Newton intended to evade the real issue. Obvious to even the most casual observer, his attitude had changed dramatically. And right now, having a deep philosophical conversation about the subject was not what he had in mind. He was where he was, who he was, because God had willed it, or so said the theologians back in England. He had given up trying to figure out why; it was simply the hand of Providence at work. "My ways are not your ways," he recalled. How many times had his mother read that scripture to him? Nor did he understand why his mind kept struggling with the concept of God's sovereignty, especially after professing his lack of faith. In the end, he wanted to put the entire matter down for good. It was delusional to think someone might come looking for him.

"You get my drift, so don't pretend otherwise." Jordan threw a piece of driftwood back into the water with a high lazy arch. "I'm talking about the blacks. To be blunt, you've gone native."

Unfazed, Newton chose to ignore the remark. "I've changed because you convinced Clow to get rid of me. If not for you, I'd still be at the Plantations, not much more than an animal."

Jordan looked at Newton out of the corner of his eye. "John, you're deliberately evading my earlier question."

"I wasn't aware that you'd asked a question. I believe you made an attempt to describe my current status here in the islands. I'll neither confirm nor deny my relationship with the natives."

Jordan turned and looked directly at his friend. "All right, is there any truth to the rumor that you've taken a mistress?"

"You mean a *black* mistress," Newton intoned. "I admit to nothing more than visiting the grass mansion of one of my favorite women from time to time. She attends to my needs, whatever they may be at the moment."

"All men have dreams, John? Don't you want to go home someday, go back to your family?"

"Before settling here, I thought of nothing else," said Newton. "I'm not sure when the dream died, but I wasn't even around for the funeral. No, Jordan, I've no plans to return home."

"There must have been something that made you give up?"

"There's no longer a reason for going back."

"Meaning?" said Jordan.

"It's like this, my father thinks I'm some kind of derelict and despises me for having wasted my life, and he would be right. I've lost any hope of marrying the woman I loved since my youth. By now, she's most likely given up hope of seeing me again and found someone else. I'm not the same man I once was. Clow broke me of that. It's better for everyone if I remain here and live out the rest of my life."

The men continued walking until Jordan found a place to sit beneath a palm tree. "This," said Jordan, changing the subject, "is the spot where I signal passing ships for supplies."

"I've seen the fires."

"And you always go to the other side of the island when sailors come ashore." When Newton remained silent, Jordan slowly shook his head from side to side. "I'm just saying, you needn't give up hope."

Newton wiped a forearm across his forehead. A breeze rustled through the palm trees and offered a momentary respite from the heat. Hope died a long time ago in a field full of lime trees. My life would be so different today if I were home with Polly. I remember telling Abigail I'd do more than make promises. I'd show her. I can hear those words as clearly as if I just spoke them. What a child I was, and she knew it. He turned his head away from Jordan, shut his eyes and pressed back the tears.

Chapter 23

Rescued

Plantains, Africa (1749)

"And you will know the truth, and the truth will set you free."
John 8:32

Captain Swanwick was sure he'd seen a wisp of smoke on the shore, but then it vanished, and he questioned his own eyesight. His mission was clear: find John Newton and bring him home. The assignment took him to every island on the map, and to some that were not yet charted. At times, he couldn't help but wonder if his friend's son was lost forever. After all, anything could happen in this part of the world. If he failed, Swanwick would be the one breaking the news to    John's father, something he wished to avoid at all costs. He had to keep looking.

Wallace Jordan, who had camped near the beach for three days while waiting for a ship to appear, ran up to the pile of dried yellow prongs and gingerly lit a match. The wind blew out the flame, and he struck another, this time cupping his hands around the blue and yellow flicker until the leaves began to smolder.

The sun glinted off the choppy water, producing listless waves of hot air that undulated skyward only to evaporate. Swanwick was sure there was something more than mist out there along the shore. He lowered his spyglass once, raised it again for one final look, and held it steady.  Just as he was about to collapse the lens back into his pocket, the vapor lifted and Swanwick's eye clearly identified a circular column of smoke ascending into a cerulean sky. He turned to the helmsman and yelled, "Bring her hard to port." In less than an hour, the transport lay in shallow water. Swanwick stood with his boot on the railing and watched a man paddle his canoe out to meet them.

"Ahoy, there," called out Jordan. "We are in need of supplies, if you're agreeable to some trading."

"We are, indeed," said the captain. "Come aboard."

Both men retired to the shipmaster's cabin and sat in two chairs across from one another. "The name's Jordan, Wallace Jordan, and I own several trading stations along this route."

Swanwick looked the man over. He was tall, lean and wore no shirt, his chest bronzed by many hours in the tropical sun. Most of all, he did not fit his expectation of a businessman.

"Oh, I can tell what you're thinking," said Jordan. "We're pretty informal around here. I've been doing this for a long time, and it's a good life. Slow by European standards, but it suits me. I'm not looking to get rich, just live well."

Both men smiled. "Understood, Mr. Wallace. As one gets older, the value of money and power diminish, while gratification is more likely to be found in making a difference in one's life."

One hour later, a firm handshake sealed the details of their trade. Swanwick took advantage of a long-established tradition reserved for the close of every transaction. "Now, will you join me for a glass of Port? This is hard work, and it can give a man a powerful thirst."

"Of course," said Jordan, rubbing the palms of his hands together.

The men toasted one another and soon one drink led to a second and more conversation. They discovered they had much in common, as well as similar values.

"Times are changing, my friend," said Swanwick. "It's hard to know who to trust these days."

Jordan tilted his glass in agreement, before taking another sip. "Especially this far from real civilization."

The glass was near empty, and Swanwick refilled it. "My goodness, I just remembered," he said, his voice urgent. "There's more to this trip than transporting goods. I'm on a mission for an old friend. His son has disappeared and may be on one of these islands. The father hopes to return him back home to England. Do you know of anyone hereabouts named John Newton?"

Jordan sat upright and tightened his grip on the glass that was slick with sweat. The last person he expected anyone to come searching for was his friend, the man who exiled himself into native culture and turned his back on his past.

"John Newton, ya say? Indeed, I do."

Swanwick's telling eyes widened. It was a question asked over a hundred times in recent months, only to receive the same disappointing answer. It was an extreme longshot, but now he wondered if he hadn't stumbled onto the right man.

"This fellow was released from a British vessel after some trouble. He won't talk about it much. Somehow or other he came here to work for Amos Clow at the Plantains and was turned into a slave. He would have died there, had I not rescued him. He's currently under my employment and has more or less turned himself over to this way of life."

"Then good fortune is mine," exclaimed Swanwick. "I've been looking for this man for months without so much as a hint of his whereabouts. That is, until a few days ago when I spoke to the man you mentioned. I believe you said his name was Clow. Strange sort of chap. Wouldn't tell me much except that a man named Newton was seen in these parts. I'm afraid he never mentioned your name."

"I'm not surprised. Clow is a bitter, angry man, not given to helping people."

"Well, your fire did the trick, or perhaps it was God."

"You say his father wants him back home? I don't want to pry, but could you tell me something more about his family?"

"His father is quite concerned, desperate, in fact, to know if his son is still alive. Despite an earlier rift in their relationship, he'd welcome the boy home with open arms." Swanwick set his glass back down on the table. "Will you show me where I can find him?"

"I'll be glad to take you to his house; however, there's something you need to know first," -

Swanwick's eyebrows lifted, expressing his curiosity. "My God, why not?" Jordan remained silent as he formulated an answer. Finally, he said, "He keeps some family things locked away. I suspect there are many reasons. The short answer is that John is a man who has lost his way."

A raised eyebrow expressed Swanwick's curiosity. "What do you mean, lost his way?'"

"Apparently, he can't imagine facing his father after making such a mess of his life. And there's a girl back home. So much time has passed; he's convinced that she's found someone else. He doesn't know that for certain, and he's afraid to find out. That's what happens when a man fails one too many times. At some point, he'll just stop trying."

Swanwick dismissed the matter with a lazy wave of his hand. "Those are things easily dealt with. His father has forgiven everything. He just wants his son back. And as for the woman, there's always someone else. He needs to get back among his own kind."

Jordan nodded agreeably, wondering if he should continue. Finally, he said, "What I'm about to say is just my opinion, if you will. John's lost his faith in God, and without God, none of us has any hope."

"All the more reason to get him back home, back to civilization. No offense intended, sir."

"None taken. I appreciate your desire to help," said Jordan.

Swanwick slowly stood up, placed a hand on the table, and shook off the effects of the port. "I'll let you in on a secret. John's father has authorized me to bring his son back, even if I have to kidnap him.

"Frankly, Jordan, I'm prepared to use any form of trickery or force necessary to get that boy aboard this vessel and out to sea. Can I count on your help?"

Jordan stood, nodded his head affirmatively and offered his hand. "He is my friend. I'll do whatever it takes to save him, even if I have to lie."

Chapter 24

Imitation of Christ

Kittam, Africa (1749)

"Be sober-minded; be watchful. Your adversary the devil prowls around like a roaring lion, seeking someone to devour." 1Peter 5:8

By noon, Captain Swanwick found himself on the small island of Kittam, seated on the front porch of Jordan's house, a white bungalow, carved out of the trees and surrounded by tropical flowers. Jordan and Newton sat across from the old sea captain, all three lounging in large wicker chairs. Introductions were in order, and then an offer of wine, followed by some small talk about the plantation. And when the conversation waned, Jordan took the lead. "Captain    Swanwick has some information for you, John. I hope you'll listen."

Swanwick took out a handkerchief and wiped the sweat from the inside of his cap. He talked slowly as his eyes followed his hands, choosing his words carefully. "John, I'm sure you recall my association with your family, and of course, I know a bit of your history. I understand you wrote your father right after they pressed you into service. I believe you asked him for help."

Newton casually crossed his legs. "How is my father?"

"He's well, and very concerned about you," said Swanwick as he took a pipe from his breast pocket. He tapped the instrument several times then retrieved some tobacco from a pouch, thumbing it in the bowl as he talked. "He wrote, but I don't believe the mail ever reached you before you transferred off the Harwich. There were unsuccessful efforts to find you. Your father eventually asked for my help, and I've been searching for you ever since."

Newton listened to the words and stoically peered off into the distance. "I suppose that I always knew this day would come. My father and I have had many differences over the years, but I never doubted his love. You are fortunate to have found me, Captain. I was set to leave tomorrow on business."

"Perhaps it was God's will," suggested Swanwick, as he lit the pipe.

Newton blinked several times as he considered the possibility. It had been some time since anyone talked of God in his presence. "You have the advantage, sir. I'm not much on discerning God's will these days."

Swanwick blew a plume of blue gray smoke into the air. "Your father would like you to come back home, John. My ship's anchored not far from here. If you accept the offer, you'll have your own quarters, and all the privacy you want. Would you like me to make room for you?"

Newton grasped the armrests of his chair, leaned forward and looked directly at Swanwick. Although his body spoke of his resolve, his voice remained calm. "Leave? I've no intention of leaving. Not today, not ever."

"Mr. Jordan explained that you might feel that way," continued Swanwick, his tone casual. "I'm asking you to reconsider before making a final decision. You're being offered a fresh start, a way to return home with respect and an excellent future."

Newton laughed, although his tone was serious. "What kind of respect would anyone at home have for me? After all, I've done nothing but destroy my life. The truth is, I've come to accept living here. The isolation has brought me some peace of mind. I can survive there, and remain separated from my past. Honestly, starting all over again isn't very appealing at this point. No, my friend, my future will be far better if I stay here."

Newton watched Swanwick, the lines around his mouth tightening with frustration. He was a sea captain, though, and that kind of man did not give up easily. "I understand how you feel," he continued. "I might have done the same thing if I were in your position." Swanwick waited long enough to take a nervous breath, weighing his next statement. "There's something more. Your father has authorized me to tell you that a relative recently passed away and left you an inheritance. A great deal of money, in fact."

Newton's eyes flickered. His mother had often joked about a wealthy member of the family, saying a distant uncle had willed them enough money to make them all rich. "How much are we talking about, Captain?"

"You're to receive four hundred pounds a month, enough to live comfortably for the rest of your life."

The possibilities stunned Newton. He let his gaze drop to floor, hiding any hint of interest.

"I have also been instructed to offer you the luxury of my cabin and invite you to dine at my table. You'll have all the amenities of a first-class passenger."

A moment ago, Newton was committed to losing himself in a forsaken land. Now he found the offer to return home irresistibly attractive. His position in society would be elevated and the money would allow him to approach Polly's parents with a proposal of marriage, if she wasn't already married to someone else by now. Her parents would no longer have any reason to object.    And if Polly was still free, his return might rekindle their romance. If there was any chance at all, he was now willing to take it.

Newton stood and smiled for the first time in months. It was a smile never witnessed by Jordan, a smile of hope. "Captain Swanwick," he said, "when do we sail?"

* * *

The return trip to England was by no means the most direct route. The Greyhound was a vessel in search of gold, ivory, camwood, and beeswax. It docked in Gambia and Sierra Leone, as well as shorter stays off beaches in numerous river estuaries. The voyage involved thousands of miles and took upwards to a year. Time stopped for Newton, and each day was bleaker than the one before. He rose at daybreak, unable to sleep with the noise of sailors moving about as they completed the routines of ship maintenance. He washed, shaved and ate with Swanwick in his cabin. He speculated that the captain delayed his meals until Newton joined him. Their conversations were brief and shallow. Afterward, Swanwick went about his duties, leaving his passenger to his own company, giving him time to think. Sometimes a man can think too much, he reasoned. It's getting me nowhere. Just a circle ending where it began.

One morning as they lay moored off another nameless harbor, Newton silently ate his food, looking at no one, daydreaming about the fortune that awaited him.

The captain poured himself a second cup of coffee and offered Newton a refill, which he declined. "I have a confession to make, John," he said haltingly. "It's about your inheritance."

"Oh," said, Newton. "This sounds like bad news."

"It is and it isn't." Swanwick blew into his cup before sipping the hot liquid. "When your father hired me, he was very clear about wanting to get his son back. There was to be no holding back; in fact, I could have kidnapped you, if necessary."

Newton sighed. "Is there a point to this? You said it was about my inheritance."

"That's just it. Telling you there was money waiting for you in England was the only way to get you back home. I hate to break it to you like this, but there is no inheritance."

Newton's throat closed, and his eyes burned. He found it hard to speak and when he did, he spewed out the words. "So, you lied to me. Is that it?"

Swanwick sipped the coffee once more before answering. "I did, indeed but for a worthy cause."

"I'll be the judge of that, sir. This is strange behavior for someone who calls himself a Christian."

"I'm sure I deserved that," said Swanwick, looking directly at his would-be friend. "As I said before, you wouldn't have agreed to come without some kind of story to get you aboard. I apologize for the lie but not the motives."

Newton folded his napkin and let it drop to the table. The truth was, I doubted the story all along, but something kept pulling me back to England. Perhaps it was the memory of Polly. I'd never admit it that my time was leading nowhere. I was barely existing, no purpose in life. I needed to come back home to heal.

"I need to think about this before I say anything more." Newton stood and walked out onto the main deck.

The captain followed and when he caught up and asked, "Can I walk with you?"

"I suppose," said Newton, looking out over the water.

The two men strolled around the perimeter of the vessel, and when they reached the side facing the ocean, Swanwick looked out at the vast body of water before him. "It's all quite magnificent, isn't it? I never tire of looking at the sea."

"Yes it is," said Newton. "I once saw the line where the Atlantic and Pacific Oceans merge off Cape Point, on the southern tip of Africa. It's quite surreal, standing there watching the two great bodies of water churning against one another, neither one giving way. You can actually see the different colors of the oceans as they push against each other."

Newton reached back into the archives of his memory and spoke as if talking to himself. "Seeing the two bodies of water, each equally matched, was a spectacular sight for a young lad, like myself. It was enough to prove the existence of God to me, at least in a roundabout way. How else could one explain it?"

"I find that quite interesting, said the old man. "I understand you have a different philosophy today."

"You must have been talking to Jordan. Is that what this walk is about?" Mockery resonated in Newton's intonation.

"Normally, I excuse myself when other men talk of religion and God. It's a very personal subject."

"Let me guess. You're going to make an exception this time," said Newton, cutting the older man off before he was quite finished. He had no intention of entertaining another evangelistic effort to save his soul. He turned slightly, as if to walk away. "Is this something that can wait till another time? I'm tired."

"I'm afraid it can't," said Swanwick, his voice still low and steady. "Your radical behavior is affecting the crew. One wouldn't expect that kind of complaint from a motley bunch like this group. Truth is, you're scaring them, John."

"Afraid? Of me?" Newton chuckled.

"Not of you, son, of the Lord. They're concerned that you're going to make God angry, and somehow catch them in the middle."

Newton balked. "Talk about hypocrisy. These are all grown men, and it's not the first time they've heard profane words."

Swanwick released a long frustrated breath. "It's true, most of them are a salty, profane collection if sailors. But you have some education, John, albeit informal. Your parents raised you to fear God. Yet, you go out of your way to find new ways to insult the very God that loves you. But it's more than that. It's as if you go out of your way to pick a fight with God."

"Tell me, what' sailor doesn't swear?" A crooked smile etched itself into Newton's cheek. "It's just a way to better express my feelings."

"Your language is only part of the problem. You seem to have a gift for revelry, as well."

Newton recalled the incident and it forced the corners of his mouth involuntarily downward. Attempting to prove that he could out drink any man aboard, he challenged the other men to a drinking contest.

"I understand you nearly fell overboard the other night," Swanwick said.

Surprised that the gossip had reached the captain's ears, Newton offered a half-hearted explanation. "A few of us were near the rail, where I was reciting a poem. A gust of wind caught my hat and blew it over the side. I was going to jump into the Longboat and go after it, but apparently someone moved the boat."

"Some might call that being blind drunk," Swanwick fired back. "If another man hadn't grabbed you by the collar, you might not be here now. How would I explain your having drowned to your father?"

Newton said nothing. The longer he waited to get home, the more impatient and angry he became. Frustrated beyond reason, liquor became his only solution; it tamped down the rage and gloom. If he understood his conduct, he might be able to justify it to the captain, but he didn't know himself. The only thing he was sure of was that he had been cycling through bouts of melancholy. In the end, he decided that this was just another round in an unavoidable and relentless fight against the rest of the world. It was a pattern that had dogged him for the past decade. As much as he tried, nothing freed him from the misery of dealing with people in general.

With fatherly compassion, Swanwick reached over and placed his hand on Newton's shoulder. "As you know, I have the authority to force you to leave, to end it right here and now. But that wouldn't change a thing." The old sea captain faced Newton and held his gaze for a moment. "John, have you ever wondered if you're under attack?"

"Attack … attacked by whom?"

Swanwick gently squeezed the younger man's shoulder. "I'm asking you to be serious for a moment. You already know the answer to that question. Perhaps you should think it over. In the meantime, I have a book you might like to read. It's entitled The Imitation of Christ, and it once meant a great deal to me. Changed my life, in fact."

"I read a book once about religion. You see where that led."

Swanwick produced the book from his inside coat pocket and turned it over, examining it carefully. "This once was a great help to me when I was your age."

"My age?

"I wasn't always a believer," he said, handing over the book. "There was a time in my life when I was lost. I lived only for myself, and only for today.

The words surprised Newton and he searched the old man's face for a more information.

"I'll leave you to your thoughts, my boy. By the way, we're setting sail in an hour."

Chapter 25

Storm of the Century

Atlantic Ocean (1749)

"Jesus was in the stern, sleeping on a cushion. The disciples woke him and said to him, 'Teacher, don't you care if we drown?'" Matthew 4:38

John Newton awakened from a sound sleep by a thunderous crash.

He rolled out of his hammock, only to find himself knee-deep in water. The ship groaned like an old woman, complaining that her ancient body could no longer endure the sea's punishment.

Out of the night's darkness, someone shouted, "Alarm, Alarm, the ship is sinking!"

Using the canvas hammock to pull himself out of the water and onto his feet, Newton looked around the crew's sleeping quarters. The room was darker than normal, save for one shaft of light descending from the hatch leading to the main deck. Other men shouted and cursed the darkness as they stumbled about, groping for something to hang onto. Newton slogged over to the stairs and worked his way up. No sooner had he cleared the doorway then he saw Captain Swanwick, both hands holding onto the ship's wheel. The wind whipped his slicker into the air behind him, and the man's eyes filled with a dreadful fear.

"Quickly," shouted Swanwick, "get me a knife."

The crisis left no time for questions. Blind, unwavering obedience was not only expected but demanded, and for good reason. One man, the captain, was responsible for the lives of all those aboard. Newton did an about-face, started down the stairs, and for reasons he could never explain, turned and looked back. In less than a fraction of a second, a man standing where    Newton stood seconds before was swallowed by a giant green wall of seawater and disappeared into eternity. The moment, although surrounded by noise and confusion, seemed strangely still.    The man looked into Newton's eyes, and then he was no more.

The salty spray and clatter of another wave lashed the deck and brought Newton's mind back to the needs of the present. With no time to lose, he located the knife and hauled his drenched body back to the main deck. He now saw complements of men all around the ship, scooping up the dark liquid with buckets and siphoning water through two-handled pumps. But that was not true of the entire crew. Some men ran about chaotically, seemingly with no purpose.

Fundamental to every ship's ability to stay afloat is the integrity of its superstructure, the skeleton of the vessel. Bonded to that is its skin, the outer planks along the hull and over the deck. Newton instinctively knew some of the Greyhound's framework had fractured. He latched onto the rigging and crossed his hands one over the other until he half-walked, half-swam to the bridge. "Here, Captain," he said, handing up the knife. The eyes of the two men locked together.   Newton could not bring himself to break free of the captain's fixed eyes.

"I warned you about this, Newton."

The ship rolled again, as if trying to extract itself from a wild animal determined to bring down its prey. Newton looked away, grabbed a lanyard for balance and for the first time saw the breathtaking crater in the side of the hull. Although above the water line, the green water continued to spill into the bowels of the vessel. Captain Swanwick pointed and shouted at his men, placing them where they could do the most good. "You there," he yelled at one sailor who stood among the chaos, eyes glazed over, "lay your hands on that pump and get to work. Bozeman, round up that motley cluster and organize a repair party on that hole." And finally to another seaman, who was overwhelmed by the turmoil and confusion, "You, find some more buckets, or anything else you can bail with."

Newton watched as the men began to settle down and work more efficiently. Swanwick encouraged, demanded, and then threatened until he got what was needed out of each man.

Without waiting for further orders, Newton reached down and caught the handle of a bucket floating past, dipped it into the water and threw the dark contents back into the raging ocean. He performed the same task repeatedly for an hour straight, until his muscles would no longer respond. His numb limbs dangled at his side as he looked up, hoping to see the morning light on the horizon. Never before had he experienced such thick darkness.

A crate drifted by and he realized the cargo of lumber and beeswax was helping to keep the ship afloat. Looking about, he waded over to a group desperately stuffing pieces of timber, hammocks and clothing into the hole. Shoulder to shoulder, they forced all manner of debris into the cavity, choking off the water. Holding the material in place with up-stretched arms, the men looked at one another and began to laugh nervously. Then lightning crackled across the sky, and Newton could see rain dripping from their faces, nodding heads and encouraging smiles. They had overcome the worst of the damage.

Newton's spirits began to lift. "Lads," he yelled, "Tomorrow we'll have a good laugh about all this and drink an entire keg of ale."

Before the sentence was complete, a teary-eyed lad standing above him on the quarterdeck solemnly stated, "No, no, it's too late for that. None of us will ever see the sun rise again."

Fear and despair are contagious. The boy's prediction invaded Newton's heart like a virus, and he began to fear that this would be his last day on earth. He saw the commander's eyes sifting through the rain until they abruptly stopped with him.

"So, Newton," the captain yelled into the wind, "You see now what happens when one spits in the face of God. We all want to know how you feel about it now, boy."

The storm carried the words across the deck and into every ear. Each man turned and grimaced at their Jonah.

Perhaps he is right. Maybe I am responsible for the storm.

John's head hung in shame, avoiding the obvious verdict of his audience.

"Maybe the sea will calm down if we throw you overboard." The captain's voice was hard, on the edge of ordering his men to carry out the task. Each man stood ready, waiting for confirmation, but it never came. Instead, the captain bellowed, "Pray for forgiveness, John. That's our only hope. Now, the rest of you get back to the work of staying alive."

Newton tried to lift another bucket of water, but his arms hung like dead pieces of meat.

Seeing his condition, the first mate grabbed him by the arm and walked Newton over to the helm. "You," he said to the man steering the ship, "go over to the port side and help bail." Then he took Newton's hand and placed it on the wheel. "If you can't lift, perhaps you can steer."

Newton nodded, too exhausted to speak.

In a few moments, the first mate returned with a length of rope. He took Newton's wrist and bound it to the wheel. "No wave will get ya now, lad. Just do your best to steer us out of the storm."

Unsteady, he leaned heavily against the wheel and noticed that the temperature was dropping, causing his body to shiver uncontrollably. His eyes lifted toward the canvas sails, ripped and tattered. Many of the arms of the masts had broken and splintered. Most of the men now had a faraway look in their eyes. Each man took is turn at the pump, their eyes empty, they movements mechanical.

*At least here, I can rest against the wheel and think. Odd, how time seems to stand still during these moments. My life may end soon, and I have nothing to show for it.*

He recalled the story of the Prodigal Son. If only I could make it back home. But given the chance, would I really do anything different? I've lost any chance for a future. My loved ones will never know what happened to me. Worst of all, I've lost my way, my faith.

When the fourth watch arrived, Newton was relieved from his post. He went to the stern of the ship and received a ration of fish. It was a safe place to take shelter, and it gave him time to rest his mind and body.

Another man, whose face Newton could not quite make out, sat down near him in the darkness. "I saw you looking out over the water a few moments ago," he said. "Don't bother looking for land, my friend. Once you accept the inevitable, the rest is easy."

Newton looked over, still unable to see more than an outline of the face. "Surely the Lord will have mercy on us," he said with an air of hope. No sooner had he said the words than her realized their utter futility. What a mindless thing to say. What possible reason would God have for offering me mercy?

He solemnly tore off another piece of the dried fish and chewed in silence. I always assumed I'd live a long life. Is this what death is like, black as ink, eternally separated from God?

In the still of the moment, the depths of his soul cried out. Please, God, save me! And before the thought was complete, Newton found himself bathed in a powerful shaft of sunlight that burst through blackness, revealing a glorious white and gray cloud carved out of a cobalt sky. The warmth of the sun pressed against the faces of the men as they turned to the heavens.

Then a voice sounded out from the crow's nest, "Land ho!" The broadcast brought forth a spontaneous cheer as men began to backslap and hug one another. Newton followed the direction of the lookout's extended arm and watched a strand faintly appear in the mist.

No longer fearing starvation, trembling hands tenuously seize the remaining ration of fish and hard biscuits. The men fed their hungry bellies, swallowing the handfuls of food in half-chewed lumps.

Then someone spoke the unspoken question that was on each man's mind. "What if it's just a mirage?"

"Don't say that," said half-dozen voices. The men quickly rebuked him with jeers all around. One even pushed the naysayer from behind, causing him to stumble.

Like a prophetic utterance, the strand vaporized before their eyes. The wind roiled itself into yet another storm, pushing the orphaned vessel further from its course and denying its citizens the salvation that was plainly visible only moments before.

"If the sea doesn't drown us, it'll starve us to death," said another, giving a voice to the thoughts of the men standing nearby.

One man standing next to Newton broke down and fell to his knees weeping. His words echoed his earlier prediction. "It's no use," he babbled. "We're all dead men."

As an invisible wind pushed the small band further out to sea, each man's heart turned inward, offering its final prayer.

Unexpectedly, and without explanation, the wind changed direction, gently pressing the damaged sails in the other direction, toward life.

"That's amazing," said one sailor. "In all my years at sea, I never seen the wind act like." The men remained silent as time passed, afraid that speaking might bring bad luck. In a few hours, the watchman peered through the mist and once again his eyes squinted when he saw a brown strip of land. He waited until his eyes were sure, then called out in a hopeful voice, "Land ho on the port side! Land ho!"

Once more, cautious laughter rose from parched, husky voices. The darkness cleared, and the men could now see how close to land they had been the entire time. Their spirits renewed and energized, all continued to labor until the ship found its way to safety.

Newton remained apart from the throng. I don't know what I should feel. I am just glad to be alive, but I'm different now, a new person in Christ. Then he whispered a prayer that summed up most of his life. "I surrender," he whispered.

Chapter 26

A New Life

Liverpool, England (1749)

"But while he was still a long way off, his father saw him and was filled with compassion for him; he ran to his son, threw his arms around him and kissed him." Luke 15:20

Joseph Manesty sat behind a well-appointed mahogany desk where he spent most of his waking hours. He had easily transitioned from sea captain to ship owner. Commanding a ship, however, offered a man a sense of exhilaration unlike anything else he had ever experienced, and he missed his life at sea. Instead, he had to settle for the mundane tasks of an administrator whose command reached only as far as the office door. His body never failed to remind him that he had grown older. Aches and pains took up residency and refused all efforts to evict them. Admitting that he was getting old was hard, but the evidence left him no choice. And admit it. That did not mean he had to like it.

The warm afternoon sun shone through the office window and filled the room. Absorbed in his work, the old man hardly noticed when the door opened. Hearing the hatch creak, he looked up just in time to see Captain Douglas Swanwick arrive.

"Hello, Joseph," said Swanwick, as he offered an enthusiastic handshake. "When are you going to oil that door? The sea dog I knew would have ordered that taken care of long ago."

Manesty jumped to his feet and firmly grasped the hand of his old friend. "Welcome back, and thank God you're safe." His voice brimmed with genuine appreciation.

"I can't tell you how good it is to be here," Swanwick agreed, a broad smile on his weathered face. "There were moments when I was certain we'd never make it."

"I imagine so. There's been talk of the storm all over the city. Some say a gale that strong comes but once a century." Manesty directed his hand toward two chairs. "Come, sit down, Douglas.    Have some port."

Swanwick sat back contentedly and watched his employer pour a generous glass of wine. He sipped the red liquid and let it linger against his pallet before swallowing loudly. After taking a moment of savoring the taste, he let the glass rest on his knee. "I've come to make my report, of course."

"I've been expecting you," said Manesty. "I'm anxious to know how things went with young Newton. Years ago, he failed to show up after signing onto one of my ships. I had even offered him a partnership on my plantation. I lost track of him after that, until his father contacted me last year asking for help. He was desperate to find out if the boy was still alive. That, of course, was when I sent you searching for him."

Manesty filled his glass again and offered Swanwick another. He nestled his back into a tall wingback chair and waited. "Newton wasn't any different for most of the voyage back home.    I seriously considered throwing him overboard in the middle of the storm."

Manesty tilted his head, and his face registered concerned surprise. "You don't mean that."

Swanwick averted his stare and looked across the desk. "I'm ashamed to admit I do, at least, at that moment, I did. It's no exaggeration when I say his being aboard was a threat to our lives."

Manesty dismissed the admission with a wave of his hand, mindful that the movement did not cause the port to spill. "Oh, that sounds like a seafarer's myth."

"It was, and it is," agreed Swanwick. "At the time, though, I seriously considered it. I didn't think we'd survive that first night. A mighty wave collided with the side of the ship and left a huge hole in the midsection. I can't explain it. I was sure there was some connection between our situation and Newton's behavior. Somehow I was felt we'd have a better chance if we threw him over the side."

Manesty measured his friend's words once he realized Swanwick making a confession of sorts. He wasn't exaggerating.

"Oh, I know, I know," Swanwick continued, shrugging his shoulders. "My better judgment hold of me at the last minute and I decided to ride out the storm. Now I can't believe I ever considered such an act."

Manesty shook his head from side to side, almost imperceptibly. He decided to push past the comment and move forward. "So, you didn't kill the boy. And I suspect you'll not sign him on again, either."

One corner of Swanwick's mouth curved upward into a half-smile. "No. . . I mean, no, that's not it at all. I'd hire him again today."

Now Manesty looked perplexed, and he knocked back the glass, killing the rest of his port.    When he looked back at Swanwick, he barked, "Hang it all, man, say what you mean."

"That's what I'm trying to do." Swanwick held up his hand, as if to plead for his employer's indulgence. "I watched Newton during the storm. One might say I literally watched him change during the four days we were lost. Afterward he became my best man. He worked when he didn't have to. His superiors never had to give him an order, and he turned from a rebel-rouser into a peacemaker. Joseph, if ever there was a miracle, this was it. He's a man transformed."

Manesty raised a troubled brow. "Wouldn't his fear of death account for all of that?"

"Normally, I'd say yes, but I think his attitude is genuine."

"So, the Prodigal has returned. His father will be quite pleased."

"Yes," said Swanwick, setting his empty glass down on the desk. "And the boy deserves the fatted calf."

Manesty stopped, reflecting, and then his eyes began to sparkle. "I don't have a calf," he said, "but if he's as good as you say, I'd gladly give him another chance. He can take command of the Brownlow, my newest ship."

Chapter 27

Home Again

Chatham, England (1749)

"The fear of the Lord is the beginning of wisdom; all those who practice it have a good understanding." Psalms 9:10

John Newton was having serious doubts.

He walked the small hills and curves of the cobblestone road, the heels of his highly polished shoes clicking against the pavement. The Catlett house was visible from where he stood, and he could see Abigail kneeling in her garden, planting the season's first flowers. Spring was everywhere, and life was in bloom.

Will the family accept me after all I've put them through, after all this time? And will Polly still feel the same way? Has she found someone else by now? The idea had crossed his mind a thousand times since starting the journey back to what he now called home.

As he neared the house, Abigail stood, turned in his direction and lifted a hand to shield her eyes from the sun. She seemed not to recognize the man nearing her home.

John had grown taller and filled out across his chest. His hair, while longer and tied in back, was well-barbered, and his face clean-shaven. And he had purchased a new suit of clothes especially for this occasion.

He studied Abigail's face for some reaction as he approached. Unexpectedly, she bolted in his direction and leaned over the fence, arms outstretched. "John," she cried, "finally." She briefly hugged him and then pushed herself back, still holding onto his shoulders. "Let me look at you. My goodness, you've changed so. We received your letter. Oh, listen to me ramble. Polly's in the backyard."

John tried to speak, but tears began to blur his vision as he tenderly embraced the woman who had taken the place of his mother.

Hearing the conversation, Polly came to the front door. It took her a moment to recognize the man to which she remained dedicated.

Newton saw that the girl he'd left behind had disappeared. Polly was a woman now, with a woman's mind and heart. The picture of perfection, she was dressed in a plain white dress with a simple blue ribbon in her hair. Her smile, tender and gentle, spoke of enduring love. Her step was purposeful and deliberate. She quickly walked through the yard until she was against him, nestled into John's strong arms. A stream of tears trickled down, and she wiped her cheek against his shoulder, unable to speak at first.

"John, my darling, John," she murmured against his cheek. "Finally, you've come back."

Newton buried his face against her neck. "You've no idea," he whispered, "how often I dreamed of this moment, of coming *home*."

They continued holding hands while walking toward the backyard, talking in low tones. At that moment, no one else in the world existed.

The short stroll concluded naturally under the shade of the trellis where they had first talked during their early courtship. They sat down, sharing little at first, preferring the quietness of the moment. It was

Polly who spoke first. "By now you know your father retired and took a position in Canada. What you might not have heard, though, is that he wrote mother and said he approved of our marriage."

Newton smiled inwardly. His father would be pleased with his son's transition to manhood. "There is still a great deal for me to accomplish before I can pledge myself further," he said. "It would not be fair for you to be bound to the man I once was."

Polly looked upward into her love's face, unable to speak for a moment. "I know you've changed. I can see it in your eyes."

"I have changed, too," said John, "but I owe it to you and your mother to prove that the change is permanent."

"John, you know I want to make plans, permanent plans that include marriage. Haven't we waited long enough? How will putting it off make things any better?"

"I need to test myself." Newton's expression was solemn. "I have so many black marks against me. I've got to build a new history, one that speaks to the kind of man we all hope I am." Newton squeezed Polly's hand and watched her smile back at him.

"Hope you are?" said Polly. "That's a strange thing to say."

"It probably does sound strange. I've had so many false starts, so many failures. For both our sakes, I have to prove that this is real, prove it to you and to myself."

"I'm told Joseph Manesty has offered to let you command one of his ships. I'm so proud, John. You're going to become a captain."

"I hope he knows how grateful I am, but I'm not going to accept the position." John could see the disappointment in Polly's face, as well as her bewilderment, and he tried to explain. "I need discipline in my life. It will be better if I serve as second-in-command for a while. Then we will see if Captain Manesty's offer still stands."

Polly lowered her eyes and leaned into John's shoulder. "Just as you say, John, just as you say."

Chapter 28

First Trial

Charles Town, South Carolina (1750)

"Blessed is the one who perseveres under trial because, having stood the test, that person will receive the crown of life that the Lord has promised to those who love him." James 1:12

Newton joined several other captains for supper at the Liberty Inn, a name that reflected the political mood of Charles Town. Like most cities along the coast, the wealthy resided on one side of town, while the sailors took temporary lodging in coastal taverns where one could get a hot meal, a sound bed and a good woman.

Newton concluded that by now, he was probably above that kind of temptation, having turned his life over to the Lord. It was the naive thinking of a man new in his understanding of spiritual matters, unaware of the ongoing great battles between good and evil that went unseen by humans. He was one of the last to arrive as the sun set, and the shops began to close. He joined several other captains who had taken up residence at a large table toward the back of the room. English mariners enjoyed good English ale, and the bartender gladly provided each man with a large mug filled with amber liquid.

"So, what took you so long?" asked the man who sat across from Newton. He gulped down a mouthful of the brew as he waited for an answer.

Newton wearily slumped back against a wooden pillar that

supported the roof. "I thought I'd get a look around the city, but all I want now is some stew and a soft bed."

The man set his mug down on the table and smiled. "Speaking of social opportunities, you'll find them here aplenty." Then he laughed raucously, holding the mug up in the air high enough for the doxy at the bar to take notice and bring him a fresh tankard.

The noisy talk and continuous laughter, the aroma of liquor, and especially the sight of the barmaids all commingled into the memory of another time when Newton was quite young and easily beguiled. Now, however, he was committed to living each day in a manner the reflected his innermost convictions.

But the man across from him persisted. He leaned on his elbows and looked at Newton through whiskey soaked eyes. His hat covered much of the gray hair that hung over his eyes.  When he spoke, the words came slow and thick. "I know what's on your mind, sir. Your reputation precedes you. There's talk that you're to remain faithful to someone back home. I salute you for it, I do." He raised his glass in a toast. "But a man can't be without a woman for months on end. It's impractical." The man downed the remainder of his mug and set the glass down hard on the table. "No one will think the less of you for it."

An uncomfortable knot formed in the pit of Newton's stomach. My personal life is none of this man's business, and I want no trouble. Perhaps he thinks Christians are judgmental think too highly of themselves.

The sailor gulped from his mug before continuing. "Some would go so far as to say that you're a slave for staying with one woman."

The accusation was like a slap in the face. Newton shot back, "And you, sir, are a slave to many?"

The remark produced a round of laughter from the surrounding tables, and the man's stare turned to stone. Seeking to dampen any hostility, Newton waved at a woman standing next to the bar. "Bring my friend another round, and I'll have one, as well."

Everyone took a breath and a few minutes later, the woman, not unlike the one of years ago, walked over to the table with two fresh mugs of beer. Her skirts swayed as she moved. She stopped at Newton's side and bent forward, letting her red hair fall across his shoulder. Glancing sideways, he took in the woman's ample cleavage. She lingered for a moment, giving her customer his money's worth, and then laughed as she raised back up.

The men joked and laughed for the next hour. There was talk of shipping, politics and, as always, of women. And the conversation allowed Newton to gaze over at the barmaid, who casually smiled from across the room. Then an unexpected yearning erupted, and Newton felt himself burn with passion. For months, he'd prayed for purity, for mental and physical freedom from lust. And God's grace had provided a spirit peace, until now. His heart thudded so loudly that he had trouble thinking. Despite his plans to eat and go to bed, he remained at the table and continued drinking.

As the night wore on, the woman leaned against the bar. Only the servings of the other customers interrupted her wandering glances in his direction. Occasionally, she would tilt her head in his direction and once she even winked. As the fire in the hearth burned down to coals that glowed in the darkness, she sauntered over to the table where many of the men were now unconscious or had wandered off with other women. She sat down on the bench, sidling in close to Newton. She rested an arm on his shoulder and tenderly pressed her lips next to his ear. "I want you," she whispered in seductive tones. "I don't know why I feel this way. But I do, and I can't wait any longer."

The woman's hot breath stirred Newton. She was pretty, and her skin was soft. He inhaled the aroma of her perfume and held it in his lungs. Then his mind snapped awake. He knew he must either run from the woman or give in. Taking in a deep breath and pulling back, he said, "I'm sorry, but I must leave."

The remaining men looked up stupidly, wondering at their friend's reaction.

"I bid you all goodnight, gentleman," said Newton, as he stood, put on his coat and without further explanation, and marched outside. He braced against cold night air and cleared his head and looked down at his trembling hands. *That was too close. I almost fell back into my old ways. Never again will I be that vulnerable; never again will I test God.*

Chapter 29

Judgment is Mine

The Plantains (1750)

"You have heard that it was said, 'Love your neighbor and hate your enemy.' But I tell you, love your enemies and pray for those who persecute you, that you may be children of your Father in heaven. He causes his sun to rise on the evil and the good, and sends rain on the righteous and the unrighteous. If you love those who love you, what reward will you get? Are not even the tax collectors doing that? And if you greet only your own people, what are you doing more than others? Do not even pagans do that? Be perfect, therefore, as your heavenly Father is perfect." Matthew 5:43

Newton stood at the helm of the Brownlow as she dropped anchor off the coast of Sierra Leone. He studied the line of white sand against the blue water. Like most days, the sun shone through a cloudless sky and a soft breeze grazed his face, carelessly lifting the collar of his shirt. The appearance was deceivingly peaceful for such a dangerous part of the world. Tribal law often resulted in small skirmishes regarding boundaries and territorial ownership among the islanders. Each man fended for himself in a world where strength and numbers determined the ultimate authority. Peace was no more than a temporary lull between the ever-present tribal conflicts.

Now a new enemy invaded the land. Arriving in ships and settling on large plantations. The Europeans used the native people against one another, capturing entire families and taking them across the water.

Newton's assignment was to barter for the slaves, install them in the lowest compartments of the ship, and deliver them safely to an auction house in England. However, he had in mind a greater purpose for this trip. After all, these are the Plantains, and I have unsettled business here.

"Make ready a Longboat," commanded Newton. He rested his hand on the shoulder of a subordinate and pointed to a tree that stood out on the shoreline. "You'll find a woman named Princess PI there. Offer my compliments and invite her aboard as my guest." Newton raised his hand and pressed his thumb and index finger together, emphasizing each word. "Make sure she knows my full name and rank, that I'm here to purchase slaves, and that I'll only bargain with her."

The seaman hesitated before asking, "But what if she refuses to come, sir?"

Newton kept his eyes on the shoreline and appeared to be formulating an answer. "Tell her I've prepared a meal in her honor, and that I've business to discuss. She can't refuse."

No more than an hour passed before Newton raised a spyglass to his eye and watched the Longboat pushing off from the shore. It contained two people, the member of his crew and a statuesque native woman, dressed in a long flowing dress that went all the way to her ankles. As the boat neared, Newton called his gunner's mate over.

"Fire off one of our cannons as a salute to our guest," he ordered. The seaman scampered off, and soon the unexpected blast of the gun sent shock waves through the still air. Newton watched as PI flinched at the sudden explosion, and then hung her head in humiliation. She quickly regained her composure, straightened her back, and remained stock-still during the rest of the crossing.

Newton collapsed the spyglass and tapped it against his palm. *She's quite regal when it's required, even under the most difficult conditions. But I know the evil that lies beneath the surface.*

When the boat thumped against the side of its mother ship, Newton offered to help PI step aboard. She took the hand but quickly released it once she regained her footing.

Newton stood, bowed low and gushed, "It is my great pleasure to see you again." As he rose to his feet, he saw the pinched expression on his guest's face. *She would blush if she weren't so dark.*

He escorted her to a table centered on the quarterdeck, where an assortment of fruits and nuts rested on top of a fine linen tablecloth. Newton pointed to a chair at the head of the table. "Please," he gestured, "sit and refresh yourself."

PI sat down and picked up a lime. Trembling fingers removed the skin, and she took a small bite. Although polite, her manner was mechanical, and she looked straight ahead, avoiding Newton's face.

"I hope you and Clow are well, and this has been a prosperous year," said Newton, opening the conversation with the expected pleasantries. Then he did something completely unexpected. He reached across the small table, placed his fingers under the woman's chin, and lifted it until she faced him. PI stared past Newton, refusing to meet his eyes. "Look at me," commanded Newton.

PI finally relented and met Newton's gaze.

"Have you had much luck with the crops this year? Has there been enough to eat?"

The princess only nodded, refusing to engage the second officer in conversation. Their roles reversed, she clearly did not like her new subordinate position.

"As you know, I am here to buy slaves," Newton continued, "and I want to deal directly with   Clow. Only him. Do you understand?"

Never speaking, PI responded with a reptilian smile, as if contemplating what the reunion would bring. With the terms clear, she quickly stood and paraded back to the Longboat. Her back remained ridged as the boat skimmed across the water. When she climbed out, every step declared her nobility, until she disappeared into the compound.

Newton watched from afar and took a moment to reflect. He had expected to find great satisfaction in forcing PI to acknowledge him as at least an equal. Instead, there was nothing but emptiness. He had anticipated the sweet satisfaction of reprisal, but it had not come. Only emptiness, a great void, lingered his soul. He could not reconcile revenge with being a Christian.   And with that realization, Newton began to understand how God was gradually shaping his life.

The next morning Newton went to the island, intending to inspect the latest captives. As soon as he stepped from his boat onto the beach, he saw Clow approaching.   The creases in his white shirt and linen pants were stiff from a combination of body oil and grime. Newton wondered how a man with countless slaves could go so long without assigning one of them to wash his clothes. Clow's greasy hair was no different, slicked back, except for an errant strand that limped across his shiny forehead.

"How good it is to see you again," said Clow, mimicking Newton's exaggerated bow from the day before. He gestured in the direction of a table laden with food, and said, "Come and sit where you can enjoy something to eat and drink."

Are they mocking me? He pulled up a chair, sat down, saying nothing.

"This is the first year we've been able to harvest these limes," Clow continued, filling his cup to the brim. "They're from the trees you planted the last time you were here in the village."

Newton blanched but let the taunt pass without comment. He had come full circle. Nothing Clow could say or do could alter that fact. His mind took him back to his last day on the island, the day he was planting the seeds that had since matured into the trees that provided him with shade from the sun, and drink that quenched his thirst. It was that day that he had been the object of a trade between Clow and Jordan, the friend who had rescued him. Newton gazed in the direction of the trees, now laden with fruit. Look at how they've grown, so tall and strong. God used my time here to change me, as well. That which was meant for evil, He used for good.

Newton knew that his former master was dependent on slave traders to sustain his way of life.    He drank his juice down slowly, breathed deeply and changed the subject. "As you know, I've come to trade for slaves."

"Good," said Clow as he signaled a native who disappeared into the bush and returned with a train of Africans tied together by a rope. "I rounded some up since I heard you would be coming."

The line of men, women and children were tied together by a leather rope, prodded along by spear-wielding natives until all stood beside the table where Newton assessed the merchandise.

It was an unexpected sight, even where slaves were common. The gaggle of humanity pulled one way and then the next. Mothers tried to reach around and cover their small children with protective arms, while the men, many of them warriors, all spoke at once, their words tumbling over one another, fierce with anger. They occasionally leaped forward as far as the rope would stretch, issuing challenges to their captors.

One of Clow's men gripped the end of the tether, shouted an order and jerked downward.    The slaves pulled back, voicing their objections in words that only they could understand. One prisoner, more prominent than the rest, lifted his chin, daring his guard to use the spear pointed at his chest. The native, obviously intimidated, pressed the tip until a red stripe ran down the slave's torso.

"Careful there," cautioned Clow, with a raised hand. "Don't damage the merchandise."

He waited for the throng to quiet down before making his sales pitch. Then he turned to Newton and said, "As you can see, the men are strong, the women will bear many children, some during the return voyage. It will substantially multiply your investment, and the children will grow into excellent field hands."

"Can't use the children," said Newton, coolly. "The captain doubts they'll survive the trip."

"And what'll I do with them if you take away their mothers," objected Clow, his voice rising. "They'll die here certain."

"That's not my problem." Newton calmly leaned forward, his forearms resting on the edge of the table. "I don't have the authority to buy anyone who looks younger than sixteen."

Clow drug his forearm across a glistening forehead and spat on the ground. "Then there'll be an additional fee for the rest of the lot. Regardless, there's going to be a ruckus when you try to move them."

"What do you mean by that?" quarried Newton.

"Never you mind," he said defiantly, dropping any pretense of respect. "Let's get started. Make your best offer, and we'll see if we can come to terms."

The men haggled back and forth for the next ten minutes. When they still did not agree, Clow said, "Come, come, Newton. Why don't you take a moment to inspect the stock more closely?"

Newton needed a break. The bartering was beginning to look more like an argument than a negotiation. He stood and walked along the line. He had never examined a human before, not like this. It was like looking at a cow or horse one bought at auction. He squeezed one man's bicep, testing the muscle. Another opened his mouth and let the buyer examine his teeth. Missing teeth signaled health problems and in some cases predicted death.       Clow bounced his fist off a third man's chest, testing the thick density. Another man, clearly a leader, defiantly stared at Clow, and the slaver glared back. When neither would relent, Clow spat on the ground.

"Be careful," he said, "that one will be trouble. Take my advice and keep his shackles double locked."

Newton took the warning seriously, and soon the men settled on a price, much to his relief. With their business concluded, Clow ordered the guards to corral the slaves onto a small transport boat and deliver them to the Brownlow.

One of the chief guards began shouting in his own language, obviously issuing orders. The others set about cutting the leather thongs, quickly separating the male slaves from the women, and the women from their children.

All at once, a great chorus of fear rose up from the mothers, who cried out, begging for their children. One woman fell to her knees, wailing as a guard tore her son from her arms. The small boy, along with the other children,   howled back, tears streaking down his black cheeks.

"Moma, Moma," they cried out, the words ringing in Newton's ears.

Newton bolstered his courage and started to object. Just as he was about to speak, he choked back the words. I'm here to buy slaves, not take up their cause. But ripping children from the arms of their mothers, even slave mother, is wicked.

Newton started to object, swallowed hard and forced the words back into his throat. At the same moment, he looked around, embarrassed that Clow might have seen. I'm here to buy slaves, not fight their battles. Anyway, who am I to judge others? I don't believe in God, and without God, there can be no right and wrong.  *

Chapter 30

One Taken, One Saved

Africa (1750)

"Remind me that my days are numbered." Psalm 39:4

The Brownlow lay anchored in the estuary of the River Cestors, some three hundred miles from Sierra Leone when the captain summoned the second officer. Newton left his quarters and found the senior officer pacing along the bow as he puffed on a briarwood pipe. He exhaled a cloud of blue smoke into the air and said, "I imagine the crew is about ready for the last leg of our journey."

Newton smiled and removed his hat. "I expect we all are, sir. We've been out for more months than I care to count."

"And you've done a top notch job of it, John. One I won't soon forget." The captain handed Newton a piece of paper. "We're going to need provisions, and it'll take several trips. I want you to personally take charge of getting that list purchased and stored below."

"Aye, Captain. I'll start work on it immediately."

An hour later Newton boarded the small craft with three other men. But before he could sit down, the captain rushed out of his quarters and leaned over the side of the ship's rail. "Mr. Newton," he wheezed, "belay my earlier order. I want you back on board." He pointed at another man seated in the boat. "You there, take charge of the detail."

Newton saw the determination in his captain's face and decided not to question his motives. Puzzled, but ever respectful, he came back

211

aboard and went about his duties.

Later that night a native rowed his canoe out to the Brownlow. Waving to the watchman, he yelled out, "I must speak to the man in charge."

"The captain's asleep," replied a bluejacket who was standing watch. "What's your business?"

Closer now, the native lowered his voice. His eyes remained steadily fixed on the sailor leaning over the side. "I cannot talk to anyone but the head man," he said.

The captain, who overheard the exchange, came out of his cabin. "It's the middle of the night, man. What's so blasted important?"

"The small boat you sent ashore," the native started, "hit a snag in the water. It turned over, and all the men drowned."

"Everyone?" asked Newton, who had taken a position next to the captain.

"Yes, sir. No one survived."

No one was more surprised at the news than Newton. The next day he approached the captain on the quarterdeck. "Excuse me, sir, but something is bothering me."

"Go, ahead," said the captain, puffing on his ever-present pipe.

"May I ask why you had someone else go in my place last night?"

The question clearly perplexed the captain, and his face turned red as he searched for an answer. He scratched his head and sputtered, "I can't say, John. I can't find the words to describe it. You know I'm not a religious man, never have been. But as the boat was about to cast off, it came to my mind that I must call you back." He turned his palms upward and said, "I can't explain it any better than that."

John Newton looked across the deck of the African, a fast sailing two-masted cargo brigantine. He had proved himself trustworthy and been appointed the ship's senior officer. He watched the crew of thirty as they busied themselves preparing the vessel for the next trip out. Watching the well-disciplined men gave him a sense of confidence in his new role. He intended to be firm but fair,\ and hoped to set a good example for his subordinates in the months ahead.

Off to his side, above the din of workers, a voice called out to him. "Ahoy, there . . . is that  Captain John Newton?"

Newton turned sharply toward the abrupt inquiry and saw someone he recognized from a lifetime ago. Job Lewis, his fellow midshipman on the HMS Harwich, was standing on the gangplank.

"Permission to come aboard, sir," requested Lewis, a large grin creasing his face.

His friend had grown older, acquiring a brush of premature grey in his temples. Lewis smiled warmly. Without a word, Newton marched over and the two men embraced, offering exaggerated insults that questioned the other's character.

"Seeing you is like a drink of fresh water to a marooned islander," said Newton as they stood back and appraised one another.

"You're not far off the mark," said Lewis. "I was scheduled to take command of my own ship, but my benefactor came upon hard times and lost his business in the bankruptcy courts. So in a sense, I am

I am marooned."

Newton's mind was already at work considering a remedy for his friend's situation, but he declined to speak. He had changed since he last served with Lewis. Two months prior, his dreams of marriage to Polly had come true. He was now fully committed to remaining faithful to her and to God.

"Will you join me for supper," asked Newton. "Unless you're otherwise engaged?"

"I'm at your service, sir." Lifting his hand to his brow, he saluted smartly.

Newton laughed at the pomp and ceremony. "Job, I'm afraid you are incorrigible."

"Indeed, I am," said Lewis with a mischievous wink.

Within the hour, the two men sat at a nearby tavern, eating a fine meal. They talked of old times and the experiences that had molded their lives in years past. As the night wore on Newton considered his plan, one that would give him a chance to make up for at least one of his past sins.

"Job," he said, "would you consider joining me on this trip? You would be fine company. Your only responsibility would be to entertain me, something you were always good at."

Lewis wiped his napkin across his lips, taking advantage of the moment to think. "Before I answer, I have a question. The rumor is that you've changed, that you're religious now. Am I going to have to put up with you trying to convert me? The idea of being trapped on a ship in the middle of the ocean with you clamoring away about God is more than I could bear."

Newton smiled. "I feel like a school boy caught cheating on an exam. I hope only to share my personal story of how God gave me back my life. I promise not to bore you."

"I warn you, John. I read Characteristics, the book you loaned me back in the day, and it changed my life. I've developed a taste for the vices of life and have no intention of turning back to the days of my youth. If you can accept me as a man of lesser character, then we have a bargain."

"With me the winner," said Newton, and the two men heartily shook hands on the arrangement.

Nevertheless, in the days that followed it became apparent that Newton's heart had trumped his logic. Lewis frequently told crude jokes and used his engaging personality to influence the other men, who acted more like boys. It was not uncommon during the evening hours to see the men in a circle, listening to his regaling accounts of his bawdy lifestyle. The stories always ended in the crowd's raucous laughter.

Newton tried his best to dissuade his friend, usually as they dined together in his cabin. One evening, he told Lewis about the vision of the ring. "I believe the Lord made each of us with a specific purpose in mind," Newton concluded. It was an invitation to discuss the deeper meaning of life and man's relationship with the God who created him. "I do with a purpose." said Lewis,   "It's to raise as much hell as possible in as many days as I have remaining." He ended the remark with a brazen laugh.

Newton did not share in his friend's deprecating humor. Instead, he said, "Doesn't any of this speak to your heart, Job? Do you not have any fear of our Lord?"

"Not one bit," Lewis shot back. For a moment, he looked serious, and then his contagious smile pierced the momentary gloom. "How am I to respond to something as radical as a vision, if that's what it was? At least, I could argue different points of theology in a normal conversation about religion. But this…there's nothing I can say. And speaking of mysticism, I might remind you, John, that it was you who convinced me that religion only appealed to weak minded people."

The accusation was hardly necessary, and it pricked Newton's conscience. He recalled the day and the hour of their conversation. He intended to mislead the young lad, to make him doubt. It had taken a good deal of convincing before he was able to build a strong enough case to convince him that a Christian's belief system was full of holes. In the end, he won Job over, something he now deeply regretted.

"Friend, I would do anything to live that one day over again. No one can prove to you that God is real, but that changes nothing."

"Then I will leave you with this, John." Lewis idly drained his glass of wine and stood. "I believe there is a God, just like the demons believe. But I'm not interested in being saved, and that's my final word on the matter."

With nothing further to say, Lewis set the glass down, wiped his mouth with a napkin and walked out.

Newton remained at the table and bowed his troubled head in silent prayer. He had done all within his power to reach his old friend and failed miserably. With every phrase that Lewis uttered, Newton saw himself. He had resisted the influence of wiser, older men, those who spoke of humility, and fearing God. Now he saw his reflection and nothing he tried could alter it. Ultimately, he concluded that he could do nothing without the help of the Holy Spirit.

Following their conversation, there was a newfound tension in their relationship. If it had been nothing more, Newton could have dealt with the discomfort, but it was apparent that Lewis intended to undermine John's authority as captain. So much so, that Newton began to wonder if    Lewis wasn't attacking him out of his general loathing of Christians. He made disrespectful jokes that came dangerously close to insubordination.

It continued for weeks, until one evening Newton watched as three men encircled Lewis on the main deck and listened to his latest story. Their heads bowed inwardly, catching every word, grinning in anticipation, and arching back with laughter at its conclusion. One man cautiously looked sideways and saw Newton watching from afar. The man's body stiffened. He hastily said something then two of the men walked away in different directions. Only Lewis remained. He looked in his friend's direction and touched two fingers to his cap. The casual salute had become his signature trademark. Newton nodded in return. Distance prevented him from hearing Lewis' words, but the outcome was plain enough for anyone to see. Newton resolved to do something about the situation before he completely lost control.

The following day he was up at sunrise. He stood at the front of the African looking out over the water while clutching a cup of coffee. The brew was hot, and Newton blew into the cup before sipping the liquid. It was a good way to start the day, surveying the ship's activity and prioritizing plans for the coming hours. When Lewis came out of the officer's private quarters,   Newton waved him over.

"Come walk with me," he invited. "Can I order the cook to bring you some coffee?"

"I'm fine," said Lewis, an edge to his voice. He kept pace with Newton but said nothing further.

"I have an offer that I hope you'll consider." They moved toward the midpoint of the deck and leaned over the rail, watching the sunrise. "I've purchased another vessel. How would you feel about taking charge of her?"

Newton could tell he'd caught Lewis off-guard. He had been a more likely candidate for the whip, even if he wasn't an official member of the crew.

"Is this your way of getting rid of me?" Lewis inquired.

"I'll speak plainly." Newton turned and faced his nemesis. "Your conduct is causing problems among the crew. You know that kind of behavior can be dangerous. Frankly, Job, I'm tempted to put you ashore and let you find your way back home." He let the words sink in before continuing. "But I think it better to let you discover what it's like to command a ship, to be responsible for your men and cargo, and get both back to England safely."

Lewis stood silently, clearly waiting for Newton to conclude his offer.

"As I said, the owner has authorized me to purchase a second ship to take care of additional matters. Are you capable of taking charge of her?"

Lewis stared back. "You know I am, or you wouldn't ask. I never expected a Christian to cast me off like this."

Newton concealed all reaction to the stinging remark. He sipped his coffee and rested the cup on the rail. Then he stood up straight, and commandingly. "I take no pleasure in what I do, but do it out of necessity. You've been treated exceptionally well, considering your conduct; and, I'm convinced that there is nothing more I can do to change your perspective."

Then Newton's voice softened. "I've prayed for you, you know, as a brother, and more often than you might expect. When I reprimanded you, Job, it was always necessary and done with compassion. You've left me with no other alternative at this point."

The corners of Lewis' mouth curved into a smirk. "What's that scripture? You know, the one that says let them who have ears, hear. Well, maybe I don't want to hear any of it. One might say my heart is hard, but I've come to a point where I want nothing to do with God or those who believe in Him. That said, if you still want me to take over the ship, I will."

Newton turned back to the water. There was nothing more to say. Without another word, Newton dismissed Lewis with a wave of his hand. In less than an hour, he had prepared his duffle bag, slung it over his shoulder and was about to disembark. With one foot on the gangplank, he turned to Newton, who stood by watching his friend. "Don't feel badly, John," he said. "I've chosen my path and have no regrets. All my tomorrows will be of my own making."

Lewis turned his back and walked into the distance, his arms swinging casually at his side, as though he hadn't a care in the world.

Chapter 31

God's Plan

Chatham, England (1752)

"In their hearts humans plan their course, but the LORD establishes their steps." Proverbs 16:9

John Newton had no way of knowing he was within moments of brushing up against death.

"What's the matter, dear?" Polly's loving fingers kneaded the dough that would soon become the warm bread that would complement the dinner she planned for that evening.

Newton could see the devotion in love in Polly's eyes each time she asked what he was thinking. Many nights he prayed, thanking God for such a fine wife. He couldn't imagine a better woman. She was physically attractive, but more importantly, she nurtured him emotionally. He had waited years for the level of comfort they now enjoyed. On one hand he resented the lost years. Yet he knew God's timing was flawless. Still, he worried about their future. "I'm sorry if I'm distracted," he said, his eyes returning to hers. "I didn't mean to be rude."

"Darling, you look as though you're carrying the whole world on your shoulders. What's bothering you so?" Polly turned toward her husband and waited for an explanation.

Newton sat in front of the fireplace. It was here that he would so often peer into the flames and work out the solutions to the problems of life. Six months ago, he and Polly said their vows at St. Margaret's, a twelfth-century Norman Church in Rochester. It was a wonderfully rich period in their lives and by all accounts, a splendid partnership that time would only enhance.

At the wedding reception, Polly reminded him that it was she who had proposed. "You said everything under the sun, John, but you just couldn't ask the question."

"I was afraid," he protested, watching her over the rim as he sipped from a glass of punch. "And why not, you brought so much to this marriage, while I had nothing to offer."

"That's not true, John, and you know it."

"It most certainly is. You have beauty. Look at me." It was a simple observation but an accurate one. Never considered a handsome man, years of rugged sea life had deepened the creases in Newton's face. "You were reared with culture and refinement. I am course and rough. My concern has always been my lack of money, and I still feel unsure about my finances."

"I respectfully disagree with you, darling. I always thought of you as quite a fine catch."

Newton frowned and said, "Makes me sound like a fish landed at the pier.

Polly peered at her husband for a long moment, her expression changing from cheerful to serious. Finally, she said, "John, would you like to have children someday?"

Newton looked over, surprised at the shift in conversation. Then he mused, "Yes, yes, I would. I've considered it, but timing is everything, and this isn't the best time with me being away so much."

Polly shifted herself in beside her husband on the edge of his chair. "Oh, John, I think about it all the time. Can you imagine a little John Newton running around the house?"

"No, but I can certainly envision a little Polly on my knee. Now, that would be something."

The conversation amused them both. They chuckled, and then Newton sighed, interlacing his fingers across his stomach and leaned back into the chair. "If I look down in the mouth, it's because we only have a week before leaving again. I can't tell you how much I miss you when I'm away."

Newton could see the same affection in his wife's eyes. Being at sea for months on end was just as hard on her, if not more so.

"Perhaps it won't be as long this trip," said Polly.

"I'd like to think so. The slave trade is changing. Last time out we had to go from port to port. Often times, I was able to get no more than a few slaves at each stop. Those delays lengthened the trip by four months, not to mention the problems that go with keeping slaves aboard ship for longer periods of time."

Polly wiped her hands on her apron, untied it, and folded it into a bundle as she walked over and sat down on the arm of the chair next to her husband. She enjoyed the momentary quietness, listening to the crackle of the burning log cradled in its iron grate. "Darling," she said, "have you given any consideration to leaving the slave trade? The

Quakers have taken an official anti-slavery position, and the House of Commons is considering changing the law."

Newton pushed himself back into the vast leather chair that was now familiar with the shape of his back. "This current debate is nothing new," he said, hoping to avoid the subject. "And you know where the church stands. Each year, slavery exposes thousands to Christianity. Without this industry, they would never hear of God."

"Couldn't the same thing be accomplished by sending missionaries over there?"

"Some were sent," he said. "But they've made little impact. The gap between the two cultures is too broad, and it's too dangerous. Africa is full of all kinds of wicked beliefs, voodoo and such. Taking them completely off the continent seems to be a better choice."

Polly sat upright, tilting her head forward, the way she always did when fixed on an idea. "The missionaries may have indeed had their problems in winning souls, but you and I both know this is about commerce, not religion."

"I believe you're right, my dear. Nevertheless, religion is a byproduct of what we do."

Polly put her hands on her hips. "What rubbish, John. How can anyone compare separating husbands from their wives, and children from their mothers, all in the name of religion? Not to mention what happens when some unscrupulous person takes ownership of them. The whole idea bothers me. It bothers me that we're involved in it at all."

Newton leaned forward, his face against the heat of the fire. "I've seen what you're describing, the tearing apart of families, and I have tried to prevent it whenever possible. They're not married, you know, not in the sense that we think of marriage. But they are families."

"I wish you would give it some thought. Can't you limit your trade to regular cargo?"

"Believe it or not, I've have been thinking about trying to find something else altogether, a profession that would allow me to stay home." Newton smiled at his lovely wife. "In fact, I asked Joseph Manesty to help me find another position."

Polly, who had been twisting her apron as they talked, threw it at her husband. "And when were you going to tell me about this?"

Newton, enjoying the playful moment, dodged the billowing weapon and jerked his head to one side. Then his face acquired the strangest expression as he abruptly leaned forward, overcome with dizziness.

Newton's hand touched his temple then clumsily dropped to his lap. His body stiffened, jerked twice, and fell to the floor.

It was an hour before Newton regained consciousness. He was aware that he was in his home, in his bed, but he had no memory of how he got there. His body ached, and he noticed that his vision was cloudy. Someone was leaning over him.

"What happened?" whispered Newton, trying to focus.

"You're a lucky man," said Dr. Anderson, a kindly physician who looked after the family. He brushed back a flip of silver hair and smiled as he looked at his patient. "Lay still, John. You've had a seizure, most likely brought on by your previous bout with Malaria."

Satisfied that Newton was now stable, Anderson methodically replaced his medical instruments in the black bag resting on the floor next to the bed.

Newton propped himself up on one elbow, before a new wave of nausea overcame him and he fell back into his pillow.

"Easy now." The doctor's command left no one in doubt as to who was in charge. "You're going to have to remain in bed for several days, at least until I can get back here to check on you."

"Well, I'm glad it happened before shipping out," said Newton. "I can't imagine this taking place while in the middle of the Atlantic."

"That's another matter altogether, my friend." The doctor shut the clasp on his bag and looked first at Polly then over at Newton. "Your days at sea have just come to an end. No ship owner will risk your commanding a vessel if there's a chance of any more attacks like this one."

Newton started to object, trying once more to sit up.

"Lie back down, John." The doctor rested his hand on Newton's chest, stopping his upward motion. "There's no debating it. You just retired."

Chapter 32

Even the Demons Believe

Guiana Coast (1752)

"You believe that there is one God. Good! Even the demons believe that--and shudder." James 2:19

The doctor's examining room was small, completely white and sterile in every respect. The curtains remained drawn to minimize the intrusive sunlight while the doctor examined Lewis as he lay in a bed. The physician noted that his patient was semiconscious, and his breathing fluctuated between shallow and nonexistent. He was dying.

The surgeon gingerly removed the cloth used to mop the perspiration from his patient's forehead and wrung it out into a pan of water. Not sure how much to believe of the first mate's story, he thought. He was told that the sea captain ruled his ship with the cruelty of a despot. One thing is sure: a captain has authority over life and death on his ship, and no one will question his decision one way or the other.

"There's more to this story," added the first mate. "I'm not against a man enjoying himself, you understand. But this man had acquired an appetite for perverse forms of sex. Depraved, you might say."

The doctor's eyes narrowed as he looked up from his patient.

"Perverse? In what way?"

"I'd rather not go into the details, sir," said the sailor, he eyes studying the floor. "Suffice it to say that some of the tavern girls refused to entertain him. 'Tyrannical', that was the word they used.

227

When his own kind turned him away, he started chasing some of the native women, and that's how he ended up with this here fever."

The doctor cleared his throat, signaling his discomfort. "You say he was heavy handed?"

"That's right, sir. I believe he picked me out to assist him because of my size. He wanted me to be his strong right arm, literally. But human decency demands certain boundaries, even under the law. I had to refuse to go alone when his punishment almost drowned a man."

The doctor's eyebrows lifted, signaling that he wanted to hear more. He returned the damp cloth to his patient's forehead, wet again with droplets of sweat.

"I think I can safely say when Lewis got drunk, I took a beating for each man on that ship," he said, pointing to a dark purple lump on his cheek. "Toward the end, not a day went by when he didn't take a pull from his flask. Yes, sir, he was a cruel master."

"And this Captain Newton you spoke of. You say he is a believer?"

"Yes, and he tried to change Captain Lewis, but it weren't no use. Lewis had a heart chiseled from stone, he did."

"I hope something reaches him," retorted the doctor, as if Lewis couldn't hear. "He doesn't have much time left."

Lewis opened his glazed eyes and blinked several times, trying to focus. His joints stiff with fever. "Water, I must have water."

The doctor picked up a glass from a nearby table, cautiously lifted the man's head and put the rim to his lips. "Slowly, Mr. Lewis, drink slowly now."

Lewis sipped the water, ran his tongue over his lips, and heaved a long sigh. "It's the damned fever, isn't it? Tell me the truth." He looked at the doctor for validation.

The doctor's hand rested Lewis' head back against the pillow. "I won't deceive you. I don't think you'll live through the night."

A smile briefly appeared then faded. "I knew it would come sooner rather than later," said a weak and raspy voice. "My destiny."

"I'll ask you again. Would you like me to send for a priest or minister?" There was a sense of urgency in the old man's tone.

"Hell, no." A spasmodic cough interrupted the sentence. "I heard what my mate told you. He likes to speak his mind when he thinks I'm out of my head. Knows better than to try that when I'm in charge of my faculties."

The doctor waited, neither confirming nor denying the accusation.

"By now, you know I'm not a pious man." The smile returned, somewhere between humor and a grimace. "I want no man of the cloth at my bedside, or bleating some senseless words over my grave."

The doctor, determined to make every effort, asked once more. "Mr. Lewis, this may be your last chance to make peace with God. Wouldn't you like someone to pray with you?"

"I've made my peace with God –if you can call it that --and I want no part of God. No deathbed confessions here, doctor. I will die as I have lived." The stress in his voice produced another spasm, followed by a long wheeze. "Don't get me wrong. I've always believed in God. I suppose you could classify me as a believer but not a Christian. I'm sure you've read the passage where Jesus said, 'Even the demons believe.'" Lewis cleared his throat and winced in pain. "I'm not a demon, but I'll soon join them."

The doctor looked up at the mate, a shake of his head signaling the futility of further conversation.

That night, one hour after the sunset, the chest of Job Lewis rose and fell one final time before his soul crossed over into the eternal darkness surrounding the realm of those separated from God.

* * *

"You were there the whole time?" said Newton.

"Yes, sir," said the first mate. "I saw and heard it just as I told it to you. Lewis died with those very words on his lips."

John Newton's entire frame sagged. "God forgive me," he whispered. This will burden my soul for the rest of my life. I planted those seeds of doubt, the inclination to separate himself from God. Believing only makes it worse. Of all my sins, this was the worst. For I robbed him of his place in the Kingdom. If only I could take his place.

Chapter 33

Grateful for Burdens

Olney, England (1754)

"For my thoughts are not your thoughts, neither are your ways my ways, declares the LORD." Isaiah 55:8

John Newton sensed the Holy Spirit pushing him from bed early Friday morning. He looked out the window and stretched himself awake. After a leisurely breakfast prepared by Polly, he decided to walk to the town square and collect his mail from the postmaster. As he opened the door to the building, he came with inches of bumping into Joseph Manesty, who appeared both surprised and pleased to see his friend.

Manesty placed his hand on Newton's shoulder and urgently ushered him back to the entrance of the building. Looking around to make sure no one could hear, he said in a low voice, "I was just on my way to your house. Have you heard the news yet?"

"And what news would that be?" said Newton.

Manesty stopped to catch his breath and began to share his story. "Something awful has happened. As you know, Captain Potter took command of your ship when you became ill. An insurrection broke out a week after picking up his first installment of slaves. The crew fought back and eventually won but at the cost of many lives. The old girl limped into port an hour ago."

Although shaken by the news, Newton stood perfectly still, pon-

231

dering the magnitude of the moment. Plainly, God had once more intervened, but for what purpose? I'm a Christian, but I have no more idea what God wants for me than when I lived in darkness.

Newton returned home, slumped into his favorite chair. It was an old friend and some of the material on the armrest was thin from years of use. He realized just how many hours his body shifted back and forth as his mind struggled to find answers. Moments grew into hours as he pondered life and its purpose. However, the destination of his mind always concluded its journey with Jeremiah 29:11. "For I know the plans I have for you, declares the Lord, plans to prosper you and not harm you, plans to give you hope and a future."

He opened his Bible and began searching for the answers. Irrespective of what page he selected, some part of the scripture always spoke to his heart. But today was not ordinary. He looked at the pages, his mind a blank. For weeks an inaudible voice was there, calling him to become a minister, just as his mother had hoped.

After pacing for the better part of an hour, Newton knelt in prayer, asking for humility and confirmation of God's will. As his words ended, an undeniable spirit of love convicted him of his role in God's work.

He once again picked up the Bible and turned to the first chapter of Galatians. He began to read out loud, his voice soft. "But they had heard only, that he persecuted us in times past, now preached the faith which once he destroyed. And they glorified God in me."

Newton couldn't help reflecting and realized how close the story of

Paul paralleled his own life. The Apostle had passionately persecuted Christians and even orchestrated the stoning of Stephen. If God could turn the life of Paul around, perhaps He could use me, as well.

If true, he concluded, I ought to be thankful for all of the so-called tragedies of life, not to mention the most recent illness. The seizure kept me home, away from the sea and slavery. Even if the events brought on by the illness were not from God, He's using them for His purposes. I've spent my whole life searching, and now that I've found meaning and purpose, it's plain to see that God's timing was perfect. I wonder what he has planned next for my life.

Chapter 34

God's Sovereignty

Olney, England (1754)

"For the LORD gives wisdom; from his mouth comes knowledge and understanding." Proverbs 2:6

Joseph Manesty patted his impressive belly with both hands, showing his appreciation for the fine meal. It seemed his waistline ground in its battle to stop growing each time Polly prepared dinner. Already this year he had made two trips to the tailor to have his pants let out. The old gent, wise to the way of growing in years, advised the former ship's captain that much of his business was with men of a certain age. Clearing the ever-present gravel from his throat, he said, "It's inevitable. Our bodies slow down as we get older."

Accordingly, Manesty was unconcerned about his ever-expanding middle as he pushed himself away from the richly polished Mahogany table. Thick beige wallpaper sprinkled with tiny blue blossoms graced the walls. The room had a formality about it, but its owners remained free of any pretentiousness. Roast beef and mashed potatoes, the food of common men, wafted through the air.

"That was an excellent dinner, Polly. You're a better cook than my Julia."

Polly's cheeks blushed crimson as she removed the empty plates from the table, but she could not keep from smiling.

"Now, Joseph, what would your wife say?" "I'll deny I said any-

234

thing of the kind," chortled the old man, "even under oath."

"And I'll support you," said John, who sat across the table from his old friend.

Manesty and Newton both smiled with anticipation as they worked their way to the door and began their weekly walk toward the center of town, where the fall colors and brisk air cleared a man's head.

Manesty slipped into his coat and said, "John, I want you to know how much I enjoy our time together. These walks feed my soul. Truly they do."

Newton walked alongside his friend, shaking his head in opposition. "Thank you, but it is I who benefit most from our friendship. It's one thing to have read the scriptures, and quite another to understand their application to daily life."

Manesty turned onto the grass of the Commons, shuffling through the fallen leaves left by an ancient elm tree, its branches heavy and low to the ground. It always began this way, with a question, an answer, followed by another question. "So," he began, "what's been on your mind this past week?"

Newton put his hands in his pockets and let his mind review the main points of the most recent addition to his growing library. He was consuming so much information, but the reading caused more questions than it answered. "Many things, but most of all, how does God's will play into a world full of pain? How can a loving God allow so many bad things to happen? It would seem that mankind deserves better than this from a loving and merciful Father."

Manesty pursed his lips together as if thinking. "Be careful when you start talking about what we deserve. You're liable to get what you wish for."

"And what would that be?"

Without hesitation, Manesty said, "What we deserve is to die and be sent to Hell."

There was a long pause as Newton considered his friend's last statement.

"Think about it," Manesty continued. "It only takes one sin to separate us from God. And that's a great description of Hell, complete and total separation from the presence of our creator. Actually, it is His patient and enduring love that saves us."

Newton walked in silence, considering how this applied to the events of his own life. He might have debated the issue a few years ago but now moved the conversation forward, speaking his heart. "I have no illusions about the sin in my life. If ever there was a man unworthy, it is I. In spite of it all, God was merciful and spared my life several times. One in particular keeps me awake at night. It was during the four-day storm."

"And how was that different from the others?"

Newton's expression grew solemn, and the cadence of his speech increased. He leaned forward when he walked, reflecting as he spoke.

"Because, I believe a man died in my place. He stood exactly where I had been moments before; he was there, then he was gone." Newton struggled. Each detail of the event was as clear as if it had just happened. "Why did God take him? After all, I was the one living like a heathen. I cared for no man other than myself. If common sense means anything at all, I should have been washed overboard, not him."

"John, this is nothing more than survivor's guilt. Don't waste your time comparing yourself to other men. He was a sinner, just as you are. At the end of your life you'll look back and know that on your best day, you deserved nothing more than Perdition." Manesty took a deep breath before continuing. "There's nothing you could have done or can do to qualify for God's grace."

"But I frequently see men who are good," protested Newton. "You for instance, I've seen you do worthwhile things for others without letting pride get in the way. Surely man's nature isn't completely evil."

"You're right," said Manesty, keeping his voice reigned in. "There is good in men. But it's not of our making. We are created in God's image, and any good found in mankind is because God planted it there. Unmerited grace is the phrase used most often to describe God's gift. He takes what was meant for evil, turns it around and uses it for good."

Newton turned his palms upward as they walked along, trying to emphasize the meaning with his body when words proved inadequate. The subject was more than a little troubling. "Well, why does God allow evil in the first place?"

"Ah, yes, my boy," chimed Manesty. "You've hit upon the question for which there is no sufficient answer. In the Bible, God tells us that he gives us enough understanding to live but still keeps secret things to himself. And this is why we must rely on our faith."

John looked over at his friend, his face a question mark. "Which begs the next question: if he didn't create evil, who did?"

"As you know, Lucifer was the most powerful angel, trusted with guarding the thrown of God. But he lusted for power. He took one-third of the angels and rebelled in Heaven. It was Lucifer – now called Satan – who was and is the father of lies. He tempted Adam and Eve, creating the Fall of Mankind. The fallen angels became demons and continued to torment mankind. They will continue until Christ returns and casts them into the pit."

Newton considered the statement. "So, are you saying God does not want bad things to happen to us, but he uses them for good?"

"Yes, I am."

"Still, why does God even allow such a spiritual war to go on, a war that causes endless pain and suffering?"

"This is a question as old as time itself, and many men smarter than I have failed to provide an answer. But one thing clearly stands out." Manesty held up an index finger to emphasize his point. "We are not the main characters in this story. We tend to think of ourselves on center-stage, but it's really God."

"I understand what you're saying," said Newton, "but I feel as if we are chess pieces being moved about. Sometimes we win, most often we do not. But it's all in God's hands.

Manesty briefly smiled. "It can seem that way because we don't understand all there is to know about God, and I'm not sure we ever will. However, we are promised that we will one day live in perfect harmony with God in his Kingdom."

Manesty looked over at his friend and smiled briefly before continuing. "What you're asking about is God's sovereignty. You mentioned the storm, and how dark it was. I believe you described it as being surrounded by absolute blackness."

"It was as if I had been stricken blind."

"Exactly. You also know of another time when the disciples were in a boat with Jesus when a great, dark storm stirred up. The fisherman thought the boat would capsize. Do you recall what they did at the moment they faced death?"

Newton considered his childhood. He had first heard the story as he lay on the floor and his mother read to him from her rocking chair. "As I recall, Jesus was asleep. They woke him, and He stilled the storm."

"The storm wasn't only calmed. The water changed from large waves to smooth as glass. But that's not the point of this story."

Wanting to understand more, Newton said, "I'm not sure what you're trying to tell me, Joseph."

"To understand this, we must consider two parts. First, the disciples called to the Master out of desperation, when death was imminent. They couldn't help themselves, so in a moment of absolute despair, they called out the only one who could save them. And that's what we all do, John, including you."

Newton's mind pictured the storm. Like the disciples, in the darkest part of the storm, he was sure that he would perish. He gave Manesty a long look, waiting for his friend to make his other point.

"The other half of this story is that Christ chastised his followers for having been afraid, told them they didn't have any faith."

Newton removed his hands from his pockets and held his palms up, as if asking for an explanation. "I never understood that part of the story. Were they not in grave danger? What would they have done if the boat was swamped?"

Manesty rested a hand on Newton's shoulder and looked deeply upon his friend. His voice was calm and even. "This is the key to understanding God's sovereignty, John. He used the storm, or adversity, to change their understanding. Regardless of how things turned out, they needed to have faith that God was in control. He wasn't surprised by the storm, nor was it beyond his control."

Newton airily waved his hand. "What else could they do, sit there and remain calm in the middle of this raging storm? You make it sound as though we are supposed to be happy about our tribulation."

"No, of course not. But we can find satisfaction knowing that God uses the pain of life to make us more like Him. He was well acquainted with pain, and he uses suffering to shape us. And we should be grateful for that, as difficult as it may be."

"I'm going to have to think about this some, Joseph. I value all that you teach me. But this is going to take some time to digest. Let's go back to where we started. What about the man washed overboard? Why him, instead of me?"

Manesty held out his hands, as if surrendering, and said, "Frankly, I've no idea. The Bible tells us that all of our days were recorded before we were even born. God does not give us all the answers. Instead, He requires men to exercise a certain amount of faith and move forward trusting that He is in control."

"Why faith, instead of knowledge?" said Newton.

"John, don't you get it? Because through faith comes knowledge. The power of faith allows us to realize what can happen when we rely on God's strength instead of our own." Newton shook his head in a circle, agreeing and disagreeing at the same time. He was becoming fatigued with all the heavy discourse. "But I didn't have any faith at that moment."

"I beg to differ. God created all men that they might have faith." Manesty turned toward his friend and spoke from long years of study. He saw no need to quote chapter and verse, but it was clear he knew his Bible. "Even the African who lives in the jungle understands the difference between right and wrong, and possesses some measure of faith. His soul calls out to a higher form, a God, even if he has never seen a missionary or read one page of scripture."

"Faith," he continued, "is unseen, the glue between the Creator and the created. We may build on that faith, but we are literally born with it. We intuitively know there is a God."

Newton's feet shuffled through a layer of leaves as he silently kept pace beside his friend. He flexed his hands inside his pockets and struggled to make sense of it all.

"Why did he create us, then, for what purpose?"

A small smile appeared as Manesty spoke. "That is the eternal question, the answer for which every man cries out. Unfortunately, most of us want to dictate to God. Man tends to think if something is good, it must be God's will for us to do that thing. Instead, we should be searching for God's purpose in our lives, whatever it may be, even if it doesn't match our own ideas. Fact is, most of us act like small children throwing a fit when we don't get our way. And if we don't understand what God is doing, we just try to explain him away. Can you think of anything sillier than trying to explain God out of existence?"

"I did exactly that for a very long time."

Manesty nodded in agreement. "And don't go taking any credit for having changed your mind, either. God gave you that change of heart, although you had the right to choose. It took a string of events and finally the darkness of a terrible storm to break your will. You're in good company, though. The Apostle Paul had to be struck blind before he could see with new eyes."

Newton smiled at the play on words. He was soaking up the lesson, trying to understand the larger picture of mankind. "Then there are some things we may never understand. You said that, didn't you?"

"Yes, I believe that. I also think that in spite of all our theological differences, we want the same thing: to obey God and enjoy his fellowship. At that moment, and only that moment, man finds peace and contentment."

Newton looked over at his friend. "I thought this was about glorifying God, not the pursuit of our own happiness."

"Right you are, but God doesn't deny us happiness in the process." Manesty caught himself, finishing the sentence abruptly. "Perhaps a better phrase would be that God gives us peace of mind. At best, our definition of happiness is too broad. Here is the key--and this is important--seek happiness, and you will never find it; seek righteousness, and you will find happiness."

Both men walked in silence, marveled at the brilliant colors, and arched their pathway back toward the house. The information was more than the student could grapple with and comprehend in one conversation. "I believe," said Newton, smiling "that we are both ready for some of Polly's apple pie."

Chapter 35

Navigating Life as a Christian

Olney, England (1755)

"Now faith is confidence in what we hope for and assurance about what we do not see." Hebrews 11:1

Five years into their marriage, John Newton sat at Polly's bedside, and for the first time in days, he was hopeful. He fluffed up her pillows and helped her settle back into them. The dark green velvet curtains to the bedroom were finally open, letting in shafts of life-nurturing sunlight. He cautiously carried a cup and saucer of cinnamon tea and watched as she stirred the brew in small circles. "You seem to be doing much better. The doctor thinks so, too."

Polly sipped the tea, hot the way she liked it, and offered a tentative smile. "It's you I'm worried about, John. Going without work is taking its toll on you. I wish there were some way I could help."

Newton sighed, pulled a chair up alongside the bed, and slouched into it. Clearly, his body magnified the recent sense of despair. He let his arm drape across his face, blocking out the light as he spoke. "All my training is in ships. Finding a job in another field has proved more difficult than I imagined. If things don't improve, returning to sea will be the only left for me to do. I'm beginning to think the seizure was a one-time event." He looked up, wondering how Polly would respond.

"What about your health, John? You're not as young as you once were. And you always disliked being gone for so long."

"You're right, of course," he said, his brows knitted together in a serious expression. It wasn't his age or health that worried him. Polly had been ill several times during the last five months.    He couldn't imagine life without his longtime companion. His love for her had flourished since seeing her the first time in the garden behind her parent's house. She was his best friend and closest confidant. She always supported him, and never suggested that he should do anything other than rely on God when making a decision.

It had been months since the seizure, yet there was no hope of returning to sea. Being out of work wasn't so bad. He knew that a new job would come eventually. But he worried about medical bills and not having sufficient money to look after his wife.

"Tomorrow's Sunday," said Polly. "Going to church always makes you feel better."

Newton smiled, warmed by his wife's thoughts of his welfare while she lay sick in bed. "There is a new minister that's stirring things up. He's one of the leaders of this evangelical awakening that is sweeping across the country, and in the Colonies, as well. If you feel well enough …"

* * *

The next day Newton found himself sitting under the instruction of George Whitfield, friend and fellow clergyman of John Wesley, both of the Church of England. The service was a three-hour Communion service, interlaced with hymn singing and the fiery presentation of the Word to a congregation of over a thousand souls.

When the time came for him to speak, Whitfield, adorned in his black ministerial robes and white collar, addressed the need to bring the Gospel to the common man. Leaning over the pulpit and punctuating his words with raised fists. "We should not become so comfortable that we overlook the working-class. Did not Jesus reach out to the fisherman who labored to eat, as well as the wealthy tax collector? Does he not call us to the same mission, the same commitment that led to the Day of Pentecost? I say yes, and I say it without hesitation!"

Whitworth brought his fist down on the pulpit with a bang, hammering home the call to each parishioner within the sound of his words. "I know what some of you are thinking." His voice leveled off to a conversational tone, and he looked across the faces that waited to hear his next sentence. "There are those among the church that say this is Methodism, sometimes referred to as evangelical enthusiasm. They will whisper that it is unseemly, and it is more suitable for a minister to conduct himself in a reserved and respectful manner. Yet, Liverpool is only a few miles from where we now worship, a place where men and women no longer attend church. I dare say that God has no place in their lives."

Newton sat in the back and recalled the many times when he had listened to such discourses, finding them dull and listless. Now the message was full of life, as was the Good News.

"I have found myself castigated by the Bishop of Bristol," Whitfield continued, "for pretending extraordinary revelations and gifts of the Holy Spirit, which he denounced as 'a horrid thing, a horrid thing, indeed. I suggest to you, fellow believers, that the very nature of Christianity is to find delight in sharing the word with all men, regardless of class or station in life."

Whitfield's voice began to rise again, the strength of his shoulders appearing as he held the edges of the pulpit tightly in his palms. "Each and every day, more and more are responding to this call, and that, my friends, is the movement and direction of God's calling."

Across the tightly packed attendees, a loud murmur of approval lifted into the sanctuary's elevated ceiling. Newton's heart began to race as the crowd grew more energized. He recalled the same thrill that he experienced when sitting at his mother's knee, encouraged to grow and one day do the Lord's work. Was this not the kind of preaching she had affirmed, bringing the message to those less fortunate? Was this not what his mind and soul longed for?

At the conclusion of the service Newton was the first to rush forward and introduce himself, the throng pressing against him, forcing him to keep his distance. When the majority expressed their thanks and moved on, Newton moved forward and offered his hand. "My name is John Newton," he said. "I found your sermon quite stimulating, sir."

"Thank you, Mr. Newton."

"I'd enjoy corresponding with you regarding this subject," said Newton. "Perhaps even collaborating on some work to be done in Liverpool."

Whitfield smiled broadly. "You, sir, are the man I have been waiting for."

In the days and months that followed, Newton responded to the need to be alone. He often enjoyed walking through the unspoiled countryside. "It is the garden of England," he once told Polly. In the midst of the lush vegetation, he would present his innermost thoughts to God in conversational prayer and seek comfort for his stirring soul. In the stillness and serenity, he made two urgent requests. The first was the restoration of Polly's health, and the second was what he called "my settlement," or the need to find a new employment. According to the Bible, God meant for man to work. Surely, God wanted him to have a job, so why did he have to go so long without one, he wondered.

Newton had just returned from one of his "appointments with God," when he observed Joseph Manesty reaching for the brass knocker on the front door. A few moments later, they walked together along the lanes of the city, discussing Newton's future.

"It must be difficult, not knowing when you'll work again," said Manesty. It was his nature to be direct. The style had served him well for many years as a skipper and businessman.

"It's been more than difficult, my friend. It's one thing to wonder if one is going to have enough money to put food on the table, and quite another when a family member is ill."

"You're speaking of Polly, of course. Is it serious?"

Newton's eyes narrowed as he considered the question. "Not at the moment, but last year you had three episodes within weeks of each other. Even then, the doctor advised us that we were lucky."

"What exactly do the doctors say?" as Manesty.

"I'd love to answer that question. So far the doctor hasn't made a definitive diagnosis. They can only confirm that her symptoms are real and not imagined. As with any illness, they treat only the symptoms." Newton held his hands, like an unarmed man surrendering to a highwayman. "I don't know what else to do. I scan the papers and check with the owners of companies in every field I qualify for, and some that I don't. Nothing has happened. It reminds me of the storm. I had no one to rely on except God. It's the same way now, only He has not seen fit to provide me with work."

Manesty hummed his acknowledgment. "I'm sorry this is going on. Let me ask you a question. Do you feel as though God is obligated to bless you with a job because you obey him?"

"I know where you're going with this. I'm a changed man. I go to church regularly, pray and read the Word; I have a desire to serve God and am open to His direction in my life. Why wouldn't he want to bless me instead of allowing all this pain in my life?"

Manesty stopped for a moment, placed his hand on Newton's shoulder. "I want you to listen to this because the answer is important. God does it because He loves you."

"Loves me?" Newton blurted. "That's a funny way of showing it."

"It may seem strange but think of it this way. Change never comes about without struggle, and that struggle is often painful. The word change is just another expression of growth."

Newton offered a frustrated sigh and fidgeted. *I probably look like a schoolboy, impatiently waiting for the Sunday school teacher to end his lecture.* He shook his head and tried to clear out the cobwebs. "Didn't we start off talking about my wanting to find work?"

Manesty smiled, and the two began walking once more. "We were talking about exercising our faith, regardless of the outcome. John, things are not always going to turn out the way we would like them to, or even the way we think they should. Regardless of the outcome, God is part of every detail. We may not understand it all, at least not in this life, but God has his purposes and his ways."

"I have to tell you, Joseph, this is not at all uplifting. In fact, I haven't been this depressed for a long time."

"That's because you are still in a kind of Christian infancy. The best scriptural advice I can offer is to praise God in all things and love your fellow man. There is a reason the Bible gives us that counsel. God is always there working. We just don't see it. Would you mind if we stopped a moment to pray?"

"Here, on the open street?"

"Yes, right here under God's blue sky."

Manesty spoke softly, unafraid of what others might see or hear. Together the men bowed their heads and sought God's blessing and comfort.

One week later Manesty was on Newton's porch, pounding on the front door. "I am told that a position as Surveyor of the Tides is about to open," he said, running his words together. "It's an excellent position, one in which you would have charge of sixty employees, should you decide to accept it."

Newton's eyes lit up, full of surprise and excitement. "Of course, I'm interested," he said, "but what are the chances of my being appointed. I understand that the process is quite political."

Manesty only smiled.

"What happened to the old Surveyor?" Newton asked.

"His father passed away, leaving him a considerable legacy which will require his full-time attention," Manesty continued. "Since time is of the essence, I took the liberty of recommending you in a letter to Thomas Salusbury, a prominent citizen of Liverpool and a Member of Parliament. He has agreed to forward his endorsement to the Secretary of State."

Newton embraced his longtime mentor. "This is indeed an answer to many of my prayers."

Two days later Manesty returned to the Newton household just as the family was about to sit down to dinner. After coming inside, he wasted no time in telling Newton the bad news. "I'm so sorry, but I thought it best to come over right away. Apparently the story of the old Surveyor's father dying was a false rumor, and he has no intention of resigning his post."

Newton and Polly looked at one another disappointedly.

"I can see how disillusioned you both are," said Manesty. "I feel terrible about the whole thing."

He returned home in the twilight of the evening, intending to write an apology and a retraction on Newton's behalf. As he walked through the center of town, he noticed that the town newspaper still had its lights burning, the employees hard at work. Clearly, something unusual was afoot.

Sticking his head in the front door, he inquired, "What's the news?"

"Mr. Croxton, the Tide Surveyor, was found dead in his office this afternoon. The mayor has asked that we print an announcement, setting off a competition for the position." The employee took a moment to wipe the newsprint from his hands with a rag retrieved from his pocket. "If you ask me, this is more about the mayor's nephew getting the job than it is a valid competition."

Manesty rushed to confirm the death, and then proceeded to contact the Secretary of State, clarifying the issue and re-nominating Newton. Agonized for four weeks, not knowing where his future lay. Finally, , a messenger arrived at his door, confirming his appointment.

"Surely, he thought, this is part of God's plan.

Chapter 36

Adoption

Liverpool, England (1755)

"How great is your goodness, which you have stored up for those who fear you, which you bestow in the sight of men on those who take refuge in you." Psalms 31: 19

John Newton ached for his wife as he watched Polly's eye's pleading for hope.

Study and time had matured him; and therefore, his relationship with Christ had taken on a new depth. He understood that his submission to God did not guarantee him a life free of the hardship. Nor did he expect to understand God's ways when they appeared illogical. After all, didn't the Bible say that life would be hard for Christians?

He had heard men say that they would get the answers to the mysteries of life once they crossed the Veil. John thought not. Instead, there would be no need to question God once a man entered God's Kingdom. But even as he believed, his heart longed to fix life's most recent challenge. I have no right to demand anything, he prayed silently. God, only you know how my heart aches for her.

"Is there no hope, no chance at all, Doctor?" asked Polly. The ragged red rims of her eyes clashed with her delicate complexion, and her fingers incessantly stretched at a dainty hanky tucked into her lap. Newton watched Dr. Robert Anderson slouch in his chair as he

253

cleaned the lens of his spectacles with a white tissue. Then he looked up and said, "Polly, I wish there was something more that medical science could offer, but in your condition…well, a baby is most unlikely."

Polly leaned forward and countered, "But not impossible."

Dr. Anderson glanced over at Newton, then back at Polly. "Nothing is impossible, of course, but don't get your hopes up. Frankly, absent a miracle, a pregnancy is impossible. And it's probably a good thing. You're well beyond the age of childbearing, my dear." He took a moment to wrap the ends of his spectacles around each ear and adjusted the lenses on his nose. "It may be too soon to ask, but have you and John considered adoption?"

"We've talked about it in general terms," Polly replied, nervously folding her hands together and trying to hold them still in her lap.

The doctor looked over the top of his glasses and waited until he was sure he had the full attention of both husband and wife. "There are many beautiful children in the world without parents, children who long for loving parents. You two would make a wonderful mother and father for some little boy or girl."

Polly sat very still and absorbed what sounded like a death. She looked down at her hands, gripped so tightly that the tips of her fingers were red. It may be selfish of me, but I don't want someone else's child."

"I know of a good contact," said Dr. Anderson, ignoring the pad. "One who will help you find a son or daughter you'd adore. Why not go home and talk it over with John before you decide?"

* * *

Spring gently rolled into summer and summer into fall. The Newtons waited, praying for a child. But God remained silent. One evening Polly came into the parlor where her husband was reading. She was prepared to speak her heart.

"John, I am sick with worry. Perhaps it is God's will that we remain childless."

"I've wondered the same thing," said Newton. "After all, I am fifty. Not exactly the ideal time to start a family."

Polly looked across at her husband with a steady gaze. "Are you saying you don't want to consider adoption?"

"It's been four months and we haven't seen a single child that would be a good match. I know how much you want to be a mother. Perhaps you want it too much."

Polly kept her voice from rising, but could not stifle the fiery blush in her cheeks. "John Newton, that's the most ridiculous thing I've ever heard, God not wanting us to take care of a child that's lost its parents." She poured herself a drink of water and tried to steady the tremor in her voice.

Newton remained calm and kept his tone even. "I really don't know what else to do. Have you considered that this may be a blessing? You know your health has been unpredictable for the past year. The whole idea is starting to worry me."

"I can't explain how I feel. I don't think any woman can, not with any clarity. You have your work, while I feel incomplete. Most of all, there is a child out there who needs us. How can we possibly say no?"

Polly started to say more, but her eyes teared up and her voice cracked. Unable to hold back any longer, she covered her eyes with her hands and sobbed.

Newton edged his chair closer to the woman who was the centerpiece of his life and placed a comforting arm around her shoulders. "I love you, more than life itself, more than God would permit. My life would change forever if I lost you." He hugged her close once more and she tucked her face under his chin.

"We'll continue to search and pray for the right child," said Newton. "But it's in God's hands now."

* * *

In late December, Polly busied herself in the kitchen mashing the potatoes she had selected from the market earlier in the morning. As she poured over her work, she reflected on her life with John. It's hard to believe that so many decades past so quickly. At this stage of our lives, we are more alike than different. He'll be home in a few hours, and we'll sit at the table, sharing the tidbits of the day in light conversation. I love those moments together.

A knock at the door interrupted her thoughts. She hurriedly wiped her hands on a white and yellow apron and released the latch.

"Yes?" she said to a young man dressed in a suit and respectfully holding his hat in hand.

"Mrs. Newton?" he asked.

"Yes, I'm Mrs. Newton," she answered, curiously. "May I help you?"

"I beg your pardon, ma'am, but I need to make sure this is the right house. You are the former Mary Catlett, is that correct?" The man shuffled from one foot to the other.

Polly interlaced her fingers and unconsciously began to rub her thumbs together. "Yes, yes, what is it?" she said, trying to control the tension in her voice.

The man squeezed his hat with both hands. "I'm sorry to tell you, ma'am," he stumbled. "There's been a death in your family. Your youngest brother, George, passed away this morning."

Polly did her best to remain calm. The line her face strained, and she did her best not to cry, not now, anyway. "Please come in," she said, a catch in her throat. She led the way into the parlor where they sat down across from one another.

"I've known for some time that my brother was ill," she continued, trying to help the poor man calm down. "But I had no idea that he was near death. We've been out of touch for some time. My family, you see, did not approve of my marriage."

"Yes, ma'am," acknowledged the messenger. "I am told it happened sooner than anyone expected. Everyone was shocked, of course."

"You know," she said, "he was only thirty-two, and he lost his wife two years ago." She contemplated what that meant for a moment. "Perhaps he simply couldn't go on without her. I could understand how lonely he must have been."

The man nodded as he spoke. "However, there's the matter of the daughter. I believe she's five. Well, the fact is, ma'am, there's no one to take her in."

Polly looked up, her eyes wide with surprise. "Oh, my goodness, I completely forgot about Betsy. Would you please inform my husband, sir? He's at the church only a few blocks away." She showed the man to the door then tears of joy and sadness intertwined as Polly offered a prayer of gratitude.

"Oh, Lord," she breathed, "I miss my brother deeply, but I know you have prepared a place for him, that you knew the hour of his passing from the day he was born. Through the gift of death, you have relieved his suffering and given us the child for which we so often prayed. Blessed be the name of the Lord."

Polly reflected on the events of the past year. I'm certain God has been a part of it all, the suffering and the joy. He planned it all. There's no other explanation. After so much prayer, so much agonizing over having a baby, he prepared a way. For the first time, I understand God's sovereignty.

Chapter 37

God's Call

Liverpool, England (1758)

"The LORD is close to the brokenhearted and saves those who are crushed in spirit. The righteous person may have many troubles, but the LORD delivers him from them all." Psalm 34:18-19

John Newton sat quietly, reflecting on what he saw as his purpose in life, and more importantly, on God's purpose for him.

"Are you going to tell me what you've been thinking about?" asked Polly.

The couple sat in the privacy of the dining room. Dark paneling covered the walls, and the windows draped in velvet curtains. The new job paid well and allowed them to move into a nicer home. Newton looked up from his dinner and across the table at his wife. "I'm not sure what you mean?"

Polly picked up her napkin and lightly dabbed it across her lips. She looked thoughtfully looked at her hands, replaced the cloth and continued. "For weeks now you've been cooped up in your office laboring over something, without saying a word. I think it's time you told me what's going on."

Newton placed his fork back into the bowl and looked over at his wife. "I didn't mean to keep you in the dark. Really, I didn't. It's something I've been praying about for some time now.

"Praying?" said Polly.

Newton folded his hands together. He felt a great peace, even if the moment was going to be difficult. "I've decided to go into the ministry."

Polly said nothing and the weight of the silence rested on Newton. He was well aware that they had never before discussed a change in employment, especially one that would reduce his income. He had worked as the Tide Surveyor for over a year and done well, and it provided more than a comfortable living. The ministry did not pay well and would require some sacrifice on both their parts.

"Have you actually applied?" said Polly.

"Not yet. I've discussed the matter with Rev. Henry Crook, and he approves. He suggested I prepare for the Church of England's ordination examination of Greek and Hebrew. He also offered me a position as his curate in the parish at Kippax."

Newton stopped long enough to examine Polly, but she said nothing, urging him on with her eyes. "There is a problem, however. Approval hinges on getting character references from three ministers."

Polly raised her brows, her eyes searching for an explanation. "And why would that be a problem?"

Newton lowered his eyes, fixing them on the sun peaking in at the far window. "I applied with three vicars here in Liverpool, and they all turned me down. I just don't know what else to do. But if I am going to get involved in this work of spreading God's word, He's going to have to open some doors."

Polly's mouth fell open. She reached over and touched John's arm.

"How could they!" she exclaimed. "What reason could a vicar possibly have for such a remarkable decision?"

Newton shifted in his chair, and the lines around his mouth curved deepened. "It's the same old issue. They accuse me of mixing too closely with Methodists."

"You mean you work with the common man. How arrogant of them," Polly said, folding her napkin in half and placing it on the table. "You are as qualified as any man in England, and ministering to the lesser members of society is an asset, not something of which to be ashamed."

"There's more," Newton continued. "I appealed to the Bishop of Chester last month, and he declined to intervene. It seems the church feels strongly that ministers should have degrees from either Oxford or Cambridge, and I have neither."

Polly leaned forward, her fists tightly clenched. "A few moments ago, I was about to argue this matter. I was prepared to say that you had no business leaving your current employment, especially without consulting me. Nevertheless, I feel that a wife should support her husband. You have a brilliant mind, and you will certainly be an asset to the church. And no stuffy bishop should keep you from God's work."

Newton folded his hands in his lap and sighed. "I appreciate your sentiments, my dear, but there's nothing left to decide. They rejected me because I associate with some rather unpopular people, people whose style of worship embarrasses the church. I believe the term the leadership used is 'enthusiasm.'"

"Is there no one else who can offer you their support?" Polly said.

Newton took a deep breath and then slowly exhaled. "Not at the moment. . Only the hand of God can change this, and I don't know if He's ready."

Chapter 38

God's Work Begins

Olney, England (1762)

"For we are his workmanship, created in Christ Jesus unto good works, which God hath before ordained that we should walk in them." Ephesians 2:10

The entire idea caught Newton by surprise.

"What I'm proposing is that you write a book of your life," said Thomas Haweis.

Newton listened intently to the younger man's proposal as they sat in a tavern eating a dinner of roast beef and red potatoes. The smell of good food was wonderful. And a crackling fire warmed their souls, as well as their bodies. This was a friendship that had flourished for years.

Like Newton, Haweis was passionate about the evangelical movement and had even started a "holy club" among his fellow students while attending Oxford.

"As I was saying," continued Haweis, "a book of your life would do wonders for the movement." He leaned back into his chair and waited for a response. Eleven years younger than    Newton, he was a stout man with an intellectual face.

"It's an interesting suggestion, but there's the question of my identity." Newton leaned his forearms against the edge of the table. "I want to help, but a biography might be the death knell of my ordination." Haweis smiled knowingly. "I've already thought of that. We could publish the story by way of a series of anonymous letters from you to me."

"I suppose that would loosely cloak my identity." Newton's brow arched as he listened.

"Well, what is it, John? You're clearly concerned about something else."

"It's an issue I've fought with for years, the sin of self."

"That's a little vague for me. Can you be more specific?"

Newton dropped his head slightly, and pushed his food in a circle with his fork. "What I mean is that I struggle with pride. Eventually, it will come out that I am the author, and there's bound to be some notoriety involved. In my case, that can become a deadly sin."

Haweis reached over and rested his hand on his friend's shoulder. "I'll be with you each step of the way, John. This has to be a service to God, nothing more and nothing less."

Newton carefully sipped a cup of tea before committing himself. "Thomas, I am in your hands," he said, measuring his words. "My only purpose in this matter is to be a tool that will help evangelize the common man, the kind of man who works with his hands, be it a farmer, blacksmith or sailor. I want to bring God out of the upper classes and down to the struggle of daily life in such a way that it has meaning. Too often, our ministers speak in obtuse phrases. It all becomes meaningless to the masses. I want to get away from formal religion and more into what it means to worship the Living God, and a

God that is part of everyday life. Do you think this book might help accomplish that?"

Haweis nodded his head, expressing his approval. "I'm sure it will," he said, pushing back from the table and resting his elbows on his knees. For a moment, he remained silent, reflecting on Newton's intentions. "You know, I practiced medicine before becoming a minister. It was not unusual for me to pray with my patients, many of whom lived in poverty. I've a pretty good idea of how hard the indigent struggle. Most are pulled away from God; that is, until someone gets sick. When all else fails, they reach out to the Almighty. I would say they are lost sheep, and the church doesn't want to dirty its hands on them. Something has to be done."

"Exactly my thoughts on the matter," said Newton, nodding his head in agreement. "With your permission, I'll write the Letters, and you will read and edit them for publication."

"Of course," said Haweis. "I suggest you set a goal of about 35,000 words. I don't want to intimidate those of lesser learning.

"Have you got a working title in mind?" "I was thinking of 'An Authentic Narrative of Some Remarkable and Interesting Particulars in the Life of (Anonymous).'"

Haweis smile was benign. "That will work for now. The day will come, though, when your signature will appear on that line. I believe that," he said with conviction. "By the way, I understand you have an ear for music. Have you ever considered writing a hymn?"

"I do have a love of poetry, and the two are closely related. I'll give it some thought."

* * *

One year later, Thomas Haweis entered the great house at the front door and handed his hat to the servant. "I believe Lord Dartmouth is expecting me," he said, bowing slightly.

"His Grace will receive you in the study, sir," replied the steward. "Please follow me."

The heels of both men clicked loudly against the burnished wooden floor of the mansion. Ornate portraits of members of one of the most prominent families among England's hierarchy lined the halls. As they entered the study, Haweis noted that bookshelves rose to meet a tall ceiling. Dartmouth, a friend of King George III, and a wealthy landowner, sat at his desk reading.

The Earl stood and greeted his guest with a smile. The fine stitching in his black coat, stenciled with gold trim embroidery, matched his dark eyes. Instead of a white wig, his thick black curls flowed to his shoulders. The features of his face were angular and intelligent. He appeared in every way to be completely at ease with the power and responsibility of his position. "Thomas, so good to see you. Thank you for coming on such short notice," he said.

"God bless you, sir. It is my good fortune to visit the man whose book has done great deal of good for our country and brought many souls to the Lord."

"Thank you," said Haweis, slightly bowing his head, "but I can take no credit."

As both men made themselves comfortable, the Earl took the lead. "Speaking of the church, what news have you of your evangelistic work?"

Pleased that the Earl had broached the subject, Haweis wasted no time. "As you know," he said, "Your Grace is one of the few patrons who are sympathetic to the small but growing evangelical bent of the Church of England. For this, we are eternally grateful. As to your question, resistance among the higher classes remains firm; however, the momentum of those clamoring to hear the Word among the working-class grows louder each day. Many are being brought to an understanding of the Lord by those courageous enough to speak out."

"And you are one of those men, Thomas. And that is why I've called you here today. It would be my great pleasure to bestow one more gift upon the people. One of the parishes under my control includes Olney. I'd like to offer it to you. It would allow you to expand your work and free you and your family of any financial burden."

Thoughts galloped through Haweis mind and for a moment, he had difficulty organizing a coherent response. When he did speak, he did so with great humility and reverence. "Your Grace is too generous. I could certainly use the money, but there is one who has greater need."

Lord Dartmouth's eyebrows peaked as he exclaimed, "You're asking me to give this to someone else?"

Haweis responded with confidence. "Not just anyone, Sir. John Newton, a close friend and colleague, greatly desires to be of service to the church. Yet, the leadership continually rebuffs him. Having proven himself worthy, he is on the verge of accepting a pastorate with the   Presbyterians. If it does not offend Your Grace, I request that the living go instead to Mr. Newton. He has worked faithfully for five years now in preparation for the Lord's work."

The corners of Dartmouth's mouth lifted into a smile. "You never cease to surprise me, Thomas, or warm my heart. Although I said nothing, I was aware of Newton and his book. Quite inspiring and most authentic. If it meets with your approval, I shall send a letter offering Newton the position as soon as I receive the necessary character references."

A short time later, the Earle dispatched a letter in support of Newton. The following April of 1764, John Newton sat in the private chapel of the Bishop of Lincoln's palace at Buckden.   Kindly hands rested on his head, symbolizing God's confirming touch. Newton humbly bowed his head and listened to the words. For the first time the scales dropped from his eyes. Now I can see that the hand of God was on me in ever life-shaping event.

# I Once Was Lost

Chapter 39

Joined in Battle

Olney, England (1785)

"For we do not wrestle against flesh and blood, but against the rulers, against the authorities, against the cosmic powers over this present darkness, against the spiritual forces of evil in the heavenly places." Ephesians 6:12

John Newton reflected on the passage of time. Slowly but surely, he came to understand the God's will. Not so long ago, all I wanted in life was to marry Polly and find my life's work. I had no idea what that endeavor might be and relied completely on myself for the answer. After all, my goals were honorable. Why would God or anyone else object? Newton stopped and smiled inwardly. Apparently God wanted me somewhere else, doing something different, and He put up walls to slow down my stubborn, childish ways. I needed time to change, time for God to shape me so that I might complete the work He created before I was born.

When I was a slave, I learned humility; when I almost lost Polly, God taught me patience and endurance; when I was unemployed, He taught me to trust and remain faithful; and when we could not have children, He was merciful and provided a daughter who needed our love. When I became ill and the sea was no longer an option, He gave me time to study and prepare for the ministry, my true calling. But I am like Paul, the chief sinner, an unworthy wretch, forgiven by a loving God.

As he stood in the pulpit this Sunday morning, he shared both the challenges and blessings of life with his flock. He was quick to point out God's constant mercy in both adversity and blessings. God had a purpose in mind for each of their days.

As he spoke, he was delighted to see William Wilberforce seated in the front pew. But this was not William's home congregation, and Newton wondered what brought the esteemed member of the House of Commons through the chapel doors without prior announcement. At the end of the service, the two men met on the steps of St. Peter and Paul Church.

"That was an excellent sermon, John, one of your best. It's been far too long since my last visit." The two men, who had been friends for many years, clasped hands for a long moment of mutual respect.

When he let go, Wilberforce continued, "You know, I always thought I knew you rather well. That is until I read your book. Your life is nothing less than remarkable, you know?"

Newton, dressed in a traditional black minister's frock, accented by a large white collar and gray wig, was by now quite comfortable with his fame and role as a clergyman. He had filled the role to the best of his ability now for twenty years. "It's been too many years, William. I wish you could come to services more often."

The men began walking down the steps of the building and began casually talking as they moved toward the bottom. "Do you remember when I first came all the way from London to listen to you preach,"

# I Once Was Lost

said Wilberforce.

"I do remember, and now you're what, a man of prominence? Your wit has become your trademark, not to mention your brilliance when taking the floor of the House. I've watched you mature into a fine man and a respected politician."

Newton watched as Wilberforce, a small frail man, adjusted his French cuff so that it extended just beyond the sleeve of an elegant dark green velvet coat. A matching waistcoat and breeches set him apart as a man of position and influence.

The two men reached the bottom of the stairs and stopped. Wilberforce looked around, making sure no one was close enough to overhear. "John, I need to speak to you in the strictest of confidence. Not even Polly can know of this." He glanced around once more before continuing. "Even seeing you at the end of a service may cause undo speculation."

Newton cleared his throat, a sign that matched the serious tone of his friend's speech. He gestured toward the courtyard. The air was brisk, hinting at the end of fall. "Let us walk," said Newton, buttoning up his coat. He was used to members of his flock coming to their pastor for guidance. He strolled in the direction of a secluded corner of the property dotted by ancient trees with large overhanging branches. After a moment of silence, he asked, "Speculation regarding what?"

"There is no lack of opposition to my political future and its impact on slaver. There are men who will stop at nothing to sully my name."

Reflecting, Newton shook his head in agreement. "I've heard the rumors."

Hair bristled on the back of the young politician's neck. "Heard! Heard what?"

Newton affectionately placed a gentle hand against the back of his young friend. He was not here to judge but to listen. "Talk of frequent visits to gaming clubs and what respectable people refer to as high living. I read the Gazette, you know."

Newton waited for a response, and when none was forthcoming, he continued, "A man of your position can't avoid gossip. I'm sure you realize that by now. There are two sides to every issue. Please tell me yours."

Wilberforce gazed across the field, organizing his thoughts. "It is true that much of my time was spent in the gaming halls. Not a place of high morality, I'll admit. And, until recently, I was very fond of drink."

Newton let his hand drop to his side and navigated through a bed of gold and orange leaves. "Recently?" he said.

"That's what I wanted to discuss with you. I'm afraid I've gone from an apathetic Anglican to a fiery Methodist. Sometimes it's hard for me to recognize my old self."

"Thank you for telling me. I'm a great admirer of Methodists."

Newton smiled warmly and asked, "So, how may I be of help?"

Wilberforce sighed deeply. "I'm beginning to sour on the business of politics. Despite the efforts of many, our government remains in a stalemate regarding the abolishment of slavery. My new conversion has changed my life in ways I didn't think possible. I am seriously considering the ministry. I believe I can be more effective from the pulpit than in the House."

Newton remained silent. The only sound in the air came from the rustling of the breeze through the trees.

Wilberforce looked to the horizon as he spoke, carefully choosing his words. "It's something I've thought a great deal about, something I believe God wants me to do. There are times, however, when I just don't trust my own judgment. Now is one of those times, John. Frankly, I need your advice before making a decision."

Newton sensed the weight of the moment and considered his response. He commanded men from the pulpit, just as he had from the quarterdeck of a ship. He had a reputation for holding the edge of the wooden frame and speaking with such force and conviction that no one dared look away. Now was just such a time, a moment of plain speech. Newton stopped walking, turned and placed both hands on his friend's shoulders. "My good friend, you've asked for my advice. I've often admired your work in the House of Commons. You have the courage of ten men. You've remained committed, even when the jackals continually nip at your heels. It may surprise you to know that's not my calling.

"Nor do I feel it is your calling to be a minister, at least not right now. We often confuse our will with what God wants. Your intentions mean little, even if honorable, if you haven't first asked God what His will is. He may want to use you for an entirely different purpose. Leaving politics would be a great loss to the nation's anti-slavery movement. Your voice will reach many more ears from Parliament than it would from any church pulpit."

Newton turned away. He was like an uncle and knew that he and Wilberforce shared a mutual respect. "You know how strongly I feel about slavery, although it took me some years to address it publicly. Why not use my personal experience to support your battle? Would you consider letting me be the invisible hand that worked behind the scenes on your behalf?"

A single corner of the statesman's mouth lifted. "You've no idea what you are getting into. This battle could last for years."

"It will last as long as God permits it to last, and not a moment more," said Newton benignly. "I suggest you pray before making your final decision."

"I've been on my knees more in the last month than all my previous years combined. If you recommend that I continue to fight from the House, then that is the course I will follow."

"Then I am honored to support you," said Newton.

Chapter 40

Witness Against Slavery

Olney, England (1788)

"Though the fig tree does not bud and there are no grapes on the vines, though the olive crop fails and the fields produce no food, though there are no sheep in the pen and no cattle in the stalls, yet I will rejoice in the Lord, I will be joyful in God my Savior." Habakkuk 3:17, 18

John Newton reflected on the pamphlet he held in his hand, stunned by his friend's words.

"You've no idea what you've done," said William Wilberforce, as Newton climbed the stairs to the auspicious structure and stood beneath an arched doorway of the church.

Holding up *Thoughts Upon the African Slave Trade*, Wilberforce chimed, "Your message has reached each member of Parliament. It's made such an impact that you've been invited to offer testimony before the Privy Council."

Newton was encouraged by the news and offered a restrained smile. "I have no doubt that the pamphlet was distributed by you, and had nothing to do with any eloquence on my part. But the invitation to the Council, now there's an opportunity unlike any other we've had until now."

Wilberforce strongly agreed, his face beaming with enthusiasm. "These men are the senior advisers and Ministers to the Crown. You are to appear at St. James Palace on Wednesday of next week."

275

Newton listened, patted his friend on the back, at the same time marveling at how God had aligned the events of his life for a purpose he could never have imagined as a small boy going to sea. He did not claim to understand God's sovereignty, only that he saw the evidence of the reality of the Master's work in the small details of his life.

* * *

Newton, dressed in his black minister's robe and white powdered wig, stood in a marble lined hallway outside the hearing chamber. Felt curtains draped around windows spanning forty feet in height cordoned off the room. The magnificence and nobleness of the lavish architecture was awe-inspiring. These were the halls from which men made decisions often affecting not only the nation but also the world.

As instructed, Newton waited on a highly polished oak bench in the elaborate hallway. Nervous, he spoke to himself. "This is where God has led you, one of the great purposes of your life. He has blessed you with the ability to speak to the hearts of men, even those who lead the government. There is no reason to be anxious, only to honor Him with faith."

He looked up and was greatly surprised to see William Pitt, the King's first minister, purposefully walking in his direction, hand outstretched. "Mr. Newton," said Pitt loud enough for anyone else lingering about to hear, "please, allow me escort you into the hearing."

"I must say, Minister Pitt, it is an unexpected honor for someone of your standing to greet an old slave trader with such warmth."

"Not at all," countered Pit, as they moved along. "You are one of the most famous church leaders in all of London. It is this body's honor to have you speak before us." Pitt gestured toward the speaker's podium and turned to face some of his country's most powerful and influential men.

"Gentlemen, if I can have your attention." The group of men who had been milling around in hushed conversation became silent as the assembly took their seats. "I am pleased to present to you Mr. John Newton, pastor of St. Mary Woolnoth, of which I'm sure you are all well acquainted." Pitt's hand again gestured toward the witness. "Mr. Newton, you have our complete attention."

There was a long moment of silence as Newton looked out over the gathering of men that literally controlled the nation and would influence the outcome of countless lives. A calming spirit flowed through his mind. Once more, he reminded himself that this was God's will.

"Ministers, Admiralty, and Gentlemen," he began, "thank you for giving me this opportunity to speak on a subject that remains paramount to our future, and one that is inextricably woven into the fabric of our beloved country."

"This morning I would simply like to share my own story and let you draw whatever conclusions you may. It is a testimony of which I am not proud; nevertheless, it is necessary. The cargo during five of my voyages was human beings carried from their homeland and sold at auction. They were no different from cattle or any other kind of livestock. I did this with impunity, for like most of my countrymen, I felt neither hot nor cold on the matter of slavery. However, with the passage of time, God directed my life toward the ministry in which I now serve. He convicted me of the sinfulness of possessing another human being, and brought me to the realization that all men, women and children belong to the one and only Creator, and to no other."

Having pointedly stated his position on slavery, Newton, as he so often did, grasped the sides of the podium, leaned forward and looked into the eyes of the men who sat in the gallery. He had worked on his brief message for days now. His voice clear and direct, he began to share not only the history of his involvement in slavery but also the testimony of his life.

"Most accounts of the Atlantic crossing are written by ship's officers or traders who record the business of transporting slaves in the ship's log. These men often congratulate themselves on the decent treatment of their cargo, a point of view that differs from my own. Most slaves had not seen a ship or a white man before, nor did they have any idea where they were going. They feared the worst, and the voyage often confirmed their suspicions.

"On my first voyage on the Brownlow, I was the first mate, responsible for a cargo of two hundred and twenty souls, one-third of which died between our middle passage between West Africa and South Carolina."

There was an audible gasp as the men regarded the number of deaths.

The Archbishop of Canterbury, head of the Church of England, raised a hand and stood. "If I may interrupt. Surely the captain was punished for such a great loss?"

"I'm afraid not," stated Newton. The deaths were regarded as both normal and acceptable, considering the conditions." Another murmur emerged from the audience. "If I may explain. It is the purpose of such voyages to get as many slaves as possible delivered to purchasing agents, who then auction off the men, women and children to slaveholders. In order to achieve this, the ship's hold must be filled to capacity."

"How was this accomplished?" called out another voice. "Surely, they moved about once the ship got under way."

"No, sir. Each slave shackled to another close beside him, as were his head and another at his feet, until a mass of humanity covered the entire deck. Slaves were positioned with no more room between them than two people might have while they rested beside one another in a small bed. These conditions, as you might well guess, were intolerable. First sickness set in, guaranteeing that those who were weak or infirmed would be the first to die.

"There are also those on every voyage who conclude that death is their destiny. They reason that if death is inevitable, then why not die fighting, allowing those who survive to take over the ship. Such insurrections must be put down with deadly force, of course, even when a loss of some of our own men is certain."

The admiral winced at the thought of losing his sailors for such a vile enterprise.

"I might say that I learned from this experience," continued

Newton. "As the senior officer on the African, I buried neither white nor black during my last voyage." Heads in the crowded room offered hopeful ears. "This, however, was not due to any moral superiority on my part. I had received orders to leave Guinea by a certain date and, as a result, had to depart before the hold was full. We had ninety slaves instead of our usual two hundred and twenty."

The First Lord of the Admiralty, resplendent in his royal blue naval uniform, lifted a cane. Newton acknowledged him with a slight nod.

"I have information of some of the slave uprisings of which you spoke," said the Admiral, "and I am aware that there is an element of danger to our seamen. Can you tell me how most captains punished slaves for acts of rebellion?"

It was important that all hear and consider the weight of his words. "I was not there to see what I am about to describe, but the story came from the mouth of the captain who committed the acts, and I have no reason to doubt him. Allow me to preface my story by stating such torture as I am about to describe makes my heart sink to its lowest level."

Even under these circumstances, the depth of the well-known minister's resolve struck the men who waited to hear his oral evidence. "There were two methods of punishment for those sentenced to die. Some of them were 'jointed'---."

"Excuse me," interrupted the admiral. "This jointing thing, could you elaborate?"

"By all means," Newton agreed. "Jointing is a slang expression.

Specifically, an axe is used to cut off the feet at the ankles. Assuming the victim does not immediately bleed to death or die of shock, he is again struck at the knee. Moving quickly to ensure the greatest damage before death ensues, the thighs are severed at the hip. In like manner, the hands, arms at the elbow and finally at the shoulder, are amputated, until nothing more than a man's trunk remains. Lastly, the head is lobbed off and rolled among the remaining slaves as a form if terror."

A great and heavy silence hung in the air. Eventually the admiral cleared his throat and said, "Thank you."

Once more Newton stood firmly and surveyed the dignified faces in the room. He began in an even tone, but his voice rose with each sentence, challenging every man in the room.

"Gentlemen, let me conclude with this brief statement. I believe that coming here fulfills a great purpose in my life. God has seen fit to mold me, having spared me from death on numerous occasions because of a larger purpose that would glorify his name. Now that mantle is passed onto this body. I implore you, remove this cursed blight from our country, that we free men, shall extend that most valued status to all those who God created. As a minister in the faith, I declare it to be His will."

There was a smattering of applause, and the Prime Minister stood. His face was flush, and he cleared his throat before speaking. "I believe we have sufficient information, gentlemen, to make up our minds. Thank you, Mr. Newton for your invaluable testimony."

Newton respectfully thanked the men, whose heads were now close together in muted conversation, and walked from the room, wondering how long a civilized nation would allow such atrocities to continue.

He made his way home, pondering the moral condition of his countryman. When he arrived, weary from the trip, he stepped down from his carriage and walked through the front door, his mind still filled with the activities of the day.

"Hello," he said to Polly, who was sitting in her rocking chair, arms folded across her lap. Even after all these years, he admired her youthful appearance. Her complexion was smooth and wrinkle free. Her hair, though gray, remained full of natural curls. She had always taken great care in her appearance, and today she wore a simple blue gown. It was one of his favorites and he wondered if she had not worn it just to please him.

She's been ill for months now. One day she says her stomach is all twisted up, and the next her neck is so stiff and painful that she can't turn her head. The symptoms are so sporadic, I sometimes wonder if she isn't imagining things. On the other hand, if they are real, neither I nor the doctor knows how to treat them. What can I do but pray for guidance and healing?

The condition remained unchanged for months until Newton arrived home one evening. He hung up his heavy coat and called out,

"Polly, I'm home, dear."

Strange, she always answers when I get into the sitting room. He stepped quietly and looked into the sitting room. She was lying on the couch, and their eyes met. Instead of a smile, her expression was quite serious, and he instantly knew that something was terribly wrong.

"You've been to the doctor again," he said, kneeling at her side." "What news have you?"

Polly's voice was suddenly small, leaving her husband straining to make out the words. "The surgeon found a tumor in my breast." She paused, apparently waiting for her husband to grasp what she had just said.

"Surely, they can operate?" Newton said, his encouraging head nodding forward.

"It's the size of a half-melon, and the doctor says that surgery would be too risky."

The words had a ring of finality, of hopelessness. Newton's took Polly's hand and clasped it between his palms. After a moment, he asked, "Can nothing be done?"

Polly rose on one elbow and struggled to speak. "The only advice that the doctor offered was to take laudanum. As the pain increases, so must the frequency of doses."

"But you are allergic to laudanum."

She lay back against her pillow and gazed at her husband. "Yes, I know."

\* \* \*

Newton watched over and did his best to nurture Polly as she valiantly fought against the disease for the next two years. Then, on the night of December 12, he scribbled out a note to his doctor.

"A change took place about half past six this evening. Convulsions in her face were clearly evident. She groaned much but did not struggle or move her hands or feet. I hope her suffering will soon be over, but the Lord's hour and minute must be respected."

By dim candlelight, he held his companion's hand for the next two hours. In silence, he prayed, "Oh God, the giver and taker of all life, watch over the one who has nurtured me for so many years. I pray that her pain will be brief and that your Holy Comforter will bless her during these final moments. And I pray that you will be with me in the days ahead, for I do not know if I can bear life without her."

Polly opened her eyes once more and tenderly smiled as she gazed at her husband. Weakly, she squeezed his hand as he palmed it in both her his. In her final moments, Newton watched as the love of his life closed her eyes, and breathed once more before leaving for her Father's Kingdom.

He stayed beside her, racked with grief and unrelenting tears. He was overwhelmed with a great sadness, and yet joy that she was now free.

In the days that followed, Newton opened his Bible to the text of Habakkuk, which he had never preached on before. There in the margin he read the notes, written a quarter century earlier, reminding him that if he should survive his wife, he would use this verse when he preached Polly's funeral sermon.

Chapter 41

The Peoples' Hymns

Olncy, England (1772)

"The Spirit of the Lord is on me, because he has anointed me to proclaim good news to the poor. He has sent me to proclaim freedom for the prisoners and recovery of sight for the blind, to set the oppressed free." Luke 4:18

John Newton sat hunched over the desk in his study, deep in thought. Weary, he removed his spectacles and polished each lens with a handkerchief drawn from the inside pocket of his jacket.

"What's all this moaning about," said Polly, as she walked into the study, cup and saucer in hand. "I thought you might like some hot chocolate. It'll warm you up."

Newton looked up and smiled at his wife. She was wearing a blue dress –the color that most favored his wife –with a matching ribbon that adorned her hair. Even now she looks young and lovely, he thought.

"Thank you, my love," said Newton. "I needed a break." He picked up the cup, blew into it and cautiously sipped the hot liquid.

"Are you working on your sermon?" said Polly.

Newton held up a sheaf of notes. Some of the lines were scratched out and replaced with new words. "I have been working on my New Year's Day sermon, but this is a hymn. And it's not going well."

"How wonderful, John. You've had such great success with your other hymns." Polly walked around behind her husband. She placed her hands on his shoulders and leaned forward as she looked at her husband's scribblings.

"Yes, but at a cost, my dear. At a cost."

"Everything worth doing comes at a cost," said Polly.

"I'm not talking about the work." The lines around Newton's mouth stiffened.

"Then you must be referring to the church," said Polly. "I wonder how long this is going to go on."

"Not long, I hope." Newton put his manuscript down on and turned toward his wife. "It's not me their criticizing; it's the people I write for, the common man. I continue to be astonished at the church leadership. There's not much difference between them and the Old Testament Sadducees. Why the average man can't understand half the words preached from the pulpit, and we'll never see the day when they pick up a copy of the Bible or Book of Common Prayer. Half of them can't even read."

"Your congregation is hardly traditional, and that's why it's grown so much." Polly gazed down at her spouse encouragingly. "Why, over two-hundred attended the first time you held Children's Church, and now it's about to outgrow the building. And with every child come more adults. The Church officials can't deny that kind of success. And it all seems to hinge on what you've been calling t the 'people's hymns.'"

"I've come to believe that hymns are simply an expansion of the sermon." Newton took another sip of the chocolate. Determining that it had cooled down, he took another. When he set the cup down, he reflected for a moment. "It's a teaching ministry. It's something the children *and* adults can understand. The numbers are not at all important. What counts is how many souls hunger for the truth of the gospel, working folk who found church beyond their reach."

"So, why are you having such difficulty with this particular hymn?" said Polly.

"This one is different." Newton picked up his notes and weighed them. "It tells the measure of my life, of every man's life really. It's the recognition of how unworthy I was and how amazing God's grace truly is."

"That's the core of the gospel, isn't it?" Polly said. "I mean, none of us can measure up to God's forgiveness."

Newton nodded and read the first line. "Amazing Grace, how sweet the sound, that saved a wretch like me."

Polly chuckled, and said, "You're not going to make yourself into some kind of a martyr, are you?"

"Far from it. As the Apostle Paul said, 'I am chief among sinners.' And I slammed the door in God's face every time he came calling. The point keeps coming back to my unworthiness. Even after all these years, it's hard for me to accept."

"He just had a bigger work for you," said Polly, and she leaned down and kissed her husband on the cheek.

"God may have had a different purpose for my life. I keep thinking of David's story. 'Who am I, O Lord God, and what is my family, that you have brought me this far?' And after all that, David later committed adultery. That event brought him to his knees."

"Well," said Polly, "you're no King David, and I certainly don't believe you're going to commit adultery."

Newton shook his head. "You're right that I can't compare with the man who had a heart for God, but no man can say he will not fall. It's happened to men much greater than I."

Polly wrapped her arms around her husband and rocked him gently. "You are one of the most righteous men I know," she cooed. "Now, tell me again why you're having such difficulty making this work?"

"I suppose it's because I'm thinking of my early years, and how hard it was for me to accept God," said Newton, reflecting as he spoke.

"Then I am going to leave you to your work. Drink your hot chocolate before it gets cold." She kissed her husband on the cheek again, and said, "I love you, John." Then she quietly walked out, closing the door behind her.

Newton leaned on his elbows and considered his life. In the center drawer laid a journal in which he recorded his thoughts. He had done so since his conversion, ten years ago. This time of year he reflected on his life, measuring both successes and failures.

It all started with the death of my mother. Never has there been a more saintly woman. I couldn't understand why God allowed her to suffer so many years and then go through such a hard death. And then my father remarried so quickly, began a new family and in no time sent me off to boarding school. That was almost my undoing. I decided that the loving God my mother described couldn't be real, not if he let us both suffer so much. Nevertheless, I wanted to believe. There was just too much anger.

Now I think on how many times God spared my life. Once in a while, I wondered if I was mistaken, and God was real. Funny to think of it that way now. Then the Navy conscripted me and kept me from Polly. I was such a child, such a spoiled child. But the darkest time of my life was when I became enslaved. I gave up all hope of ever returning home to my former life.

In all this I learned to fear God, learned to let go. But I also learned that he was my shield. Once I stopped fighting, peace and joy gave my soul rest, regardless of the flesh. I learned that this earth will dissolve like the winter snow, and that the sun will shine through the darkest clouds. I learned that I am forever his.

Newton began to write, short plain words that expressed his heartfelt emotions. He gave no regard to the rhythm or tempo and was amazed at how freely the words flowed onto the paper. When he finished, he read the work out loud.

"This is it," he murmured. "Just a little more work and it's finished. I hope it touches others the way it has warmed me."

# I Once Was Lost

Chapter 42

The Final Years

Olney, England (1807)

"Although the Lord gives you the bread of adversity and the water of affliction, your teachers will be hidden no more; with your own eyes you will see them." Isaiah 30: 20

Newton sat in front of the fireplace of his home beside the hearth; at last, his soul was at peace.

He wrapped a shawl around his shoulders and shivered. He wondered how the lingering cold could penetrate his bones right to the marrow, while at the same time burning embers crackled and split near his feet. The outside of his body was warm, yet no coat or blanket, and certainly no fire, could warm the core of his being. And why should it be any different? I read somewhere that the average man lives to be about forty-five, yet I am an in my seventies. Strange that the Lord would give me this much time.

He often dreamed of Polly, especially of the years when they were young, just starting the marriage journey. Betsy, his adopted daughter, visited every day, preparing meals and nursing him when needed.

Despite his infirmities, he continued to preach the message of salvation. His voice spoke to the hearts of men and women, who filled his church to capacity.

"Why not give up the pulpit, John," suggested a friend.

"The old slaver, give up?" thundered Newton, leaning on his cane.

"God has taken my eyesight, but not my voice. I'll not stop while there is yet breath to exalt His name."

At home, he sat back into the chair that had comforted him for so many years, taking the first sip of warm tea prepared by Betsy. There was a knock at the door, and when she answered, Newton heard her talking to William Wilberforce.

"Aren't you going to invite me in?" he teased, clearly in fine spirits.

Betsy smiled and gave an exaggerated curtsy. "Uncle Wil', how good of you to visit." She took his coat and said, "I'll leave you two men to your conversation."

Seeing Newton in the chair, Wilberforce walked over and stood beside his old and dear friend. "John, how are you?"

Newton looked up toward the voice. "It seems God thinks I've seen enough of this world," he said straightening up. "I honestly believe he will call me home soon."

"Perhaps, but not before I share some excellent news. I am pleased to announce that at 4:00 this afternoon the House of Commons abolished slavery. What do you think of that?" he said, and enthusiastic smile on his face.

Newton could hardly contain himself. He began to rise, faltered until Wilberforce lent a steadying hand. He shook his head in disbelief. "This is your greatest achievement, William. God bless you, son."

"Can you believe it? It took twenty years, but it finally passed. By a vote of 283 to 16 Parliament passed the Slave Trade Act."

Wilberforce patted his friend on the shoulder, watching the

satisfaction is his old friend's face. He was touched by the warm memories of their years laboring side by side for this worthy and Godly endeavor. "John," he said softly, "let us sit and talk for a little while."

And the men did talk. They enjoyed their tea, a cozy fire and the memory of the challenges they had met.

"John, I know you won't take credit for this, but you had as much to do with our success as any member of the government."

"Not I, my friend," said Newton with a wry smile. "It was God who saved the wretch, not the other way around. He used the great blasphemer's sin for His own good."

Newton sat back into the chair and considered how God had smiled upon him throughout his life. The fire warmed him now. He was tired and his Betsy took the teacup and saucer from his hand, just as he drifted off to sleep.

# I Once Was Lost

Three weeks later, John Newton, once a slaver, a man who refused to believe, and who counseled others to do likewise, a man whose life had not only been saved countless times, but was formed into the likeness of the one who breathed him into existence, went home to his Father's Kingdom. His last words were, "I am still in the land of the dying but will soon be in the land of the living."

Although he had been the author of much poetry and countless hymns, Amazing Grace remains his best-known work.

When originally written, it is unknown what music, if any, accompanied the verses. The hymnbooks at that time did not contain music and were simply small books of religious poetry. However, sometime between 1789 and 1799, four variations of Newton's hymn were published in the U.S. in the Baptist, Dutch Reformed and Congregationalists hymnodies, all set to music. By 1830, Presbyterians and Methodists also included Newton's verses in their hymnals.

The hymn is still popular two hundred years after its author put pen to paper. The words represent the summation of Newton's life as he saw it. Although completely unmerited, God sought out a lost wretch, expressed His unending love, and forgave him for all.

*Amazing Grace* is the most sung, most recorded and most beloved in the world. No other song, spiritual or secular, comes close to it in terms of numbers of recordings, frequency of performances (it is said to be publically sung millions of times each year), and international popularity across six continents. The first stanza best captures John Newton's recognition of the depth of God's love.

# I Once Was Lost

Amazing Grace

Amazing Grace, how sweet the sound,

that saved a wretch like me.

I once was lost but now am found, was blind,

but now I see.

T'was Grace that taught my heart to fear.

And Grace, my fears relieved.

How precious did that Grace appear the hour I first believed.

Through many dangers, toils and snares

I have already come;

'Tis Grace that brought me safe thus far and Grace will lead me home.

The Lord has promised good to me.

His word my hope secures.

He will my shield and portion be,

as long as life endures.

Yea, when this flesh and heart shall fail, and mortal life shall cease,

I shall possess within the veil, a life of joy and peace.

When we've been here ten thousand years bright shining as the sun.

We've no less days to sing God's praise than when we've first begun.

Printed in Great Britain
by Amazon